What Readers Are Saying about *The Poor Man's Guide to Suicide*

"...a beautiful portrait of a decent man at the end of his rope. Andrew Armacost's writing is wonderfully funny and sad, and I will be reading whatever he writes from now on."
—*Scott Phillips, bestselling author of The Ice Harvest.*

"A somber yet hopeful walk along the ledge."
—*Kirkus Reviews.*

"Armacost's fictional depiction of depression has an alarmingly real feel."
—*Library Journal, Douglas Lord, Books for Dudes.*

"Funny and well-conceived."
—*Dan Fante, author of Chump Change and Mooch.*

"...true grit at its best...a powerful read that will satisfy any who like dark, gritty noir writing..."
—*D. Donovan, eBook Reviewer, Midwest Book Review.*

"The descriptions of Wesley's shifts and prison routines are gripping. This is a rare opportunity to see prison life from a guard's point of view."
—*Galina Roizman, Portland Book Review.*

Also by Andrew Armacost:

Space Bush

THE POOR MAN'S GUIDE TO SUICIDE

Andrew Armacost

Moonshine Cove Publishing, LLC
Abbeville, South Carolina U.S.A.

This book is a work of fiction. Names, characters, places and incidents are products of the author's imagination or are used fictitiously. Any resemblance to actual events, locales or persons, living or dead, is entirely coincidental.

ISBN: 978-1-937327-446
Library of Congress Control Number: 2014937932
Copyright © 2014 by Andrew Armacost

All rights reserved. No part of this book may be reproduced in whole or in part without written permission from the publisher except by reviewers who may quote brief excerpts in connection with a review in a newspaper, magazine or electronic publication; nor may any part of this book be reproduced, stored in a retrieval system or transmitted in any form or by any means electronic, mechanical, photocopying, recording or any other means, without written permission from the publisher.

Book interior design by Moonshine Cove; cover design by Andrew Pederson, used with permission.

DEDICATION

This book is dedicated to my indestructible brother.

ACKNOWLEDGEMENTS

I would like to thank Gene at Moonshine Cove, who gave me a second shot, Rachel at RMA Publicity, who remained dedicated as well as mercifully patient, and Joe Michaels, who helped me as a writer, generally, and with this work, specifically.

On a very personal note, I would like to thank my wife as well as Detective Ingram, Special Agent Foster, and Officer Jones, "O.I.C. of South Dorm," friend, father, brother, bad-ass, mentor, protector and *survivor*.

About the Author

Andrew Armacost studied literature and writing in Scotland at the University of Edinburgh after serving in the U.S. Navy, during which time he worked at sea and overseas, with long-term assignments to both Afghanistan and Singapore. Formerly a Corrections Officer for the State of Indiana, Mr. Armacost has also resided in Illinois, Ohio, Georgia, Florida, Japan, California and, most recently, Virginia , where he currently lives with his family.

> "Stone walls do not a prison make,
> nor iron bars a cage."
>
> —Richard Lovelace

ns Guide to
The Poor Man's Guide to Suicide

Merry Christmas, 2004!

FOR a long time now, I've wanted to kill myself. The closer Christmas gets, the worse I feel. About everything.

Just to add to the spirit, my monitor went to hell this morning. Blanked out during some last minute shopping. My computer is about the only thing in my dilapidated shitbox of a house that's worth anything to anyone but me. I mean Jesus...this house is a urinal with windows. And it's coming apart at the seams.

Well I picked up a new monitor from Best Buy...a cheap one...the cheapest...but first, I wrapped three gifts for my son and three gifts for my daughter. They live with their respective mothers.

I shoved a few gifts beneath the bed, and stacked the rest under my wobbly-ass coffee table, managing to knock over a wooden replica of a Christmas tree, a wooden tree with tiny plastic bulbs that light up, or should, if I ever plug it in.

Mom made the tree for me last year. She's blind, but still pretty good with her hands...creative, I should say. She lives nearby...in a slightly larger shitbox, the one in which I was raised with my sister...It's just a couple blocks away...one street over.

Mom refers to this neighborhood as 'working class.' Three years ago, while heading out for her morning walk, she tripped over something on the porch—a body...the result of a drive-by shooting, said the next day's paper. Apparently, this guy had been seeking shelter...in a hurry...he was trying to break into Mom's house when whoever wanted him dead caught up with him. That guy's no longer a member of any class, working or otherwise.

I can't wrap gifts worth a damn. The whole ordeal was further complicated by my mutt, Cleo, who kept stepping on the paper, kept jamming her nose into my crotch, pleading for attention. Cleo resembles a black lab but she's a tad smaller and doesn't like to fetch.

Back when I lived with my first wife near the speedway—that's where the Indianapolis 500 takes place every May—I usually took Cleo for a morning jog along a narrow wooded trail that would've been somewhat scenic if not for the tangle of power lines overhead.

I've since grown lazier, my environs more precarious. She gets a daily walk around the block and her weekly trip to a city park. That's if she's lucky.

DIVORCED, non-custodial fathers maintain a much higher tendency to bump themselves off, or so the Internet tells me. I can see that. It's not surprising, really. I'm thirty-three...two kids, two moms...already bald...and twice-divorced.

My father, Dr. Edmond Weimer, that dickhead still has a full head of white, greasy, slicked-back hair...might be fake, wouldn't put it past him.

Dr. Weimer D.D.S. was never really in the picture...at least not for long. He left Mom for Linda Elpers, his assistant, or whatever they call those helper people. Technicians, I guess.

For thirteen years, Mom enjoyed a somewhat happy second marriage until my stepfather died on the bathroom floor, bleeding from both ends, as they say, because an ulcer had perforated his stomach.

Nobody saw that one coming. For years, I blamed the EMT guys; they didn't exactly hustle up the porch steps...

SO I'm thirty-three and bald and suicidal and the father of two children and the son of a creative blind widow named Sunny Lee Vogel, originally from central Florida, who kept me alive through two divorces, quite literally, by giving me a roof and two meals a day.

Poor Mom. She's stuck in the Midwest forever, looks like. She abhors cold weather but won't start complaining until the holidays have finally passed.

Then she'll really start in.

'Wesley,' she'll say, 'When are we moving to Florida?'

And I'll say, 'Whenever you want, Ma.' But nothing will ever change. We'll both end up dying here, unlike my younger sister, Wendy Ann, a successful environmental lobbyist who lives in Boston—Plymouth, to be exact—with her three daughters, an irritating beagle, and her perfect handsome husband, a federal prosecutor named Jake Arnold.

Jake's a good guy, although I know he considers me an absolute loser. As well he should. Even so, he tries pretty hard to conceal his disdain for me, which I certainly appreciate.

Wendy's out there saving the whales. Literally. Her last project had something to do with reconfiguring lobster traps in Maine so as to keep whales from getting rope burn, which leads to a painful bacterial death of sorts, or so I've been made to understand.

Until I was thirty, or thereabouts, Wendy and I were close. But we've slowly drifted away from each other, as you do, when you grow older while living far apart.

WELL I wasn't always bald and sullen and hopeless.

When I fell in love with Claudette, my first wife, I was on the football team, and the wrestling team, and the prom court, and I helped organize student dances, and so on and so forth. I even maintained pretty good grades. In short, I had in my possession all the necessary passports to the often despised, furtively coveted, Realm of Popularity. But, in spite of any teenaged angst, I was also nice to everyone and optimistic too (at least outwardly). I was funny, pleasant…a real pleasure to be around, I don't mind saying. Not only this…My body, said Claudette, could've been chiseled by Michelangelo himself. Oh, and I played the guitar and composed bad poetry during study hall.

All true.

My only point here is, I once exhibited a range of characteristics that a few women might find attractive.

That is, at least I can see what Claudette saw in me. I honestly can't see what anyone would see in me now…my life has all the charm of a Third World luggage turnstile…

Today, my body is neither hard nor soft, neither large nor small. It's just a body. And its main purpose now, apparently, is turning the beans and rice, the cans of tuna, the jars of generic pasta sauce and other easily made cheap food, into shit, to be flushed down the toilet like so many wasted years.

None of this matters.

FOR me, the notion of self-mutilation, or any mutilation for that matter, holds no appeal. Neither does the slightest degree of physical pain. I think some folks, when they snuff it, are out to punish themselves for something, or else out to make some kind of a statement. Not me. I just want it to end. I wanna go out like a light, just that quick. Click.

My initial suicidal ideations were pretty straightforward but have recently grown more elaborate, more ambitious, more demanding on the imagination. At first, I considered swallowing a bunch of pills. Simple enough. I could wash them down with bourbon while flipping through the channels. Nightie-night. But the Internet tells me this doesn't always work. One young gentleman, having graced who knows how many people with his presence, left this astute observation in a chat-room for me and whoever else wanted to read it.

Then I was like dude I'm still alive. Shit! Plus my liver was fucked. Don't go with pills!

And so there's that. But I'm not sold. I'm certain it's a matter of dosage. What really gave me pause was the fact that, inevitably, somebody would have to clean up the mess. I mean, I'd hate to stick my mother with a bloated body...the stench alone would be too much; she's had a very strong sense of smell, ever since her vision went south. I bet the house would stink for weeks.

So. Perhaps I could circumvent such a spectacle by renting a motel room, I thought. But then again, those poor maids...they really don't get paid enough to walk in a room and find some stiff slumped over the tub, sporting an empty gaze. It just wouldn't be a nice thing to do to an ill-prepared stranger, or to anyone for that matter.

So the proper thing to do, I figure, is to drive your ass over to a funeral home, swallow what you need to swallow, and then curl up in a sleeping bag on the steps with a note pinned to your chest, along with a check already made out for the cost of cremation. As long as the cops don't catch you, you should be fine. Besides, a mortician—or even the mortician's secretary—shouldn't be shocked by the sight of one more stiff. I would even remember to wear an adult diaper, so when I shat myself, the mess wouldn't be much of a problem.

Courtesy is underrated.

EVENTUALLY my fantasies grew downright greedy. I thought about the child support I pay, which equals about forty-percent of my post-tax income, and over which I have no discretion once those checks have been mailed.

Hell, my money could be paying for French manicures, could be paying for men's ties and silk boxers or trips to warm places. Could be. Who knows. But I know it would impact my children, financially anyway, if I snuffed it. So, I thought perhaps I could take out a sizable life insurance policy, which I've already done, and pay someone to kill me.

For most people, it might be pretty hard to find the right person, to find someone both willing to act and yet competent enough to do the job without suffering the paralysis of contrition, without botching the whole affair. True, most people don't know many professional killers but, lucky me, I'm a prison guard.

◎

THE Greenborough Correctional Facility is a Level-4 prison located three miles west of Greenborough, which, due to the intractability of urban sprawl, most folks regard as a suburb of Indianapolis.

Level-5 prisons are classified as 'Maximum Security.' Before the name change, Level-1's used to be called 'Minimum Security,' to give you some idea of where a Level-4 fits into the picture. The National Correctional Industries Association, for what it's worth, considers my workplace a 'Medium-High' institution.

How do you wind up in the GCF, as opposed to some other prison? Well, you could first do something terrible and then, once the inexorable passage of time has whittled your sentence down to twenty years or less, you could be transferred to the GCF, provided no one caught you breaking too many rules at the Level-5 prison from which you came. This works in reverse, of course, and you could likewise get transferred to the GCF after fucking up at the Level-3 prison to which you'd been assigned initially (fighting, drugs, the usual).

You may also land yourself inside the GCF if you're initially sentenced to less than twenty years. This might require you to steal a car, to molest a child, or stab someone (without killing them), or else maybe sell one kilo of cocaine, to provide a few examples.

Now bear in mind that, in the State of Indiana, if you're sentenced to twenty-years, you'll only serve ten of those, so long as you stay on your best behavior. The average time served at the GCF is nine years and I've done about nine years myself, on the other side of that blurry blue line.

In order to reach the prison each night by five-thirty, I typically speed as much as possible down Washington Street, also known as 40 West, part of the old National Road, which runs all the way to California.

Washington Street, for the entire length of my commute, is flanked by garish strip-malls and dreary parking lots. I'm assigned to the night shift...so, on my way to work, at least in the wintertime, the storefronts usually appear dusky, save for the neon squiggles and backlit signs advertising all the usual franchised crap.

It's depressing.

I went to Canada once. I went to Windsor for my best friend's bachelor party. His name's Chris, Chris Cooper, but I don't think I've called him Chris or Christopher in years. It's always Coop or Cooper. Probably a holdover from the high school football and beer bong days of our half-wasted youth.

Now aside from that trip to Canada, I've never been outside America, though for years I ached to see the world, or at least some other part of it. By now, I may've idealized all the places I want to go. They probably don't exist in the way I think they do. But when I picture Milan, or Sydney, or Edinburgh, or Singapore, or Buenos Ares, or wherever...these cities in my mind never appear even a fraction as ugly as my drive to work, which to me seems representative of an average American city...In terms of culture, or aesthetics, or whatever, Indy is basically interchangeable with Cincinnati or Columbus...

Or even Saint Louis
Kansas City
Louisville

And on, and on. Midsized McCities of the Middle West. It's all the same.

I mean, I've always imagined that over in Europe, all those besotted old buildings might reassure those who live among them of the eternal connectedness of human history, of something if not permanent then at least substantial, unlike the ephemera, the junk, the disposable boxes we so rapidly slap up to house our mass-produced dreams. Maybe I'm deceived by the Internet, deluded by foreign films. Maybe things are getting just as bad over there.

I guess I'll never know.

GUSTS of wind and icy rain whip against my rusty blue hatchback Honda Civic as I downshift and vie with other metal insects for the passing lane.

Damn, I wish I had a CD player in here. It's hard to shift gears and change stations while whipping through traffic. Advertisement...advertisement... advertisement... Where'd all the music go?

Up until a year ago, I really liked NPR. Public radio. But I no longer care about the news...current events...what's going on in the world...After all, it doesn't really affect me and I certainly don't affect any of it.

So here we go...ah, yes...the classical music station...not that I'm cultured or whatever...I simply don't like popular music any more...it's the lyrics, I guess...all those the wistful, sugary hooks that booby-trap most popular songs. I'd rather feel nothing. I prefer white noise, or at least noise that avoids primary colors.

Thrashing through a yellow light, I head south down Sun Road, past the warden's home there on the left. Barren, shadowy cornfields lie to the right, separated from the grayish sky by a thin red strip on the horizon. For most folks, the day is almost dead. For me it's all just beginning...another undead day, something between life and not life.

My cell phone rings. Christ, I hate my phone. It's so intrusive. STOP WHAT YOU'RE DOING, it says. I got this phone, this expensive piece of plastic, so I could stay in touch with my daughter and my sister. Like I said, my sister's in Massachusetts. Gretchen, my daughter, she lives in Portage...about four hours north, door to door.

With my work schedule, I have every other weekend off. Every other weekend, or thereabouts, I'm up in Portage. Gretchen's mother should, according to the legal paper work, drive my daughter down for every other visit. It never happens. If I had the heart and the balls and the money to hire an attorney, I'd take my ex-wife to court and make her share the burden of those freeway miles.

It'll never happen.

So during the two weekends I have off each month, I'm up in Portage, a town you'd never go to if you didn't have friends or family trapped up there. During my other off days, I'm here in Indy with my son or else helping out my mother. If I'm not otherwise obligated, I take part-time security gigs, just to make ends meet. Or at least make ends share the same zip code.

My phone is still ringing. I yank it from the pocket of my black, Department of Corrections jacket. This will be Mom calling, or Cooper, or Gretchen, who's a sweet young woman of fourteen years. Okay, she's an unhappy teenager with a major 'body image' problem, as it's now called. But a beautiful person, I think. Though I really don't know anymore…

We're drifting apart.

I guess all teenagers drift away from you, but I mean we're really drifting. Two weekends a month, it's just not enough. We hug like strangers, I think, and often times, now that she's getting older, she wants to use my designated visitation days to spend more time with her friends. Not that she has a ton of friends…two or three that I know of, but they must be close.

It's not her calling. It's Cooper. Better not pick up.

THE prison parking lot is filled with pickup trucks, modest sedans, and decrepit SUVs. Beyond the parking lot, two orangey brick buildings sit side-by-side. The smaller of the two serves as the entry point to the Level-4 prison where I work.

The larger, six-story building is the Greenborough Diagnostic Center; it's the Level-5 prison where I used to work. It's called a 'Diagnostic Center' because inmates there are screened and then—based on their crime as well as their behavior over a thirty-day period—they're assigned to one of Indiana's many long-term facilities.

It's a growth industry.

Both prisons are surrounded by two chain-link fences, ten feet high, capped with razor wire and guarded by watchtowers. Hence, a potential escapee would need to make it over not one but two fences.

History shows that it *can* be done.

I kill the engine and pat myself down for any prohibited items...like my cell phone, for example, or my pistol, which I always keep under the car seat, despite written policies here to the contrary. I don't really like touching or having guns, but who knows when some pissed-off ex-con might spot me in a parking lot somewhere, or else jump my ass while I'm pumping gas into my rusty piece of shit.

I step out of the Honda and into a brisk wind. It nearly takes my breath away. I stretch out while yawning at the same time. My dark-blue pants, along with my light-blue polyester shirt and clip-on tie, conspire to lend me the appearance of a mall cop, only with a Russian soldier's cap.

I look ridiculous.

A mumbling blue herd mills about the lobby, each guard waiting his turn to grumble through the metal detector before having his bag lackadaisically rooted through by another guard, some doofus named Dreyfus, who's asleep on his feet. I drop my keys, two pens, and my fraying wallet into a plastic tub.

'Hey Professor,' a voice startles me, yanks me from whatever train of thought I'd been on. It's Tyson...a short, kind, thinly mustachioed oaf, a man with a face like a jelly donut. We went through training together...ten, eleven, must be close to twelve years ago. He seems like such a nice person...it saddens me.

I should've accepted his friendship when he offered it. I know that goodhearted slob must be rotting away behind four walls of loneliness...oh, he totally missed the bus, never had kids, and can't overcome his shyness. I bet the few friends he had are married now and couldn't care less about him. He has that pitiable Saint Bernard aura.

Like a lot of the guards around here, Tyson still calls me Professor or Doctor because, back in the day, years and years ago, I was always spouting some useless nonsense like 'Did you know that the fable of the flood actually dates back to the Sumerians,' or 'You know, an insect's skeleton is really made of sugar.' No one cared, of course. And now? I don't care either. About any of it.

It really is all trivia.

I have just enough time to get my shoes shined. Shouldn't take long. I walk in and flop down on a barber's chair. Wait my turn. Six other guards crowd around a televised football game. Two of them prattle on about landscaping. The rest, who knows. It all blends together, forms an almost non-existent, dingy sort of white noise. I space out until it's my turn.

Now a young white kid with broken teeth and broken glasses—an erstwhile burglar, I think—he shines my shoes and, while doing so, attempts to make conversation. He tries football, professional wrestling, stock car racing. None of it works. I don't know what he's talking about. I've detached myself from the entirely pointless minutia that can bind human strangers.

So this kid finishes up the toe of my boot and looks up at me. I guess that means he's finished. Maybe he said something and I just didn't hear it. I hand him a muttered thanks, then yawn into the hallway and wait for roll call...

THE rank and file form three rows, but not very evenly...seems like an unintentional parody of the military. Captain Karfa creaks in on his number-2 pencil legs with his chest stuck out and a salt-and-pepper mustache concealing his upper lip. He's an okay guy. Not an asshole really. Not a windbag, like the last guy. Worships Willie Nelson. Loves his bass boat as well as the innumerable children he's managed to sire. We don't talk much anymore. We've said it all, I guess.

A heavy-breathing sergeant walks down each row, halfheartedly scrutinizing our uniforms. We are not faced with any sort of military regulations that actually matter, that have a purpose. You can have a belly as big as you please, but your shoes had better be polished. Anyway. The Captain calls out our work assignments, which rarely change...then he tells the parking lot guard to keep an eye out for a disgruntled former employee, Brett Rose, who yesterday threatened Sergeant Williams in a highly creative fashion.

'All right,' says Captain Karfa. 'Let's go to work.'

It's six o'clock at night. And so begins the sloppily choreographed fugue of passing strangers. Day shift out, night shift in...

The structure of the prison resembles a college campus. In fact, it's referred to as a campus. There's a chow hall in the center of this campus and, next to it, a school that just had its funding slashed. I walk past the recreational facility and the warehouse until I finally reach my post, the F-Dorm.

Here I work with two other officers and Sergeant Johnson, whom I used to supervise when I was a sergeant at that diagnostic center I was telling you about earlier. I'm just a plain old officer now. Rank and file, baby. Because things happened. As they do. As they do.

JOHNSON, the guy in charge of this circus, used to be a marine. And although he spent his entire enlistment working on trucks and fixing tanks, his demeanor would never suggest this. You'd think he was a special forces guy. RECON. Rangers...whatever they call themselves.

Once a marine, always a marine. That's what he'll tell you anyway. He's a little short, just under five-eight. Still, he maintains the ability to intimidate, which is important here at times. He knows how to look you in the eye and tell you No, which is also important. His cropped black hair, longish in the front, refuses to recede and despite the well-fed paunch he's working on, his baby-face makes him look much younger than his thirty-plus years.

I've heard so much about his five years in the military that I almost get sick when he opens his mouth. I can even predict with great accuracy what he'll say next. I can finish his stories. I know all his punch lines. Without a doubt, the man's dumber than Bisquick...but he knows his job.

Johnson's not the only former marine around here. I'd say maybe half the officers have military experience. Not me, but I'll get to that.

IT seems to me that novels and films both tend to ignore or at least gloss over the great preponderance of Nothings that populate our decaying planet. I'm a Nothing. And I certainly work for a Nothing. On a scale of one to ten, I'll give my boss a score of, I don't know...

Personality? 2
Integrity? 7
Looks? 6
Rectitude? 5
Brains? 4

Yep, all in all, just below mediocre. In a word, a Nothing. Neither an asshole nor a saint...not a genius or an imbecile. About as memorable as your first diaper change, your second step, your third word. Yes, a nothing. As am I. Air. Dust. I am a cloud surrounded by clouds.

F-Dorm is comprised of two primary units, Alpha and Bravo. Alpha currently holds 184 inmates, which we now call 'offenders' because the government of Indiana, like most governments, has a penchant for euphemisms.

The Alpha 'offenders' are a hodge-podge of kitchen-workers, GED students, and 'idlers,' which means they've not signed up to do anything useful with their time. We can't make them. They watch television and masturbate.

Bravo is the Protective Custody Unit, or the PCU. Now here's how that works. When you fear for your life or even for your safety, you can then request Bravo and be transferred to a solitary cell. Let's say you steal something, especially from the wrong person, you can request Bravo to avoid taking your lumps. Or if you owe somebody money, say, for a pair of sneakers, you can also request Bravo.

Of course, in both instances, you'll be written up for breaking the rules, which means you'll end up spending a bit more time with us, but it's better than having your nose bitten off or having your neck sliced open while you sleep. That sort of thing.

Most inmates request Bravo following a negative interaction with a known Security Threat Group, which is a drawn out way to say *gang*. Granted, as soon as you enter into protective custody, everyone on the camp will laugh and call you names (including the guards) but at least you'll be safer than before.

Bravo Unit (Protective Custody) is made up of individual cells...what you see in the movies, what you probably think of, typically, when you imagine a prison.

It's a different world in Alpha, where I usually work, where men sleep in an open-air barracks with four rows of bunk beds in one room and another four rows of beds in the room across the hall. The average ratio in Alpha is 1 officer to 92 inmates, each carrying an average sentence of eighteen years, though again, they'll only serve around nine or ten years of that.

The prisoners, well, they can take this dorm from us whenever they want it. And then what? No food, no water.

That's why the cafeteria is always the most dangerous place to work in any prison; it provides the prospect of sustainable rebellion. But everyone here knows that eventually we'd take the prison back and that, in the chaos preceding and during the takeover, hundreds of human beings would be injured or killed.

Even so. If the sentences being served here were longer, this kind of open dormitory would never work. See, it's not that the prisoners here can't kill me. Of course they can. And it's not that they don't want to kill me. Sure they do. Certainly. Certainly many do and certainly more than one prisoner here has killed someone on the outside. Or even on the inside.

But, as for killing a guard...it's simply not worth doing more time, at least not to rational men who can see themselves as being free within ten years or less. But then again, not everyone here is rational.

Not everyone here is sane, for that matter.

WHEN I walk through the door of the dorm, I get rid of my jacket and hook up my radio... then I count all the prisoners in the Delta Wing of Alpha. I count them in their bunks, row by row. It's full, so there should be ninety-two men in here. Hmm. Ninety-one. Someone's missing from the third row. There's an empty tangle of sheets in one bunk, A3-4U.

I poke my head into the day room, where I find two night workers—one mopping the floor, one watching the smaller guy mop. I've already counted those guys. Someone's still missing.

I go to the restroom where I find a thin, sallow-skinned black man taking a dump on one of the four open toilets. I look him in the eye.

'Whittaker,' I say, 'Count time.'

'Count me from here,' he says, glaring angrily, 'Shit. Can't you see I'm busy?'

'Count time,' I repeat, with no more emphasis than before.

He furiously wipes his ass and shuffles to his bunk.

I could write him up for 'interfering with count,' for insolence too, and vulgarity directed at an officer, to mention nothing of his initial failure to follow a direct order. But I would never do that. Well, unless he pulls the same routine on me tomorrow night.

For one thing, it's not like what a lot of people think. I mean, there aren't a bunch of lunatic guards running around here with nightsticks, whipping the piss out of prisoners...looking for the next power trip. Very rarely do guards here beat the prisoners and even more rarely can they get away with it...not with lawsuits growing faster than the national debt. It happens, sure...but it's anecdotal, not the norm. Not by a long shot. Those days, as they say, are over.

Now consider this. A cop's most tangible power, in my opinion, is the ability to haul people off to prison. *Officer, no! Please don't take my ass to jail!*

Well where I work, the criminals are already in jail. There's not much we can do. Are you kidding? We can't even call them filthy names—they can file a grievance for that.

Let's see. We can make them mop the floor, wipe the windows, clean the toilettes. And we can cut off their phone privileges for a week or two. We can send them to 'segregation' but we only have fifteen 'holes' in which to stick men, so you'd better have a good reason to cart someone away in cuffs. A really good reason. Besides, many prisoners don't mind going to the hole. For some, it's a nice little break...a change of scenery, replete with three hot meals and a serviceable bed.

Time. It's the only significant weapon we have. The only means of recourse. They screw up...we write them up...they stay here longer. But, as everyone knows, our prisons are overcrowded, so the chain of command will throw out your paperwork if it looks the slightest bit frivolous.

And there's one more reason I don't fuck with the prisoners; there's a good reason I don't write them up for every little thing, don't shake down their property without provocation...there's a very good reason that I never rock the boat...

NOT long after I came here, to the GCF, after nearly being fired at the diagnostic center...one Sunday morning I was working the visitation room with Ricky Moore, self-touted playboy and avid deer hunter. Lots of hunters work here.

Well the visitation room is just that, with five rows of beige-colored plastic chairs and people sitting in them, holding hands, gabling, laughing, crying, and so on. As you'd expect.

Each prisoner can have up to five visitations per week. But the same visitor cannot return more than once every fourteen days. Those are the rules.

No glass barrier, as you see in the movies, separates the visitor from the visitee. We permit one embrace at the beginning and one embrace at the end of each visit. These are the rules. From time to time, we must put a stop to excessive groping and/or mutual masturbation.

When a prisoner finishes his two-hour visit, he must enter a tiny annex to be strip-searched because the visiting room is where weapons and drugs and tobacco are most frequently passed, despite two apathetic officers being posted there and despite a camera that records everything (we review the footage only if something suspicious has been detected). Personally, I think a lot of contraband comes in on babies and young children, whom no one, including me, really wants to search thoroughly before a visit.

SO here's what happened in the visitation room that day.

Harold T. Manfred, or 'Big H,' as even the guards referred to him, was in the visitation room, waiting for his visit to begin. To fully appreciate what I'm about to tell you, two things must be understood. First of all, Big H was a big black hairless Yeti of a man. I mean the word huge is a puny adjective next to this guy.

The second thing is this. The Central State Mental Hospital was shut down by the governor around 1990 or so, due to funding shortages as well as staff incompetence, as I recall. The mental patients, poor and crazy, segregated themselves and struck out on one of three paths. The first path was homelessness. These are, in part, the people you see downtown, cadging pocket change and sleeping on park benches. The second path, I guess, could be called the Happy Ending—they wound up living with relatives and perhaps working some menial job. The third path of course was a life of crime. The GCF houses hundreds of crazy people whom, from my experience, should be looked after by some sort of medical staff, not prison guards.

Big H was crazy. Looney Tunes crazy. He used to rub toothpaste in his armpits. Once in a while, he'd jam a pencil down his urethra...we called him Pencil Dick behind his back. Each day, Big H was given two shots of thorazine, which is tantamount, I'd say, to a temporary chemical lobotomy. He needed it. When he was twelve, he slashed his mother's throat and wound up in some juvenile correctional facility that turned out to be nothing more than a stepping-stone to the big house. His mother forgave him, from what I gather. The state did not. He was on his third bit already when we had our rather memorable encounter.

So anyway. Big H finished a visit with his well-fed mother, who had a nasty box-cutter scar down her neck from when her son tried to kill her, and then I called him into the visitation room's annex to be strip-searched. It was like sharing a walk-in closet with a rhino.

I followed all the steps. I did everything by the book. Strange, but that's how I used to be.

'Open your mouth,' I said.

He bent down so I could see inside his mouth. His breath stank of curdled milk. I backed away.

'Check it out,' he said. 'You know cereal?'

'Like...breakfast cereal?'

'Yeah, yeah. It a gift.'

'How's that?'

'Think about this shit. It come in a box. And it be lookin all pretty and shit. Just like a gift.'

'Lift up your tongue,' I said. 'All the way. Okay. Pull your ears forward. Now run your fingers through your hair. All right. Take off your clothes.'

'I'm goin to Bible Study,' he said, stripping down, his baritone voice reverberating off the cinderblock walls.

'Good for you,' I said dismissively, rifling through the pockets of his fusty trousers.

'Uh-huh,' he said, 'But I gotta go now.'

I looked at my watch, some plastic piece of garbage that my second ex-wife had given me. Meanwhile, Big H threw his piss-stained underwear over a chair.

'Big H,' I cautioned him, 'that's a no-go till six-thirty. You need to get back to your dorm for count. You know the drill. So lift up your testicles. All the way.'

Big H was proud of his manhood. He was a huge beast of a man and everything was proportional. He hoisted up that great, menacing, gnarled tree root of a cock as he grinned like a kid with some filthy, irresistible secret. He stroked that monster while staring at me. He gave himself a semi. I viewed this as a veiled threat.

'Goin to church *now*,' he insisted. 'You hear me dawg?'

The visitation room was busy. Many more asses and many more balls required my expert scrutiny. So I ignored him, and got on with the task at hand, looking for drugs and weapons.

'Turn around and bend over,' I said, peering into his asshole, searching for hidden contraband, 'Spread your butt cheeks a little wider.'

He complied without another word, or even a hint at the gathering storm.

'You're good to go,' I told him, yanking off my latex gloves, 'Get dressed and go back to your dorm. I mean when you walk out that door, Big H, I better see you take a right, not a left. Understood?'

'Quit playin. I'm goin to church, dawg. See what happens, you try to keep me.'

Big H routinely attended every single church service offered by every faith and denomination. Either he was wisely hedging his metaphysical bets, or he was milking the system in order to escape his dorm and wander around the camp. Or he was just plain crazy. Or all three. Who knows.

Regardless, I didn't enjoy being threatened. It's a slippery slope, I thought. I didn't like the inmates getting over on me so easily.

'Let me get this straight,' I said, probably adding a few hand gestures by this point. 'Are you trying to intimidate me? That's a class B offense, just so you know.'

'I said I'm goin to the chapel.' He stared me down, still naked and brandishing three quarters of a hard-on, by the way.

'And I said you're going back to your dorm. Have I made myself crystal fucking clear?'

Big H, as I would soon find out, didn't give a damn about whatever administrative discomfort I could cause him. Not at all! Before I knew it, with one quick flick of his Yeti wrist, that crazy giant had locked the door, a door to which Ricky-the-playboy should've had a key but, as Chance would have it, didn't.

I ducked just in time to avoid that great, terrifying paw of his, sailing toward my face. And, in so doing, I landed on my ass with a jolt that jarred my spine. The only thing I wound up using from those 'personal protection' classes was that fetal position they tell you about. I curled up on my back with my arms over my body, my hands over my face, while Big H beat me like a madman, which he was.

By the time the Quick Response Team finally crowbarred through the door, I had damn near gone unconscious. Sergeant Kaniewski, the first guy through the door, he was tossed against a row of chairs in the visitation room. Two full cans of pepper-spray later, they had made some progress against that crazy Yeti bastard.

Did they shock Big H with a stun-gun after he'd been subdued, as two civilian witnesses later claimed? Doubtful. I'm sure it looked bad on tape when, with the retrospective luxury of frame-by-frame analysis, Big H's mother, or rather her attorney, could carefully dissect split-second decisions. Excessive force? If motives factor in, I'd say no. Not that it matters. Sergeant K. was fired and the state had to pay out...I forget how much. A lot.

Personally, I don't think the old shock treatment had been the byproduct of some sadistic instinct embedded in the guards. I think everyone was just plain scared, scared to death. Even after he'd been sprayed and shocked and cuffed and shackled, I was later told, Big H refused to move unless someone asked him nicely.

'Big H,' Ricky had said, catching his breath, 'Will you please get up? Will you please come with us to segregation?'

'Man, all right. But I need my shot. I need my meds dawg, else Imma go off again.'

The thing was, Big H only had six months remaining on a two year bit for his third battery charge. His job on the outside had been to batter people with bad debts, usually shmucks who owed money to crack dealers. Six months, that's all he had left. He ended up serving two more years for breaking my arm and my collarbone as well as permanently disfiguring my right pinky finger, which had a metal rod running through it for six weeks.

Rationality, in the case of Big H, had no appeal. So I'm more careful today about pushing buttons, about being alone when making a stand or else delivering bad news to men much larger and meaner and tougher than myself.

JESUS, was my pride ever wounded. I had always fancied myself if not a 'tough guy,' for the lack of a better term, then at least not the kind of guy who'd end up prostrate on the floor, balled up uselessly in the fetal position during a physical confrontation.

Growing up in a part of downtown that I've heard described as a "white-trash ghetto," I had presented myself as an athlete, a jock, a meathead, simply because it had behooved me to do so much more than if, for example, I had joined the choir—I did love to sing—or auditioned for a play with the drama club, where I probably belonged.

But rather than obeying my true nature, I convinced myself that I was tough, merciless, strong, brave. Macho to the nth degree. I wonder, sometimes, if any of it had ever been true...or if I had merely manufactured a convenient myth for myself.

Clearly, I'm no tough guy today. I, like so many others, am just trying to get through another day without bumping into the unexpected.

BACK to the present.

Once the count has cleared, that is, once all of the dorms have called in their count and the 'Master Locator' is happy with the numbers, then the off-going day shift bolts for the gate.

Tootles.

I walk back to the Alpha Unit, open up the blue metal door, and yell.

'Count's clear! Rec call! Rec call!'

So as the prisoners, swaddled in khaki pants and shirts and jackets, hurdle through the door in a disorderly fashion toward the recreational facility, I count them one by one, then call the Yard Officer on my radio.

'Twenty-two,' I say, 'Eighty-seven here.'

'Go ahead eighty-seven.'

'You got a hundred-and-two on the walk to rec.'

'Clear,' he says, meaning 'Ten-Four,' or what have you.

While noisily scratching his nuts, Sergeant Johnson records that same number in a finely ruled log at his desk, which sits between Alpha and Bravo, the latter being shut off by two locked metal doors.

I've known Johnson for five years and can't remember his first name. His brass nametag includes a first initial, J.

Um...Could be John, I guess. John Johnson? Doesn't sound right. Sounds too much like Don Johnson. Christ, I've been to this guy's house before. Oh well. Like I said, he's a Nothing. As far as I can tell, *J* has no interests, no passions, and the summation of his world view could fit on the back of a lottery ticket. I wonder if Johnson has likewise forgotten my first name. I'm not far from forgetting it myself.

At least I'm in the dorm instead of the gym. The daily recreational period for the prisoners here is a total time-bomb, with pool balls and pool cues for gunpowder. Ever seen a bar fight? What do they always go for first? The sticks. The balls. But clearly, their morale is more important than our safety. Why not just put a game of darts over there...or better yet, an archery range? Or even a skeet shoot.

Granted, inmates don't need wooden sticks and porcelain balls to pose a threat. Last week, some kid was stabbed almost to death with a pencil. A pencil! It pierced his colon. Apparently, this kid had stolen tobacco from a member of the Aryan Brotherhood.

Tobacco is prohibited here, and so the black market has driven up the price of cigarettes inside to fifty dollars a pack or more, depending on whether the prison is 'dry' or not. I didn't believe it either, the first time I heard it.

WITH half the inmates at rec, and the other half in the day room watching football, I can now surrender to my neurotic dependence on coffee.

Brenda Ray, or B-Ray, as everyone calls her, she pours me a styrofoam cup of some brand-name stuff she brought in from home. I know from experience that I better thumbtack a smile to my face, or else she'll mother me to death, ask me intrusive well-intentioned questions and beseech me tenderly with her auburn eyes. She's a true sweetheart, which is a quality I find highly annoying when I just want to be left alone.

'Howdy stranger,' she says, smoke-throated.

'How do,' I say, playfully mocking her Oklahoma accent as I creep away from the break room before she can latch onto me. B-Ray's my age with three of her own and has every right to be more depressed than me.

Her first husband left her destitute in some small town...somewhere in Alabama, I think it was. She then married the first decent man who'd have her, a diabetic who's twenty years older. Roy. He works the day shift here. Good guy.

Roy had been a farmer like his father...somewhere west of Plainfield, I gather. For some reason, Roy had to sell the farm. Anyway, I guess Roy was just passing through Alabama from somewhere, Florida maybe, and he stopped off at the diner in which B-Ray had been working. They were married two or three months later.

From what I can tell, B-Ray truly loves Roy. And I know for a fact, with her evangelical upbringing, that she's not the kind to fool around, to compensate herself for what a few innuendos have told me is a failing love life. It's obvious that, three-kids-and-a-million-bottles-of-wine ago, she must've been pass-out beautiful. Her face still is and, though her skin looks rather hardened, her curly reddish-blond hair allows you to envision the golden pageant of her youth.

I spend most of each night in a long, wide, low-ceilinged, brightly-lit corridor with haze-gray paint bubbling up and cracking here and there, to reveal the white primer coat beneath.

Christman works the Echo Wing, to the left. I work Delta, to the right. We share a tall, podium-like desk that sits in the hallway between both units.

You look through one giant Plexiglas window and see where the prisoners sleep and sometimes read or stab or fuck each other. You look through the next giant window and see the day room, where prisoners watch one of two televisions, or else play cards or chess, or maybe plan ways to stab and fuck each other.

The next window shows you the showers and the toilets—if you stare too long, the inmates might get pissed. Moving down the hall, you come to the sergeant's desk and the break room. Keep going, and you'll reach the Protective Custody Unit where B-Ray always works. So that's it, more or less.

Occasionally I do my rounds, walk around, and peak at the blind spots to make sure no one's smoking or screwing or beating anyone. But mostly I gawk at them through one of these three windows. It's a bit like working at a zoo, in that it diminishes everyone involved.

Silent prisoners go unnoticed. The others seem like muscular children with ADD and violent tendencies. I mean, I spend the first few hours of every shift nagging them about the same old shit.

'Tuck in your shirt...Where are your socks? No, you can't go off your unit...then find someone in your own unit who can braid your hair. No, laundry's only issued during the day shift, Monday through Friday—I told you that yesterday...No radios in the hallway. Medical Call goes down at eight, same time every night.' And on, and on.

I sit at the desk and space out while Christman bellows 'Chapel call! Chapel call!' Johnson doesn't mind too much if I read for pleasure, that is, once the prisoners have gone to bed. But for now, I can't get away with it. Technically, I'm only allowed to read official publications put out by the Department of Corrections. But whatever. The State of Indiana pays me just enough to stay awake and count prisoners...anything else I give, that's pure charity.

Sitting at the desk while listening to the furnace, I think about Cooper's phone call and start conjuring up believable excuses, ways to get out of whatever social entanglement he's going to thrust on me.

Coop and I have been friends since middle school. He was my best man. Twice.

'Better luck this time,' he had threatened to say during the formal toast at my second wedding, which cost me a lot more than my first because my stepfather, who'd been a minister, was dead by then, and so he couldn't arrange the church and do the wedding for free again. The second time around, I had to fork it over.

Cooper is a cop, a narcotics detective. He works on some special task force for IPD

(I still call it IPD, even after the merger). His wife Sarah, an uncomplicated and currently pregnant redhead, is a speech therapist at Ron Collie High. They're not raking it in, but they're doing quite well for themselves. Big house. Big cars. And a rambunctious four-year old named Jeremy. He calls me Uncle, which is nice, and he runs to me, which is also very nice.

Sarah cooks and cleans. Looks after Jeremy. Her husband cuts the grass and fixes things. Drinks beer.

Works on the car. It's all very 1950. Not exactly 'progressive' but it seems to work for them.

So we live in different worlds, do Cooper and I. He has what folks call disposable income, whereas my income arrives pre-disposed. He frequently calls me up, with nothing but good intentions, I know, and tries to haul me out for the night...to a Colts game, or a Pacers game, or some outdoor concert. He asks me to meet him out in Broad Ripple for a drink or else he begs me to join him on a boys' trip to Vegas, offering to pay for my flight when I refuse. His generosity is both bottomless and strangely repugnant. No, not repugnant. More like telling. His generosity highlights my failure; not only can he do what he wants to do, he can pay to bring me along as a witness and paid-for sidekick.

It's just that...Well, Coop can't get it through his head that it's not like before, like when we were kids...we're not equals anymore...I can't afford to play in the adult world. I can pay child support. I can eat and put gas in the tank. And that's about it.

Nothing can divide an adult friendship like an income gap. Money is more important than religion or politics or even education.

In fact, I was always the more studious of the two, with huge delusions about my future worth, yet Cooper's the one who graduated from college and then did a few things he's actually proud of. He was a dispatcher for the police department straight out of high school...a little lost...drifting...trying to find his way. His old man hooked him up with that job. His dad, an irascible Vietnam veteran, has been a cop for as long as I've known him.

Cooper, by taking that dispatcher job, had been killing time until he was old enough to apply to the police department. But when Sarah graduated from high school and went to Bloomington, lovesick Cooper followed after. He picked up a criminal justice degree while he was down there, almost accidentally, knowing that formal education had little to do with how he wanted to live, or what he wanted to do.

Anyway, he never gave away my Best Friend title. I went to a few of his frat parties, and when I did, Coop would always collar this guy or that and say 'Hey man, this is Weimer. My best friend. The guy I've been telling you about.'

Circumstances may've excluded me but Coop never did. Oh, he has his flaws. Who doesn't? But loyalty is not among them. I've always appreciated that.

Still, it was tough to go down there for a visit, to walk across that utopian campus with its tree-lined brick paths leading students from one majestic limestone building to another, and not feel as though perhaps I was missing my destiny. It was difficult to see Kirkwood Avenue bustling with carefree youth and not feel some sense of betrayed entitlement.

I was on the outside looking in.

This feeling of being on the outside has magnified and solidified itself with the passing years. When I first started working in the good old corrections field, I was inwardly arrogant, a muffled Raskolnikov, biding time until his undiscovered genius became obvious to all. I didn't make that many friends, not good ones. A couple maybe.

And most of the guys I went to school with were one by one taken up by the ghetto life or else they joined the military. Cooper went away to school. I was alone, except for Claudette and the baby. We had each other, which seemed like enough at the time.

And meeting people hasn't gotten any easier. I always have one of the kids on my days off. There's no time for anything other than maintaining the status quo. In short, I have failed to cultivate and sustain meaningful friendships, a fact altogether incongruous with my youth.

So now, when I do interact socially, which is rare, I inevitably find myself with Cooper and Cooper's friends. I orbit.

But that's too much of a simplification...It fails to illustrate my complete inability to fully connect with anyone. I can't connect with white-collar people because, well, first of all, I rarely meet any, but more importantly because I don't have the same stuff and don't share the same values. Not that I wouldn't share the values if I shared the stuff—who knows, maybe I would. As it stands, I can't connect with my brethren here in Corrections, or with Cooper's friends, or with anyone. I don't fit anywhere. I used to fit a few places. I remember that. Now I don't. It's a weird feeling.

I've even lost the basic language of sports, of trivia. When Cooper's friends rattle off scores or when Johnson says 'Hey Doc, you see the game last night?' I don't even know what to say anymore.

After all, what is conversation? I mean what do most folks talk about? Sports, work, current events, travel, other people...or perhaps what they did over the weekend, I guess. Well I don't travel. I'd love to do something more exciting with my time, to sail, for example, or ski, or learn how to scuba dive. But I don't have the time or money. I can't talk about my investments because I don't have any. I sure as hell don't want to talk about work and my family life, if you can call it that, is a wreck. I'm not dating anyone. What is there for me to talk about aside from the books I read or the thoughts I have? And who wants to expose themselves so wholly as to share their undiluted thoughts? Besides, honesty just puts people off.

So. I have this fantasy where I'm woven into a circle of friends who talk the way people talk over dinner in Woody Allen films, with that sublime witty banter and those heady insights into the crevices of life while names like Kierkegaard and Robbe-Grillet get sprinkled like croutons over the conversation. I'd like to be around a few people who actually enjoy thinking or at least don't scoff at it. I'd like to dwell in the land of ideas but the bridge that could lead to a place like that has already burnt down so long ago that it's nothing more than the memory of smoke and twisted metal.

THE prisoners seem to have themselves occupied, so now I'm working on my taxes, which, apparently, I screwed up and have to redo. I pay taxes on money that I give to other people who don't pay taxes on that income. I pay it for them. It's another benefit of joining the Non-custodial Fathers Club.

While I'm adding the same column of numbers for the fourth time in a row, Johnson walks up to my desk with a clipboard.

'Hey, Doc, you get that in-house memo from the Captain?'

My face must tell him I don't know what he's talking about because he says 'From now on, we gotta search at least one property box. Every shift, is what the memo said. So...'

Each officer, according to DOC policy, must perform six searches on his or her shift. Of course, it has to be documented. Everything here is supposed to be documented.

Many of us are pretty lazy and so most officers usually do pat-downs instead of strip-searches or instead of shaking down an inmate's personal property, which takes a lot of time. But if the Captain wants me to hit some property boxes, then okay, it's not like I have much else to do on the night shift.

A new inmate just checked in yesterday...Mumford, Jamal. What's Mr. Mumford all about? I go to his bunk. He's not there. He's probably in the day room. His bed is perfectly made.

I unlock his property box, a gray plastic carton about two-by-three-by-two. I strap on latex gloves and get to work.

You can make somewhat educated guesses about an inmate's character by rooting through his property box. This particular box, judging from the photo album here within, belongs to a black male around twenty years of age...from a lower-middle class family, a single-parent family with no father figure. A feebly written unmailed letter to his mother, which I scan but do not read, tells me that he's poorly educated in the formal sense, or at any rate, his spelling and grammar are both shot. There is, however, a GED study guide in here. So I guess that's good.

This young man has ripped several pages from various porn magazines to make one composite folder, having thrown away all of the original magazines, except for the photos, which are pretty raunchy, even for porn.

Beneath the porn folder is a photo album. In one picture, Jamal is leaning against a new white Cadillac parked in front of an Eastside house that looks ready to fall down if someone so much as throws a rock at the door. Another photo shows me a big screen TV inside this home. His photo album is full of shitty durable goods and yet high-end consumer goods such as watches and sneakers and so on...I'm guessing he's in for selling drugs.

In the next picture he's holding his little niece, who seems mesmerized by her uncle. His eyes look kind. Soft, and Bambi-like. Yes, I realize features like eyes can deceive, but there's something adoptional about this kid...like, one little push in the right direction and he'd be on his way.

His mother and sister appear in nearly every picture. Everything is neatly organized. This box is stuffed with packaged food items, which can be purchased at the commissary store once a week, using a prison account...Yeah, so this prison account is funded by relatives on the outside or else by taking a job here on the inside (the kitchen is always hiring).

The abundance of comfort foods, the oatmeal cream pies and so on, may only indicate a sweet-tooth. Or this may point to a state of anxiety. He's probably never been locked up. The fact that he hoards tons of ramen noodles and packaged tuna, tells me that he's trying to live out of his box, that he doesn't go to chow with the others, that he's attempting to divorce himself from the prison life as much as possible. He's scared. That's my guess.

I find an untouched bible. The spine has never been cracked. A gift, then. I find no crosses or any other religious paraphernalia. I find no gang paraphernalia. No letters from friends, no pictures of friends. He's a loner. The only thing that matters to this kid is his family, his mother and sister and niece.

How far off am I? I don't know. I'll find out later when I chat with him. Often, it's a dull job. These pointless games can help.

In any case, I found no drugs, no tobacco...neither tattoo guns nor shanks. So I'm heading to Johnson's desk to fill out the paperwork that my search just generated when it becomes apparent that we may have a situation on our hands.

Johnson's alto voice rises to match that of a short, slender inmate—a fiery-bearded, skin-headed white supremacist of some sort (judging from his tattoos) who goes by a rather unoriginal moniker, 'Red.'

Apparently Red, an epileptic who has seizures occasionally, has been instructed by our medical department to go to Wishard, the downtown hospital we always use for inmates. I don't know if he's HIV-positive or what. I always think about that stuff when a physical confrontation is on the horizon. It'd be nice if we could have that kind of information. But apparently an inmate's right to privacy is more important than our health, than our own right to life.

Well it looks like Red doesn't feel like making that trip down to Wishard. As I draw near, I can hear Red saying, 'I told you, Sarg. I ain't goin.'

'The fuck you're not,' Johnson fires back.

'Write me up then. Like I give a shit.'

Johnson growls, 'You can stop eyeball-fuckin me right now.'

'Whatever. I'm goin back to my bunk.'

'You wanna play that game Red? Stop right there.'

'I ain't took a step. You can quit that yellin.'

'Go in the laundry room and get butt-naked. *Move.*'

We're allowed to strip-search the inmates whenever we feel like it (wait, that didn't sound right), without probable cause. Well, there is some probable cause. They're in prison and, as several old hands around here are fond of saying, none of these guys are in here for singing too loud in church.

Now then. As I mentioned earlier, thankfully, we can't get away with wantonly beating on these guys. As I also mentioned, it's hard to send a prisoner to segregation, especially if they're getting full over there. However, there's one notable exception. If an inmate refuses a search of any kind, the worst is assumed and that same inmate is promptly escorted to segregation by any means necessary.

So Johnson, by ordering Red to strip amid a swelling dispute, may have been driven by one of two motives (or both). First, he could be reasserting his authority...After all, other than beating a man, what greater exercise of immediate authority could there be, I mean, to make a man get naked against his will in front of other people? Forced nudity is to rape what foreplay is to consensual sex.

Secondly, Johnson might want to goad Red into a confrontation...not, necessarily, with the intent to hurt him—I've known Johnson too long to think he'd do that—but with the hope that Red will resist or refuse and therefore land himself in the hole for quite some time.

I never do this to inmates because, if for no other reason, I've had my ass beaten tremendously and steadily over the duration of several long minutes, as I spelled out earlier. Regardless, I don't think I'd do it anyway. It can be effective, don't get me wrong. I've seen Johnson get bad apples to the hole, bad apples who desperately needed some time alone but had remained just savvy enough to skirt the rules. Still, when you go around pissing off prisoners, they're bound to get even. And Johnson, although certainly no scholar, must know this at bottom.

Regardless, I back Johnson up and step into the laundry room. It stinks like gym socks. Red's already naked. Johnson's moving through all of his rehearsed lines, most of them plagiarized. My voice is about a thousand decibels softer than Johnson's.

 JOHNSON - This your first bit?
 RED - I been to County.
 JOHNSON - County? County? That ain't a bit. That's a country club for losers. I asked if this was your first bit. So is it??
 ME - The sergeant asked you a question.
 RED - Yeah, it's my first bit.
 JOHNSON - How long you been down?
 RED - Three months.
 JOHNSON - Three months?? Jesus Pig-Fuckin Christ! Young man, you're still shittin Big Mac's! Hey, quit ballin up yir fists. That's what they call a threatening gesture. Read yir rulebook. Now keep yir hands wide open, or I'll cuff yir ass right now. Fuck it, just turn around and face the wall. Face the wall! That's better. Now how much good time you got left?
 RED - Good time?
 ME - If you act up, how much time can the fine State of Indiana take away from you?
 RED - Three years.
 JOHNSON - You feel like doin *all* of it?
 RED - Course not. Man, I was just—
 ME - Red, you ever hear that little platitude "actions speak louder than words?" Ever heard that one?
 RED - Yeah. Everyone's heard that before.
 ME - You wanna die in prison, don't you?
 RED - Die here!? Hell no I don't wanna—

ME - Hold up. Wait a second. I have the floor now. You *do* want to die here. Despite anything coming off your lips, that's what your actions say. Fuck home. Fuck freedom. Fuck family. This dump is home for you, that's what your actions say.

JOHNSON - Did you see a sign for Burger King outside this prison?

ME - I think you heard the man.

RED - Yeah, I heard him all right.

JOHNSON - Did you?? Did you see a sign for Burger King flashing out front?

RED - No, I didn't see no sign. Look Sarg, I don't like your sarcasilasm.

ME - First of all, that's not even a word. I think you meant sarcasm. Have you signed up for a literacy course yet? They're free, in case you wondered.

JOHNSON - You know why you didn't see a Burger King sign out front? It's not there, because you don't get things your fuckin way. Guess what, you're incarcerated!

RED - Goddamnit I know that much.

ME - Really? You don't act like it. This can be a short bit...or a long one. That's up to you.

JOHNSON - Turn around. You see this? You see this son? This here is a pen. If you can't learn to respect this uniform, you better damn well learn to respect this pen. Because kid, it can *seriously* fuck you up...

THIS went on for a while.

Anyway, Red went to the custody building, then to medical, where he signed his medical refusal chit, as

Johnson had asked, shortly after Johnson had made it clear to him that if he didn't go and sign the form he would,

'...tear your shit up, then I'll tear your bunky's shit up and let him know why,' meaning, Johnson would search Red's property box, perhaps violently, and then extend the same favor to the ogre who sleeps above Red. From here, prison justice would unfurl in favor of the guards. It's all pretty stupid, I know, but if you don't set boundaries for new inmates, then your entire class of muscular kindergarteners will go berserk and people will wind up hurt.

As soon as Red gets back from medical, I can see that he looks shaken and rattled from what we just did to him. I feel bad. I don't want to, but I do. So I pull up next to him at the water fountain, entering into a classic good-cop/bad-cop mode, even though his affiliation with a white supremacist group, on a certain level, makes me want to slit his throat.

'You seem like a decent kid, Red, with a whole lot of life in front of you. The thing is, you're surrounded by prisoners...so you start to think their behavior is normal. It's not. That's why they're locked up. The goal isn't to act like a bad-ass...the goal here is to get out as soon as possible, right? Now let's go over a few ways you can get some education, pick up a trade...get some time-cuts and get out of here. And hopefully not come back. You gotta keep your eyes on the prize,' I say to him, quoting MLK to a white supremacist who merely shakes his head with vigilance, as if each word had been created for him.

AT nine-thirty, we count the prisoners and get the cleaning crews going. At eleven thirty, we call 'lights out' and count them again. This is when the shift really starts to drag.

I stare into space. I stare so hard it's a form of sleep. Now Christman comes back to the desk, sidles up to me, and proceeds to talk about the same old shit. He's fifty-something but looks sixty-something, with a scarecrow body and a thick horseshoe of silvery hair. At least I have the dignity and good sense to shave my head.

Christman is one kooky bastard with too many quirks and facial tics and speech aberrations to describe. I would genuinely like him if he wasn't so annoying, if he could make his sentences cohere more than fifty percent of the time. It's like I can tell that he used to be intelligent but then something seriously fucked him up...Whether quickly, like a small stroke, or slowly, like chemical dependency, I don't know. But something is definitely off.

I often get short with him. And then feel guilty. That's the cycle. It's easy to feel bad for the guy. He's a widower who looks for aged love on the Internet and claims to have a psychology degree.

His children, they don't want much to do with him...that's the impression I get. Regardless, Christman's dream is to buy an extended RV when he retires, then haul the grandkids from Disney World to the Grand Canyon, if I have that right. At least he has a dream. I guess that might be enough to keep you breathing in and out for a while.

Christman was a Baptist minister until a crisis of conscious caught up with him. Namely, he's a non-believer. But not an atheist, he'll have you know...He's now a mystic, he claims, whatever that means.

I sit in my chair and try to read my library book, *West of Rome*, but Christman keeps staring over my shoulder.

'Doc,' he says, 'Picture yourself on a sunny beach.'

'Sure thing,' I say, already growing irritated.

'See, you looked up. That means you were using the visual part of your brain to imagine it, understand? If you'd a looked left, then I woulda known you were using the recall part of your brain. Know why? I'll tell you why. It's cause of a thing called the grai—'

'I looked up because I was thinking...how many times is he going to tell me all this?'

'Nope. Now that there's cognitive. You woulda looked down.'

'I'm getting some coffee, you want some?'

It's been a long time since I've seen the ocean. Yeah, I can imagine a sunny beach all right...some place foreign, ideally, where some shirtless, swarthy young man with white teeth brings me an endless supply of chill-beaded Corona with lime, or whatever they drink there, while some honey-skinned angel incessantly rubs my feet as I slowly get burned and listen to the ocean hiss while debating whether or not to call up that wealthy divorcee, the one with a mink bra and a Finish accent from the night before.

Things were a lot better before I killed that poor bastard. Have I mentioned this?

AFTER the 2 a.m. count, the cards come out...Johnson heads up a round of euchre at his desk. Right now, a card game sounds perfect. Not mentally demanding. Far from. But it does require you to pay attention to colors and numbers and shapes and so on. It's a welcome distraction...For a while, I'm able to forget what a complete fucking train wreck my life is. Playing cards is like talking without talking.
'You won the deal.'
'Pass.'
'Pass.'
'Pass.'
'Pass.'
'Aw, what the hell. Hearts are trump.'
'Then it's your lead.'
'Lord, I'd be in good shape if we was playin poker.'
'Tell me about it.'
'Who laid that ace?'
'B-Ray.'
'Okay, who's got the right?'
'Uhp, must be buried.'
'Damn.'
And so on. No personal questions. Nothing is required of me other than a few perfunctory comments. Time passes.

I look across the desk and wonder...Maybe I could talk B-Ray into bed. I say this only in a fit of vague curiosity and languorous bravado, the kind that makes a man wonder if he can seduce a woman, even if he would never wish to do so in earnest. Do women do this too? I don't know.

If I'm still able to read such signs correctly, then, well, the way she looks at me….so often, so long…I can't think of it as purely benign.

Okay, here's what would happen. She'd only do it once, first of all. And she'd be ruined forever by the subsequent guilt. I bet she'd change over to the day shift, just to get away from me. Hardly seems worth it. Even if she weren't punctured by guilt, which, I know, she would be…any amorous involvement with B-Ray would reduce to rubble her maternal appeal. In fact, I feel curiously incestuous even entertaining such possibilities.

Besides, maybe I'm a complete fuck-up in life…in fact I know it…but I've never screwed anybody's wife except my own. Okay, ruled that one out. Moving on…

AT five-thirty in the morning, dehydrated from all the coffee, I count the prisoners again, recording their presence on a square piece of paper called a count slip.

Most of them are sleeping. I take my time, study their faces…I'm trying to determine which of these convicts might be kind enough to kill me for two thousand dollars, which is all I have.

On the back of a blank count-slip, I scrawl out a top-ten list, using only their initials. Now I hand one count slip to Johnson and put the other one in my pocket.

A PRISON YARD is never a cheery place.

But at six in the morning... in December, in the middle of Indiana...with moonlight bouncing off the razor wire...and with your frozen breath heaving out before your watering eyes as you make your way to a nondescript brick building, wondering just how fucked-up the holidays will be this year...well, it's a tad bit depressing.

We go through the usual rigmarole with the electronic doors, then bolt for the lobby. Out in the parking lot, people mutter good-byes or else shout them from their cars.

'See ya back in paradise.'
'Take it easy. And drive safe.'
'Merry Christmas, Ed.'
' Later.'
'Later shithead.'
'Tell Jemma I said howdy.'
'See y'all next week.'
'See ya fucker!'
'Merry Christmas.'
'Hey. Shoemaker. Don't forget to bring in that Earnhardt DVD.'
'Bye now.'
'Not if I see you first.' BlahBahBlah.

As I approach my piece-of-shit hatchback, I can hazily sense that I'll need to jack off soon. Not that I've been aroused by anything. Not that I'm looking forward to the ritual with any rapt expectancy. Not at all. I mean it's like the way you can sense a full bladder, for example, or when you know you need to shit, or when you could really use a bite to eat...yep, I can see a nice meaningless tug in my near future. It's about the only thing I look forward to any more, and I don't look forward to it very much.

Ah, fuck me running. I still haven't bought a scraper...so I set to work on my iced-over windshield with my state ID. Then I realize, there's nowhere I need to be, particularly, so I just start the car and let the defroster work while I read a book by dome-light. Having finished that book by Fante, I'm trudging through the first few pages of a Thomas Wolfe novel, *Look Homeward Angel*. Two things work against me. One, my mind's not been functioning so great, as I may've mentioned previously. And two, I'm battling a three-point font here. It's terrible. There should be a law against small font. Don't publishers know that reading is a visual encounter? That the layout of a page can make or break a reader's experience? I love the way this guy writes but I hate the actual physical book I'm holding.

So I throw the book in the back seat, knowing I'll never finish it. Because of the font, I mean. It's not Tommy's fault.

I check my phone. Four missed calls. All Cooper.

BY six-thirty in the morning, I'm rolling into the mostly empty parking lot of Dancer's, a strip club catering to firemen, cops, bums, and prison guards—horney men with irregular schedules.

The 'dancers' here work one of three shifts, morning, afternoon, and evening. You get the idea.

They close at 2 a.m., and open back up at six...just in time for guys like me, coming off the graveyard shift.

Outside, the sun's probably coming up by now. But inside this hopeless urban grotto, it could be midnight.

I don't go in much for titty bars. Personally, I don't think of strippers as the only victims. Some are predators who view us, the loveless men of Indianapolis, as their prey. Long ago, I lost the suspension of disbelief one needs in order for strip clubs to do what they're designed to do. Once the illusion is gone, it's gone. There's no getting it back.

Among these young, tight-skinned sexual athletes, not even one fosters the slightest desire to feel me jack hammering away between those nubile thighs. And I can't deceive myself, even though I'd like to for a while. They want what little money I have left, and that's all. It makes me feel pathetic, used, a victim.

On the other hand, these women seem to love Cooper. There's something about cops and strippers. It's true. A cop uniform does something strange to them...it directly serenades their ovaries. But why? I don't know. Safety? Security? A lot of scumbags hunker down in titty joints. Besides which, maybe cops earn a decent wage compared to most patrons. Who knows. But strippers sure go in for cops. Especially Cooper. His face looks a lot younger than it is. Plus, he's fun. Witty. Smart...but able to communicate with them effectively, on multiple levels. He's up on the music, up on the lingo.

There's nothing to do while I wait for Coop except watch the lone dancer on stage. She's black, like both of my ex-wives. There's no specific reason I can think of for that, other than proximity. Or maybe luck. I love blonds and redheads and Taiwanese and on, and on. In this department, I am a truly Equal Opportunity employer. Yeah, so I've only slept with two black women...I just happened to marry them both.

Actually, I never thought of my first wife as black. Or white. Or any particular color. Claudette was just Claudette, the woman I loved. Her features, as well as her deportment and parlance, rebelled against classification. Her lips weren't simply full, they were gigantic...yet her skin was rather faint, even for a mulatto, if I'm still allowed to use that word. She never knew her father but her mother, a curvaceous though idiotic redhead, had given her a patch of freckles on each cheek. Claudette's tear-shaped hazel eyes seemed redolent of ancient Egyptians; or rather, of how ancient Egyptians depicted their nobility through art.

I remember one time, it was right after we'd finished making love—gingerly, because she was five months pregnant—she rolled over and whispered,

'Baby, might sound crazy but...sometimes, I forget you're white.'

'What do you mean?'

'I don't know.'

But I think maybe I do know what she meant. If you truly know and love someone, over time, notions of race and ethnicity seem so trivial and idiotic and, finally, damn-near non-existent.

AS I wait for Cooper to show up, I reply to a text message from Big Ed Smithe, a big-hearted bad-ass brother I used to work with at the joint. When I met Big Ed, he was a struggling entrepreneur and only did the prison gig to keep a stable paycheck and some health insurance for his family. Autonomy, that's what he burned for above all else. He detested the very concept of a boss. He bristled. He loathed the idea of being ruled and he never went very far to hide this fact from anyone, including sergeants and lieutenants and captains.

Well his seafood restaurant flopped. So did the coin-operated car wash. But he made it, eventually, and now he runs a lucrative second-hand sporting gear store over on Georgetown Road. He also runs a security company on the side. He's humble, so it's hard to tell, but I sort of get the idea that he's filthy goddamn rich, what with all of his kids going to Park Tudor now. I used to pop into his shop once in a while. But, as with most of my old friends, we've lost touch.

Even so, I still think about Big Ed quite often. I guess you could say I miss him. In a way, he's dead. I mean dead to me. When he left the joint to strike out on his own, Christman filled his spot and that was that.

More than anything else, I think friendship—and any other love, for that matter—feeds itself on time. Pure and simple. And I spent heaps of it with Big Ed. There was a period during which I felt closer to Ed than to any other human on Earth. Twelve hour shifts. Night after night. We talked about everything. We got into a few scrapes. Helped each other out. I was with him when his father got cancer, whittled away to nothing, and died. He kept me going during my second divorce. I suppose...well, I suppose I loved Big Ed.

But I called him up a couple months ago and it was like talking to a stranger. I guess friends come and go, while loneliness accumulates. Our friendship has been reduced to the occasional text message or E-greeting card.

NOW I look up from my phone and see Cooper hovering over me with a long-neck Bud in each hand. He plunks one down in front of me, reaches over the table and gives me a one-armed hug.

'Holy Ass! You actually agreed to meet me out!"

Coop looks like a drug dealer, like a heavyset drug dealer in his late twenties with silver rings in both ears and another one protruding from his left eyebrow. His head is also shaved...like mine, only not so close. He's not going bald. And he keeps enough stubble up there to tell you that. His goatee looks thicker than usual. I wish I had a goatee. I'm not allowed to have one at the prison. A bald man grows facial hair to communicate something to the world, 'I'm not a cancer patient or anything like that. See, I can grow hair...just not on my head.'

Like me, Cooper once had a pit-bull body. We used to hit the weights six days a week. We were serious with it. Egg whites. Spreadsheets. Vanity, sometimes of the enjoyable kind. Weird smelling farts due to supplements from GNC. And while I've slimmed down to the point of frail androgyny, he's kept his bulk, though a good bit of it has turned to flab. Our bodies have both devolved, though in opposite directions.

If I had to summarize this guy, which is never fair, I'd say he's a young John Belushi with features rounded by overeating and too much booze. Yet not a single wrinkle on his face! He's a genuine wild man, but never in a malicious way. His closets are stuffed with Elvis costumes, with afro wigs and fake beards, with Village People outfits and retro-clothes...fake poop...whoopee cushions. The whole bit. He's a committed prankster, always ready to spring a shameless gag on the unsuspecting.

In a lot of ways he never grew up. And because of this, I think, children absolutely adore him. My own son seems more enamored with Cooper than he does with me. Coop often goes with me, and whichever kid I have, when we go to the zoo or the mall or wherever. Needless to say, some people give us sideways...or rather backwards looks; like we're gay, like we're out with our adopted kid or something. I don't get offended. It's not that. It's just...I find such assumptions ignorant of our times and therefore irksome.

This morning, Coop looks pretty beat up. Like he could use some sleep. He pulls up an ashtray and gets to work on a fresh pack of Marlboro Lights.

He smiles, 'So talk to me.'

'You called me,' I laugh a little. He wants to talk. But, like me, he's a reticent bastard. He smiles some more. We both know the deal. Something's on his mind. Finally, he coughs it up.

'State police called me yesterday. Middle of the day...'

'Yeah?'

'Yeah, they picked up my old man again.'

'How uh...how bad off was he?'

'Falling down. Said he almost hit a guard rail.'

'Jesus. Any paperwork? Is he...?'

'Of course not. Cop-to-cop. Professional courtesy. But here's the good part. The kicker. I get home, you know, just hoping to chill for a minute. But Sarah, she'd left some mail on the bed for me. So, to cut it short...they turned my package down.'

'What, the DEA?'

He nods in the affirmative, still maintaining a smile somehow.

'How could...You're so...so qualified, brother. I don't get it.'

'I don't know if you'll remember,' he says, 'don't know if I told you, but back in the day I was VP of my fraternity...'

'Yeah, I remember that. I remember the photo with the...'

'We got busted with kegs once. By the cops. The president was gone somewhere. I was the man that night. So we got raided, right, and whatever...my name landed in the report. Like, forever. It's there. I wasn't prosecuted or anything. Like it really matters...I was still arrested for contributing to the delinquency of a minor. The DEA's out. FBI's out. I'm stuck.'

'Jesus that..That fucken sucks.'

'Yeah.'

'Just because you got busted at some frat party a million years ago?'

'Yeah,' he says. 'It's like the crayon that gets left in dryer...you forget about it...you think it's harmless, but when it turns up...I don't know. What can you do?'

'What a...Jesus, what a stupid thing to hold you up.'

'Yeah and the deal is, if I would've remembered it, I would've reported it. But like... the way it went, it looks like I lied.'

His smile evaporates and though his tone of voice isn't grim, it's grim for him.

'Bro,' he says, exhaling a cone of bluish smoke, 'I'm suffocating. To death. With the...the job, man. The whole thing. It's like this. I don't want to brag, I don't want to...'

'Coop, just spill it.'

'It's...I've whipped this city's baddest asses. I've done all the big cases, federal cases. Everything's...everything's starting to repeat. Know what I mean? Blah blah blah blah blah blah. Groundhog Day. See what I'm saying?'

'Sure. So...switchover. Try homicide.'

'Yeah...no man, I've thought about that. Fuck that. In Indy? You know who's killing who? Drug dealers are killing drug dealers. Why move downstream? I don't want to sound like a dick but...one drug dealer kills another...who cares?? In a way, you know. You know what I mean, I mean why not stop the drugs? Constrict supply. See what I'm saying? Stop kids from getting hooked, see what I'm...Murder? In Indy? That's all downstream. Know what I mean?'

'Of course. What about...I don't know, what about sex crimes?'

'Well sure. No doubt, you're doing the right thing, right? But I just, with kids, you know how it is...it's not the kinda job I could leave at the office. Not hardly bro. I know those guys. It fucks them up.'

'I can see that...'

Coop sighs deeply, involuntarily. But again, with a smile. I root through my brain, searching for some best-friend mumbo-jumbo. We've been friends so long, I have to stick to some version of the truth, which dwindles my ability to say anything that might be life-affirming or at least reassuring.

'Coop. Listen. You have a great life. Great wife. Great son. Another one on the way. Great house. Good money. You made it, brother. You left the ghetto way behind you. There's nothing left to worry about except staying alive on the street. That's your problem, you won't let yourself acknowledge that you've really made it. I'm being objective here...Don't get greedy...you have a great life.'

'It's...yeah, I'll admit that I...It's not...Yeah. Yes. Yes, it's a great life. But it's not exactly the one I want, know what I mean?'

'Yeah but....'

'I've never left Indiana. My whole life, right here in Indy-fucking-Anna. It's like I'll never...'

An over-tanned blonde comes over, a blonde with nipples long enough to tie into granny knots. She throws her scrawny ass in Cooper's lap.

'What's up sugar?' she says with a wink in her voice.

'January, sha*zam*! Damn, I like the getup, the way it...it's on-point.'

'Had to buy it myself. The cheap-asses here won't help out with your wardrobe. You wanna private dance?'

'Can't. I'm working.'

'Seems like you're always working, ainchya?'

'More or less. You still cribbin over in Stringtown?'

'Yeah, for now.'

'You ever heard of a cat named Tom Morrow, goes by Tommy Two-Thumbs?'

Her sweat-laced perfume, mingling with the musk of her tiny black thong, makes this stripper smell like she's already been screwed within the last ten minutes. Her scent mixes with our beer and Cooper's smoke and manages to turn my stomach. She's all over him.

He won't do anything. He's never cheated. Never will. He's had plenty of opportunities, given the liberties of being an undercover cop. But he just bleeds these women for information and maybe a little self-validation...then he goes home to his wife...raring to go, I'd imagine.

I worry about him. He's been drinking more than usual since he found out about his dad, Harold. Turns out Harold isn't Cooper's father. Not biologically. His real father was a drug dealer who drowned to death in the White River. Quaaludes, I think. While pregnant with Cooper, his mother married Harold, who raised Cooper like his own. So he recently found out that half of his uncles and so forth aren't even related to him, technically speaking.

'It's all pretty Jerry Springer,' Cooper admitted.

I asked him why all this came out after so many years. It happened like this. Harold cheated, so his parents separated. A banal enough story. Except that, during some kitchen sink argument, his mother had said to Harold,

'...then you'd better tell Chris the truth before I do,' or words to this effect.

His folks are back together. They fight constantly. Coop and his two sisters are stuck in the middle. I imagine that's another compelling reason to go fed, to get with the FBI or whoever, so he can leave Indy for a while and get away from all this shit, all the family drama.

Not a good scene for Cooper, maybe, but here's why I think he'll be okay. First, permit me to digress. I used to work the 'Control Room' with an old prison guard named Sylvia Watkins. From time to time, she'd bring in her ceramic bric-a-brac. And that's how I think of it, of Cooper's character. See, once a clay poodle or a cat has been shaped and fired in the kiln, it's a poodle or a cat forever. Ditto for a statue or for an ashtray and so on. It's done. Sure, you can paint whatever it is you've made and alter its appearance just a tad. But a poodle, once the clay's been fired, will never be a cat.

And so Cooper had a good childhood, despite the neighborhood. His parents were loving, even though Harold was gruff. Coop and his sisters, they were always close. At least one set of grandparents always lived with them. Everyone pulled together. He never wanted for clothes or even for a car. Coop always had pocket money. His mother loved him to death. He was happy.

His earliest perceptions told him that the world was a good place or, at a minimum, a good time could be had here. His young adulthood, his happy marriage, the ease with which his career ascended and accelerated...it all reinforced this perception. He is formed.

I could be wrong, certainly. But I think when bad things happen to him, they're always filtered through a prism that spits out rainbows. Bad things are reduced and neatly fitted into this world of his that ain't so bad. He'll be okay. He'll always be okay. Some people are just like that.

◎

MY tenuously existing hovel, with its leaking pipes, dripping faucet, imploding roof and thin drafty walls, serves as an accurate picture of my soul...if I have a soul.

My address is 22 ½ North Holmes Avenue. How, might you ask, does a house—mind you, not an apartment—end up with such an unusual address?

Mr. Demes, who originally built the house I'm 'living' in for his son, resides at 22 North Holmes

Avenue. He built this house in his backyard, with its front porch facing the alley. When I look directly out my front window, I see a garbage can next to a rusted garage door. It's quite a lovely view at sunset...especially on weekends, when teenaged drunks decide to brown-bag it in the alley, right in front of my house, pissing and puking everywhere but in a toilet.

Anyway. Mr. Demes worked for Olin Brass until he retired. His son Derrick moved to California to be an actor. He was blown to bits in one of the Triple X movies. Not in reality. Just for the part. So far, this one bit part remains his only claim to fame, I gather.

Now when Derrick left home, Mr. Demes sold the house to someone who then sold the house to someone who sold the house to someone who rented it out for a while, before allowing it to be foreclosed upon. I can't see how that happened. The mortgage payments had to be something like three hundred bucks a month. Or less. Regardless, it was foreclosed upon.

And then the city government, in a feeble attempt at gentrification, had for some time been purchasing such eyesores from credit unions and banks. After my divorce from Cassandra, my second wife, I lived with my mother for almost two years. Then the government sold me this house for a dollar, on the condition that I put at least ten thousand dollars into this dump before selling it. But I've already spent more than that just trying to keep this lemon from falling to pieces.

My house, if I can call it that, is basically one room. There's the family room—again, if I can call it that—

where a TV that Coop gave me sits on top of a stereo that snaps and crackles because the speaker wires are screwed. No cable TV, it goes without saying. This room is paneled with some slapdash, paper-thin bullshit. And there's a used couch that stinks of mildew, plus some cheap flimsy shit from Value City, the surfaces of which tend to collect dust, and some yellowing magazines that my beloved father sends me as birthday gifts.

Well, the bedroom contains a bed all right, but it's little more than an offshoot of the family room. The shotgun kitchen, distinguished as such only by appliances, is the first room into which anyone would step upon entering my sty.

I look around this dump and have to ask myself why the fuck I ever moved in here. Clearly this goes on the list I keep, that is, the growing list of amazingly dumb life choices. This house ranks somewhere in the middle, I guess.

The truth is, I enjoyed living with my mother. She's blind, as I said, so I constantly had to wipe up messes she didn't see, and she smoked all the time, but I was never really that bothered by it, since that's how I grew up anyway. Claudette, my first wife, she picked up smoking after she'd had Gretchen. She turned out to be a nurse. She quit eventually. Smoking, not working. She's still a nurse, a cardiac nurse.

Anyway. The point is, Mom and I got along well. And I think we both benefited from living with someone too. But pride got in the way. To me, there was something inherently creepy about a man in his thirties who still lived with his mother. I felt like a loser, like some kind of Norman Bates character. The Internet tells me that in Asia, as well as some Mediterranean nations, it's common to live with your parents if you're not married. Or even if you are married. But, in America, this seems to be the hallmark of Loserdom.

So anyway. The problem with me buying a fixer-upper is, I'm not a very good fixer-upper. Further, I hate asking anyone for help. The light Pergo flooring, for which I ran out of money, clashes with the original (now rotting) hardwood floorboards in the family room. A quarter inch gap separates the two. I lose change through it sometimes.

The gray tile floor in the kitchen was laid unevenly and, when it rains, if I don't put out buckets and bowls in time, it gathers puddles from the numerous leaks in my roof.

I don't have a shower, just a yellowing tub with one of those pathetic rubber hoses you shove against the faucet. Oh, and the heater sucks…so, in the winter, all you get is a lukewarm trickle, more like a Labrador pissing on your head than anything else. It's like the Third World, I swear to God.

Coop helped me wire the electricity…well, he wired it while I kept him company and replaced his empty bottles of Bud. I don't want to tell him that a light bulb can't survive longer than a few hours in there. Something's not quite right, I guess. Too much amperage? Voltage? I don't know. I shave my face and head every other day using only the light that spills in from the kitchen.

If I were overseas, Down and Out in Paris like Orwell, say, with a foreign culture as my life's antagonist, then there might be something redeemable about my squalid hovel here.

But I'm not. There's really no point to this...it's certainly not building toward something. If there was a lesson to be learned, I learned it long ago.

And if I were peripatetic, I wouldn't mind living like this...if I was backpacking through Europe, or living some Zen lifestyle like the dude from Kung Foo or whatever.

Such is not the case. My present state feels pretty permanent, if permanent's the word.

If I were suffering for my art, as in the novel Hunger, or like Van Gogh in that dingy fucked up apartment of his, then at least I could feel that my life of squalor could be exchanged someday for a work of art, something durable, worthwhile, with its own intrinsic and irreducible value. But that's not how it is. I'm just trying to hold on—to what or why, well, I just don't know.

IT'S nine in the morning and I just got home from Dancer's after driving quite illegally, having achieved this illegal status by drinking with a cop all morning.

Cleo jumps up, hooks a paw on each of my hips. I used to discourage this practice yet it so resembles a human hug that I let it pass. My mother kept me alive through my second divorce. My dog kept me alive through these last few months. Pathetic, really, but there it is.

When Coop called, I forgot about the dog, so there's a hot pile of shit in front of the couch. Not her fault, so I don't even mention it to her. She must've been in pain. I take her outside in case she has anything else to get rid of, in case she needs to go into extra innings.

My yard, if I can call it that, is sectioned off from three backyards and the alley by a chain-link fence that Cooper helped me to put in. The fence is in remarkable condition relative to the house itself. Cleo's piss audibly splatters off the frozen earth, not yet covered with snow. And now, while she paces the .001 acres available to her, searching for the one swath of worthless tundra that she's not shat upon already this week, I call Cooper to see if he's okay. No answer.

I could go to bed, I guess. I usually do around this time. But I think I'll stay up, since I need to drive to Portage tomorrow morning. Better get on a somewhat normal sleeping cycle. Besides, Cleo could use a walk.

◎

As I round the corner, coming back to the house from walking the dog, I see something so unwelcome that I don't know whether I'm supposed to go lion or go ostrich. So I just...I don't know...I just freeze, staring at this thing the way a future meal might stare at the bright light offered by an angler fish...Is that really what I think it is???...Yep, Dad's Volvo, parked in the alley, in front of my shit box of a house. I haven't seen this prick for a year, maybe two. And I'm not exactly thrilled with the prospect of a reunion.

I walk into the house, my house, and there he is, seated at the head of the table with his reading glasses on…his feet propped up on the kitchen table…thumbing through my paperback copy of *A Brief History of Time* by Stephen Hawking, which I read on the toilet, so…

Cleo growls. The black hair along her neck stands up. I pull on the leash. My father is the only human being she has ever bitten. She nipped him, once, during Thanksgiving, about three or four years ago.

He looks at Cleo, not moving an inch, simply staring her down, because he's a dick who thrives on confrontation. I think about letting her go but instead I lock her in the bathroom. She maintains a low steady growl through the paper-thin door.

I return to the kitchen and throw my keys on the counter.

'So when'd you start breaking into people's homes?'

'Good to see you too, son.'

'Why are you here?'

'To wish you a Happy Birthday.'

'It was last week, but thanks."

'I was out of the country.'

'Would you mind taking your feet off the table? That's where I eat sometimes.'

'I don't know how you do it,' he says, removing his feet and then his glasses, 'This coffee is pure swamp water, if you ask my opinion.'

'How'd you get in?'

'The key was under the mat.'

'Yeah. For me, not for you.'

'Look, I just want to talk.'

I pour myself a cup of coffee. I thought I was out, so Dad must've rooted around in my freezer and found something way in the back. I take a good look at my father, so dashing and dapper...Dr. Weimer...he looks great for his age, which is fifty-nine.

He's still taller than me, the bastard...still has more hair, too, albeit gray. Muscular and well-groomed, impeccably dressed, wearing perfectly creased J-Crew khaki pants and his tailor-made electric-blue dress shirt with its funky fly-away collar, a crisp new shirt further embellished by French cuffs boasting sterling silver cufflinks with diamond studs...all of this, no doubt, had been picked out by my stepmother, Linda, who has no qualms about spending my father's money, which is more or less the glue that keeps their childless marriage together.

'You blocked my phone number.'

'You kept waking me up. I work the night shift. This simple fact has never fully penetrated your mind.'

'You also blocked my email address.'

'Did I?' This I say with mocked surprise as I sit down across from this aging czar of a man, feeling like there's a bat or a rodent in my house, and I just want to get rid of it somehow.

'I had no choice. I had to drop in on you like this.'

'No choice, eh?'

'I've been worried about you.'

'You? Worried?? Not likely. Unless you have a brain tumor or something. Do you have a brain tumor?'

Dad slides a gift-wrapped object across the kitchen table. 'Happy Birthday.'

I shake my head no.

'Will you just open it?'

Curiosity gets the better of me. For the last ten years or so, he's given me a hundred dollar check for every occasion that called for a present. Plus a magazine. But a gift, an actual gift....well, this happens to be a new one on me. So, okay, I open the package.

It's a picture. A big a framed picture. In this picture, I'm nineteen-years-old and shockingly attractive, I have to say. Handsome. Strong. Happy. Still married to Claudette. Still looking cheerily toward the future.

Dad and I were on top of a snow-covered peak when this picture was taken, down in Paoli, one of the only places in Indiana where you can ski. Back then, he and Linda had been arguing. They had separated for the first time, which was the only time that divorce seemed like a real possibility. This period in our history was swollen with possibilities; for a while, he was a model father and grandfather. It lasted about six months. Promises were made and broken. Lawyers got involved. He and Linda got back together and that was that.

Hunched over the kitchen table, I study this photograph, feeling strange…and angry, and sad, and sick with nostalgia. It had been a happy time, a time of closeness. But the reason this singular photo remains so potent is because there are no others like it. It was, after all, an isolated event...our only father/son trip.

Dad reads my face, reaching the wrong conclusions; namely, that I am pleased and touched.

'Wish we could've had more moments like that.'

'I used to wish that too, Dad.'

'Used to?'

'I quit thinking about it. The past is immutable. Everyone knows that.'

'When'd you become such a defeatist?'

'The past is immutable. That's a statement of fact, not opinion.'

'And look at this place. It's a pigsty! My only boy is living like a pauper!'

'Technically, Pop, I think I *am* a pauper.'

'And whose fault is that?'

'Mine I guess. But I had some help. Or rather, I didn't have any.'

'Help? You mean from me, I suppose.'

'For example.'

'That's the kind of weak mindset that got you into this mess. That's the language of your commie left-wing victocrats. Listen. What Mao and Stalin did through bloodshed, the Democrats have accomplished without ever firing a shot.'

'Oh, give it a rest. If you came to talk politics, you may as well know...I'm completely apolitical now. *Completely.*'

'I don't believe that, that anyone can truly be apolitical. But no, I didn't come to talk politics.'

'What then? Please, please tell me all about your safari, or your sailing trip, or wherever the hell you just got back from. I'd love to hear all about it.'

'Look at you. You're a mess! A prison guard? At your age?? With your potential? What have you done to yourself?'

'Well, if you really wanna talk about it...It might've helped, you know, if you would've paid for college. Like you said you would. I might've been someone. Maybe not. But maybe...'

'Hey look...When your grandfather got kicked off the farm, he nearly starved to death. He nearly froze to death in that cabin with his brother. But he pulled himself up by the bootstraps. That's what's wrong with your generation. You stand on street corners, looking for alms...Men like you, you're always looking for a handout.'

'First of all, Grandpa was rescued by the war. Nothing else. When he came back, he had the GI Bill. And before you pontificate any further, he also put your ass through school. He paid for your undergrad degree. He paid for the first year of med school...and, when you flunked out, he paid for dental school too. I mean, Jesus...'

'I didn't flunk out...I got hit by a car!'

'Either way, he paid for every bit of your school. He set you up with your practice when you left the Army. What else could you want? He even paid for your first plane!'

'Is that a crime?'

'And Grandma told me he gave you a stipend until the day he died. A fucking allowance? For a grown-ass man?'

'Hey. I put a lot of hours in, to get my practice going. It didn't grow itself, you know. Give me some credit, okay?'

'Of course. Of course I'll admit that you've accomplished a lot...not as a human, maybe, but as a professional.'

'Ha! Here we go. What else?'

'It's just....Just don't give me that bullshit about pulling yourself up by your bootstraps. You're a cosseted only child who never passed the torch...'

'The torch? What torch? Let's be clear.'

'I mean you had a silver spoon. Mine was made of, I don't know, scrap metal! It wouldn't really bother me that I went to the shittiest school in the entire state of Indiana....Except you had all the support in the world, when you were growing up. A kid expects his father to give him as much or more support than he received. Not less, or a lot less. You know?'

'Oh, boo-hoo.'

'Just get out,' I say, feeling like I'm seventeen again.

He doesn't budge. His face hardens.

'I mean it, take off.'

He stands up to his full height. Instinctively, I also stand up. Clearly, we would like nothing better than to strike one another, than to cause one another physical harm. This seems obvious. We should've done this ten years ago, when we were closer in age, when I could've knocked his teeth down his throat and not felt guilty in the least about doing so. God knows I owe him for enough beatings.

'Well,' I say, deciding that I lack the fortitude to strike an older man. 'There's the door. Don't let it hit you in the ass.'

'You're emotionally spoiled. You know that?'

'Emotionally *huh*?'

'Your mother spoiled you. That's your problem.'

'Maybe. But you did quite the opposite.'

'Ahhh... So now you blame *me* for your complete failure in life. Is that it?'

'A little, yeah. I spread it around. But sure, I blame you quite a bit. You're number two, right after me.'

'You think you hate me, but you don't...'

'That's the funny thing. For a guy like you, for a guy who's never loved, you wouldn't know what hate is. Because those two things are mirror images. All you know is selfishness and survival. Oddly enough, the older I get, the more I respect that about you. But I don't have to like it.'

'Jesus Christ, Wesley. You are such a *weakling*.' He says this word with such verve, making it sound like the worst insult in the English language, puffing up his chest, and then saying the word one last time, as if to remind me that I am nothing and that nothing is his fault.

'*Weakling*.'

'You're probably right, Daddy dearest. Maybe I am a weakling. The thought has certainly crossed my mind. But me, I would never let my second wife get in the way of my relationship with my kids. You're such a brute...you're so fucking macho but...But all you do is win the battles. You've lost the war. You're just another Hannibal, but instead of an eyeball, you lost entire...

'I don't see the connection. Nor do I see why you insist on speaking unclearly, in clumsy metaphors.'

'No one loves you! That's the bottom line. Can't you see that?'

'Okay, things got all turned around. I'll admit that much. But you kids, you weren't exactly accommodating. Both of you were very cruel to Linda. You were a couple of real assholes, if you wanna know the truth.'

'I wasn't cruel. I reacted to her cruelty. And anyway...I was eight. If things got off on the wrong foot, I hardly think it's my fault. Or Wendy's either. The thing with adults is, they're supposed to try to be adults.'

'I thought I'd get more understanding from you. After all, you're not exactly an award-winning father yourself.'

'Probably not,' I admit, feeling stung by the truth of his ruthless attack. 'But I try. I *do* try, believe it or not. And there's the difference.'

'So what now? What do you want, son? What do you want from me? Spell it out!'

'Dad, I want you to listen. Now listen...I've said things in the past that were intended to hurt you. Back when I used to care. Back when I thought that by hurting you I might provoke a reaction...a way forward, or whatever. But I know it's hopeless now. And you should too. So....So, I'm telling you, and I mean it, that all I want from you is nothing. I never want to see you again. Not because I want to hurt you, but because I really just never want to see you again. Okay?'

'Oh you're just being maudlin...As usual.'

'No. I mean it. I just want to be left alone. Okay? Not because I hate you, even if I do, but simply because I detest your company.'

Pause.

'You *ungrateful* son of a bitch.'

'And I should be grateful for...what? Child support?? The court made you fork it over and we still wound up on food stamps.'

'No one told your mother to marry a bum. And no matter what, I'm still your father.'

'Father??? You're a fucking sperm donor. That's how Wendy and I refer to you. Did you know that? She'll call me up and say hey, heard from the *sperm donor* lately? And I'll say no, Sis, I think he's off on another cruise to..."

In typical Great Santini fashion, Dad decides to throw a tantrum...he picks up my birthday gift, and he bashes this thing on the kitchen table, shattering it into a thousand shards of glass...par for the course...and then he pulls from his leather wallet a check he had written out to me...Now he rips it into pieces...His rage is so much greater than the resistance offered by that paper check...the effect is mildly comedic.

On his way out, he slams the door so hard he splits the doorframe. I wrangle the door open in order to castigate him as he fumes toward his luxury sedan with its heated seats, sun roof, and dual air bags.

'You broke my door, you fuckin prick!'

'You're no son of mine! You are no son of mine!'

The car door slams shut. The Volvo tears down the alley. I can still see him screaming and gesturing.

I go back into the house and sweep up the glass, going back over the whole scene in my head, wishing I had done or said this or that.

Then I open the bathroom door and give Cleo a can of tuna to calm her down as I piece the check back together. Just as I had guessed, the check had been made out for one hundred dollars.

Feeling numb instead of upset, I think about calling Wendy and relaying this event. But I don't have the energy. She would expect to put things into context, to discuss the whole history of our shared past. No. I just don't have the energy for that.

Instead, I'd really rather have some time alone, completely alone. Or rather...

BRIANA Banks and Nikita Blonde meet me for a sultry rendezvous, along with Christine Young, Bobbi Eden, Asia Carrera, Jada Fire, and countless other queens of the Internet.

Welcome to my love life. God bless the World Wide Web. Because I'm too cheap to pay for a quality site, I pass desultorily through various short clips, torn between the insincere misogyny and the howling lonesomeness that predicate the nature of my unattainable fantasies. With no Kleenex in the house, I reach for a dirty t-shirt on the floor, and then...

NOW that I've wrapped up that unrewarding project, I click on different sites about suicide rates. Lately, that's been my routine. Porn, then suicide.

So. Who's committed to doing themselves in? Apparently, Eastern Europe is way out in front. Especially Ukraine. France is up there, which I find surprising. Socialism must be as flawed as raw capitalism. Sweden just about ties with the U.S., which I also find surprising. Must be the weather, the lack of sunlight in the winter. Japan weighs in of course. They can barely resist jumping in front of those bullet trains! And I can see why New Zealanders snuff it, so isolated, so cut off from the great human current. Yeah, well, they just don't know how good they have it down there, how lucky they are to be cut off from the rest of us.

A lot of poor countries actually have low suicide rates, Brazil, Thailand, Mexico, Tajikistan. I'll go out on a limb here, make a wild guess and say the cultures in those countries must have anodynes to palliate the great disease of lonesomeness, time-tested anodynes like extended families, like vital communities and so on.

I don't know. I'm not a sociologist. I'm just a prison guard. But I think if you ranked nations according to their suicide rates, words like 'greatness' would certainly carry a different meaning.

AROUND three-thirty, I pick Mom up from work and take her back to her place. I've turned out to be such a needy, worthless, contemptible son. I actually let my mother, a blind woman, walk to work alone through this neighborhood.

Mom answers the phones for a state vocational rehabilitation center down on Sixteenth Street, next to a pawnshop. Years ago, when she could still see well enough to drive, Mom directed plays for the Edyvene Theater. *Glass Menagerie, Joseph and the Amazing Technicolor Dreamcoat, Raison in the Sun*, to name the few I remember off the top of my head. She was a respected director. Now she answers phones.

Mom uses her cane to get to work. Her dog, Chip, died of cancer last year and she can't bring herself to get another one. If she had to be at work even thirty minutes later, I could take her every day.

I always assumed I'd make a good living someday, that I'd take care of my mother in her old age. Hell, she wound up taking care of me

As we walk into her house, which I cleaned up yesterday, Mom bolts for the bathroom and I see that she's decked out the place with handmade Christmas decorations. I said she's blind, I know, which is more or less true. But she can still see light. And she can make out the rough outline of shapes.

She has this super-duper magnifier in the basement, where she makes her arts and crafts. She spends a good chunk of time down there, especially in the winter. Otherwise, she sits up here on the couch, croqueting afghans or else knitting sweaters while listening to audio books.

Mom is one-quarter Cherokee. She could easily pass for half. She has high cheekbones, very little gray hair and blank, searching blue eyes that rest in hammocks of darkened flesh, the only indicators of her advancing years other than her widening rear-end, which of course would tell you nothing unless you knew her as I did during her racquetball heyday, when she and my stepfather would drag my sister and me to the New Life gym every Saturday or so. She used to be very pretty and quite full of life.

Something's odd. The house doesn't reek of tobacco. I pour myself a cup of coffee and sit beside her on the couch. I have to admit, it feels nice to be in her presence, to be near.

'Hey, Ma, you quit smoking or something?'

'Oh, yes and no,' she says with an ornery tone.

'Ah, a duplicitous answer…just like a woman.'

She opens her mouth, shows me some bridgework and a yellow piece of gum under her tongue.

'It's not the unleaded kind.'

'Ah, so it's..."

'Nicotine replacement therapy,' she says.

Therapy? Again with the euphemisms. What in the fuck, pray tell, is happening to our language? What about, I don't know, Gum for Addicts?

'What made you finally pseudo-quit?'

'Um, cancer?' She says with a screwed up, ironic face.

'I know, but I mean. Why now?'

'I had a dreadful dream. Oh. Oh. Don't forget to take my presents up to Gretchen. They're on the counter.'
'Got it.'
'I do wish we could've had her for the holidays.'
'Yeah. Me too.'
'But if frogs had wings—'
'They wouldn't bump their butts.'

I shouldn't have completed her line. She'll never use it again. I rattle my keys.

She gives me the guilt-gaze. 'You plan on coming to the midnight service? Say yes, say yes, say yes.'

'Maybe. I don't know. Maybe...let me re-check my work schedule.'

'Katy Laird was asking about you last Sunday.'
'That a fact?'
'Mmm-hmm. Positively. My, she is such a darling.'
'I'm sure she is.'
'She is.'
'Not interested,' I say, with an air of finality (I hope).
'Are you ever going to settle down?'
'Ma, listen to your question...I did settle down. *Twice.*'
'Do I hear a broken record?'
'It's not a record that's been broken, Ma, it's...' then I stop just short of a dreadful cliché.
'Son, sweetheart, you need someone special in your life.'
'I have Cleo.'
'Dogs die awfully young.'
'Women leave.'

A long silence drops as Mom tries to outmaneuver me, searching for reasons I should be happy or at least reasons I should reasonably hope for happiness. Here's what I imagine she wants to say, 'I'm a divorcee and a widow myself, Wesley boy; you think that was easy? And look at me, I'm happy,' which is true I guess. But then again, she's on Prozac and she has her church. Don't get me wrong, I'd love to believe. It just never feels right when I try. It doesn't feel like a turning away. It feels like impotence.

Regardless, I'm not really scheduled to work on Christmas Eve. I have the day off, but I don't want to go through another matchmaking session with Mom's latest pick.

AS Mom opens the front door to let me out, tiny bells along the base of a homemade wreath jingle and reflexively I think of that old Jimmy Stewart flick, *It's A Wonderful Life*, which growing up had been part of our family's Christmas ritual. My mother must've had a similar thought. She's looks up with those searching blue eyes and says 'Another angel just earned her wings.'

Out on her tiny box of a porch, I bring Mom's head to my chest and hug her for a good long while. I kiss her on the forehead. She kisses me on the cheek.

As I slouch toward my piece of shit car, parked along the curb, between two other pieces of shit, she calls to me.

'Give Gretchen my love.'

'Of course.'

'Drive safe. Buckle up!'
'Don't worry.'

While scrapping my windshield with a debit card, a realization occurs to me...I love my mother, but it's just not enough. Not enough to keep me going, or rather, from leaving. It's not enough for me to justify hanging around here penniless, hopeless...utterly uninspired and stumbling over broken monuments in search of happier days that'll never be here.

I can feel the portentous strain along those last few mooring lines that so tenuously hold me to this world, to humanity, to the consumption of cheap processed foods, to the forty-minute commute through strip-mall hell, the paying of child support, the sleeping alone, the dilapidated house, the senseless masturbation, the withered friendships and my continual failure to reassign any meaning to my daily existence.

These mooring lines sing beneath their strain. They sing a plangent song of expectation, ready as they are to snap at a moment's notice. And I look to their snapping with remorse about my children, yes, but almost entirely without fear, without reservation, and with little doubt that, even allowing for the most minimal of standards, my life is simply not worth living.

MY car's heater must've died. I can see my breath in here. My cell phone rings. I hope it's Gretchen. It's not. It's Cooper.

'Hey,' I say.
'You gotta come over tonight.'

'What's up? Everything okay?'

'We're having some people over, sort of a pre-Christmas thing.'

'Naw man I—'

'Dude, I'm hooking you *up*. Sarah's got a new girlfriend...a math teacher. You should see this chick's ass. It could burn up a wet elephant. Sarah's been talking you up big time, told her all about you bro.'

'Jesus, I hope not. I know Sarah has the decency to lie.'

'Be at my place around nine. Earlier's better. Don't worry about booze I got it—'

'I can't.'

'What? You're off. I'm looking at your schedule.'

'Yeah, but I'm driving up to Portage tomorrow. I'll need some sleep.'

'Oh...That's cool...Tell Gretchen I said Merry Christmas. Hey, hey...Tell you what, just pop in for a drink. A quick one.'

I really don't know which is more irritating, my mother's attempts to foist women on me or Cooper's. Mom keeps introducing me to people who are in some way or another cracked or completely broken and clearly incompatible, like Katy Laird, who sings each hymn with vibrato conceit. I think embedded in her various potential mate selections lies the unspoken or even subliminal acknowledgement that her son is damaged goods, that he's a no-load broke-ass recluse with nothing going for him and little prospect of anything *ever* going for him.

Coop lands me in completely different yet equally difficult terrain...I always find myself outclassed. He lines me up with these attorneys he knows through work and once in a while Sarah corrals a teacher for me...hot chicks with education, self-esteem, and, worst of all, standards.

At least Cooper understands the shallow nature of initial attraction, which is to say, the women he tries to set me up with are invariably attractive, at least to some degree. More attractive than me, at any rate. But do you honestly think an attractive attorney wants anything to do with a twice-divorced prison guard? Give me a break. Only in the movies.

And besides, must every spiritual rescue come in the form of romantic love and romantic love alone? There has to be another way. If not a way in, then at least a way out, which is pretty much the way I've been leaning.

◎

HOLIDAY traffic has a chokehold on I-65 North. The center lane, the one I'm in, is barely moving. My rickety wipers form streaks of melted snow flurries across the windshield of my Civic. Looks like we're going to have a white Christmas after all. Comfort and joy. Comfort and joy.

Naturally, being trapped in this tiny metal box for the next four hours, I'll have to mull over last Christmas, just for fun. What a fucking catastrophe. I was up in Portage, of course, parked at the end of a cul-de-sac outside Claudette's Mac-mansion when the stage was set.

Over the course of six months, I had coordinated work and school schedules to bring together my son and my daughter and my mother. Granted, my kids aren't close. With the age difference and the distance, my daughter is more like an aunt to my son. Still. Okay, it wasn't the Cleavers, I'll give you that. But it was pleasant and I'll chalk it up as a minor triumph...I mean, to have summoned my small contorted family under one roof for a weekend. Over at Mom's we ate, and ate, and romped, and played the Disney version of Trivial Pursuit. The next day we went to a 3-D Pixar movie. All good fun.

That night, I slept on the damp, hard-ass floor of my mother's basement next to my kids, who slept on a futon. Already, at the age of thirteen, my daughter Gretchen snored. I don't think it's a stretch to say that it was bliss, truly bliss, to see my children sleeping four inches apart. So rare!

Well soon enough, Gretchen awoke with abdominal cramps. My daughter had her first period when she was eleven, so I knew it wasn't that. It was different, the way she described it. By around one in the morning, it became clear that my daughter needed medical attention...

'Appendicitis,' said the yummy blond ER doctor.

My daughter, though among the kindest people I know, isn't exactly stoic. She didn't take the news well but she took it. What choice did she have? No choice, so it's under the knife you go Sweetheart.

The bill came to seven thousand bucks. Okay, fine. I'm not an idiot. I have insurance, I thought. But I didn't. My policy with the State had changed, and no longer covered my daughter because she lived outside some arbitrary radius. I didn't panic. I called her mother.

'Claudette, listen. Don't freak-out but...'

As it turned out, Claudette and her husband—a doctor himself, by the way—had gone out of their way *not* to purchase a health insurance plan that extended its coverage beyond Portage because they were certain, as was I, that Gretchen, being a child, would rarely find herself far from home...unless she happened to be with me. And of course I had insurance, didn't I?

In short, we got stuck with the bill, which is why Claudette, on the 28th of December last year, walked outside her great big house to tap on my car window and talk things over. Generally, I try to avoid much direct contact.

It was night. I was sitting there in my car, idling, wallowing in self-pity, which is a habit I picked up after my second divorce. I'd been watching the green illuminated dials of my car radio, totally mesmerized, so Claudette's TapTapTap startled me. Relieved to see Claudette and not a stranger, I rolled down the window.

'What's up?'

'Feel like coming inside for a sec?'

A light rain had pasted her bangs to her forehead. Normally her bangs were poofy. She smelled great.

'What's up?' I repeated.

'What are you doing out here? Come in for a cup of coffee.'

'No thanks,' I said. 'Long drive ahead of me.'

'I have some Bailey's...Come on, don't make me stand out here getting soaked for Gods' sake. Come in.'

'Really, thank you. But no,' I said. I may've smiled. It was a matter of pride. I was still in love with Claudette and so I refused to view her perfectly rebuilt life. Pillar of salt, you know that old biblical fairy tale.

Laughing wryly at my stubbornness, she climbed into my piece of shit and shuffled old newspapers and coffee cups along the floorboard to make room for her tiny feet.

I shot her a quizzical glance, just hoping to be left alone. 'What are you doing?'

'What's it look like?' she said, raising her eyebrow theatrically.

Over her blue medical scrubs, she wore a funky trench coat made of horsehair; it wouldn't work for many people but it worked for her. Everything works for her.

Claudette's face, the most expressive I've ever seen, draws you in immediately...it magnifies words, nullifies others...goes where words can't go...provokes laughter, empathy, wistfulness and giddiness. In short, it captivates you beyond all hope of rescue.

She riveted her hazel eyes on mine. Her pupils, always large, looked enormous.

'Tell me. How are you doing, Wes?'

'Dandy.'

'Be honest with me, please. I need to know.'

'Why? Because you want to see how much better off you are...or because you'd like to know how sorry you should feel for me?'

'Wes...'

'Let's just skip it, okay?'

'I only wanted to talk. Maybe this was a mistake.'

'Oh, ya think?'

She reached for the door.

I grabbed her coat sleeve, almost involuntarily.

'Wait,' I said. 'Hold on. So...so I don't know, what've you been up to?'

Failing to contain a smile, she released the door handle and rummaged through her pockets for a piece of gum. Her coat filled the car with a faint animal scent that mixed with a smell left behind by the cucumbers that she'd recently removed from her eyelids, in keeping with her nightly ritual.

We chatted for a bit, initially resigned to safe topics. We talked about people we knew, mostly our families, and about her job at the Portage Community Hospital, where she worked with her husband, C.J. Swain, a bearded cardiologist who strikes me as rather effete and who, this particular evening, had been called back to work.

'I'm down to weekends,' she said. 'I only work Sundays and Saturdays.'

'Must be nice.'

She said it was, that it gave her plenty of time to spend with Gretchen and with her two younger daughters, Zoe and Bijou.

'That's great,' I said.

'And I've learned I actually have some talent. I can draw, did you know that?'

'Yeah, you used to make me those *amazing* birthday cards.'

'No. I mean I'm truly good. I've totally surprised myself...I'm taking a class on painting now, and we're about to move up to oils.'

'Sounds a bit more complex than those collages we used to make.'

'Oh, I loved our collages! Weren't they awesome? I still have them, actually...not all of them but...'

'Yeah. Hey, well I guess I should take off.'

'Not yet,' she said. 'Please. I need to talk to you. Talk talk.'

Instinctively, I put my bucket of shit in first gear and pulled away. Claudette gave me a suspicious glance.

'Where are we going?'

'I don't know...I thought it'd be better if Gretchen didn't see us out here. You know how she'd react.'

We idled at a truck stop until Claudette ordered me to go inside and pick up a six-pack. We hadn't talked like this in years, hadn't had a beer together since the divorce. So I was stunned to hear her casual proposal, to say the least, or to say more than the least...My heart was a nervous rodent, caged between my ribs.

'Let's go somewhere else,' she suggested.

'Where?'

'Turn left out of here...we bought a piano, did I tell you? Right; turn right...you know I always wanted to play but...okay, turn right again...park over there,' she tapped her fake red fingernail on the windshield.

A light rain had subsided and the ocean-like sibilant hiss of Lake Michigan could be heard spilling over the dunes, stained with moonlight. Claudette undid her seatbelt and turned to me, all pupils, with a wry puff of laughter. Her manner of speech, once a curious hybrid, now sounded pure suburban.

'You're not getting lucky here, buster. I only want to talk.'

'That's fine. Pass me a beer then.'

My eyes moved from her tiny hands, with their chipped fake nails, and involuntarily latched themselves to a confluence of wrinkled blue fabric between her slender legs...I couldn't help but think 'Jesus, our daughter came from there.' This thought was followed by another... 'So has the seed of another man.' It was an unsettling realization.

Claudette, after several divagations, finally started in. 'Wes I...I've been holding something for a long time...for an awfully long time...longer than I care to think of, really...And it's ripping me into pieces. It's like it's burning inside. That's not right. Poor choice of words. It's...it's not burning, it's smoldering...and it's always going to smolder. What am I trying to say? What am I...There's something I need to tell you, not tell you exactly...there's something I need to verbalize and it turns out you're the only one who could understand.'

'Shoot,' I said.

And then she told me...

She told me she loved me more than anyone else and that even though she could never be with me again, that she'd go on loving me forever. After I got over the shock, I started weeping. For the first time in ages. I wept moronically...uncontrollably. I clutched the steering wheel and shoved my face into it.

'I hate to say it Wes, but if you could've done that years ago, it all would've worked out.'

'Done what?' I asked the steering wheel.

'Cry. Let it go. Let it...let it out.'

'Yeah. I guess you're right.'

BACK in high school, Cooper and I had been tacitly bullied into a degenerate contest the summer before our senior year. We never should've played along.

A bunch of us were playing wiffle ball at night, under the lights at the Rodius Park tennis courts. When the game was over, a kid named Yellow pulled out a plastic liter of Dark Eyes vodka. No chaser. Just vodka. He took a pull and handed it to Cooper.

Yellow was a certified bully, an asshole's asshole, but a charismatic sort of ghetto thug. Having flunked twice, he was two years older than most of us, which, in retrospect, might explain why he towered over us and was the first to shave and so on.

After the wiffle ball game, Yellow huddled us up and delivered a mandate. 'Next year's our senior year. We gonna have us a pussy contest.' A what? That's right. Yellow's idea was that boys from our neighborhood would compete to see who could bed the most girls, one point each, with certain girls receiving and extra points if they were exceptionally attractive. In retrospect, yes, I am disgusted with myself for not walking away. It's well documented that the average American male, when young, suffers irreparably from the oppressive hegemony of peer group politics.

At the time, in any event, I lobbied to assign extra points to Claudette Cassidy, who was ultimately awarded five points, rather than the ten I'd asked for, not because she wasn't the sexiest girl in school, which she may've been, but because she wasn't exactly chaste or squeamish and therefore did not present the same challenge that others might. Before those award-winning tits had even stopped growing, Claudette had worked her way through all the popular older boys—black, white, brown, hipster, athlete, whatever. Quite the omnivore.

Early onset promiscuity. We certainly had that in common. I'd been broken in, if you will, by Paula Flandamire, who'd been a senior, the pervert, when I was still a freshman. Welcome to the ghetto...our parents are generally nowhere to be seen and therefore yes, we fuck young.

Now then. Washington High was an absolute dump with metal detectors and drug dogs and a uniformed security force and all of that amusing, inner-city stuff. However, someone or something—an arts endowment, perhaps—had installed a television set in every classroom so that the school could run a local televised news program, which it did. The Continental News Network.

We had a yearbook, a school paper, and a morning show. Not bad for a school with a fifty-percent dropout rate. Oh, we also had a brilliant Journalism/English teacher named Mrs. Benson. She's dead now, but it was in her Advanced Journalism class that I got to know Claudette Cassidy.

None of this coy, bullshit, damsel-in-distress stuff. She had a decent left hook. She was out-and-out hilarious. She could lower her voice and do a perfect impression of Clinton with some extra smarm thrown in. She had it down pat. She could sort of do Nixon, too, and the entire Malcolm X speech about Plymouth Rock.

Filming the morning news, we'd sabotage each other's shoots to no end...What I wouldn't give for those out-takes. She was also sharp as a tack and, like me at the time, interested in nearly everything...history, science, literature, whatever, you name it.

Under the auspices of friendship, Claudette and I began doing things outside class. We took long walks along the canal...went horseback riding a couple times...we pretended to know what the hell we were talking about at the Art Museum, and we spent an unwholesome amount of time blabbering with one another on the telephone each night. Meanwhile, of course, I repeatedly assured her that her far-away college boyfriend was cheating on her.

So. The day after Homecoming, we drove down to Brown County and went for a hike. The leaves were changing and the colors of the forest were so intense that the image is forever burnt into my picture memory. She led me from a side trail by the hand. With our fingers interlaced, we negotiated a steep incline. She led, I followed. We had never held hands before. It felt so nice.

'Where are we going?' I asked. She didn't respond.

Long story short, we consummated our friendship on a bed of fallen leaves. She then said something that only youth can get away with saying, something that today would fold me in half with histrionic laughter.

'It's never felt like that before.'

'I know,' I said. 'Maybe it's better if you actually have feelings?'

'Damn,' she said, peppering the side of my neck with light kisses, 'It's like Nagasaki down there. There's a mushroom cloud between my legs. I feel...I feel like maybe I'm falling...you know.'

'Yeah. I know.'

'Like, you don't sound too happy.'

'I am, I am. I mean, I am but I'm not,' I said.

'What's the matter?'

'We're in love, Claudette. This messes up the plan. This wasn't supposed to happen till I got to college. What if we end up at different schools? Won't that suck? And what if it turns out that even though--'

'Turns out there's a glitch in your master plan? You're a fool. You know that?'

'Of course,' I said, running my fingers through the loose curls of her hair, which grew around her face like bunches of grapes.

We did it again, without having separated in the first place. There were times, as we discovered ourselves and one another, when the symmetrical placement of her kisses and the studied measure of her caress seemed to emanate from the same mechanical, academic impulse that one might find in a laboratory, where some committed student might be carefully measuring a certain reagent into a beaker, for example. At times she tried too hard. At first, her attempts were a bit too studious, too measured, too academic and clinical. And then she learned to let go. Claudette excelled most as a lover when she simply allowed herself to be in love, when she wasn't trying to be sexual.

After that first afternoon in the woods, we started using rubbers, which, back then, didn't kill the mood. We did it constantly. Jesus, young appetites are gruesome, insatiable, fed by a boundless reservoir. Where'd it all go?

So much for Yellow's so-called 'booty contest,' I decided. Oh well, I wasn't the only one who flopped. Cooper seduced a redheaded junior named Sarah Davis. She'd also been worth five points. All it got him was a happy marriage. I don't think Sarah ever found out about the contest. As for Claudette, I got drunk at a Pacers game and told her the whole story, and all she said was, 'Damn! Five points…that's all?'

Anyway, let me say this. Okay, scratch that. Let me *first* say this. Proust, that depressed Frenchman, once wrote that the only paradise is the paradise lost. However lyrical his work may've been, I'd like to disagree with Proust, even if he's dead and can't defend his thesis.

From the time I fell in love with Claudette, until the time I killed a man, life was damn near rapturous. And I knew it. It didn't take retrospect for me to say, THOSE WERE GOOD TIMES. Nope. At the time, while in the moment, I said to myself as well as others, I AM HAPPY. I AM BLESSED. I LOVE MY WIFE. I LOVE MY LIFE. IT IS SO WORTH LIVING.

Claudette wasn't just my lover. She was also my best friend. I wish that on everyone. Sure, I used the money I made from bussing tables to buy her flowers or take her to a restaurant every chance I had. And sure, the mere sight of her silhouette in a summer dress was enough to make me pass out with cum in my shorts. But she was also my pal. She knocked books out of my hands and ran away snorting. She competed with me in and out of class. She whipped me at tennis. She made fun of my pimples, naming them on occasion. We were chums, pals, buddies. It all felt pretty close to perfect.

GETTING back to the story, if such things matter, we celebrated Thanksgiving together that year. We'd only been dating a short while but it was pretty obvious that only a bizarre, unpredictable outside force, like an asteroid or something, could separate us any time soon.

My family loved her instantly. I don't mean they approved, I mean my mother—as well as my sister, I think—would've remained in close contact with Claudette to this very day if I hadn't been so petulant, if, for the sake of my ego, I hadn't forbade them to keep in touch.

The day after Thanksgiving, Claudette and I went to the *Rocky Horror Picture Show* at a movie theater behind Lafayette Square. Sleet and freezing rain had kept away even the most diehard fans, which we weren't. It was the first and last time we ever watched that film together.

A middle-aged hippie couple sat four rows down from us. There may have been a few others, I can't remember. We started kissing and that led to what it leads to when you're seventeen and sitting in the back row of a nearly vacant movie theater. Like I said, Claudette wasn't what you'd call pure, or unsullied, or whatever. Certainly no angel. She was wearing a plaid pleated skirt to a rundown movie theater. No underwear. We're lucky we didn't get arrested.

After the movie ended, out in my Trans-Am, I was thrashing into her once again. But that wasn't enough. Jesus, we were insatiable. Later that night we drove to the stadium and did it on the fifty-yard-line. We both caught colds.

Okay, fast forward...the day after New Year's, around noon, we checked into a motel on Lafayette Road. We sniggeringly referred to this dump as The MO because the TEL in the neon MOTEL sign had burned out long ago. This wasn't our first time. We knew the place all right. But this time we weren't there for sex...we were there because of it.

Inside our usual room at The MO, Claudette left the bathroom door wide open, said she didn't want to be alone. I fought off the urge to vomit. As soon as the first droplet of piss hit that tiny cotton nub, it turned the brightest blue. It was like a PA announcement. Girl, You Are Pregnant!

We used protection every time, although I did, on occasion, treat myself to some unsheathed, preliminary prodding, which almost certainly was to blame.

'I knew it,' she said, her face fixed to the broken floor tiles. 'Why'd we even bother with this stupid test?'

'What do you want to do?'

'Not be pregnant.'

'I know but...what do you want to do *now*?'

'I don't know. What do you think?'

'I...what's on your mind?'

'Nothing.' She smiled.

'What? What're you smiling about?'

'Can you imagine telling our son that, like, he was conceived at a Rocky Horror Show?'

'Could've been in the car, I guess.'

'Or on the football field,' she said.

'That's true,' I said.

'Maybe he'll be an all-star quarterback.'

'Yeah, if it's a boy.'

'Or even if it's a girl,' she said. 'Times have changed.'

'So...What are we gonna do?'

NATURALLY, being broke and desperate, I went to an Army recruiter. Dad and Grandpa had both served, so it sort of made sense.

But my absentee father, a former Army dentist, was appalled to hear that I was going to be, in his words, a grunt. See, serving as a grunt, a foot-soldier, required only a three-year enlistment, and yet I would still be eligible for the GI Bill...that is, money for college. Not to mention free housing and medical care. Made sense to me, to us. If there was a better option, we didn't see it.

However. When I was fifteen, I crashed a dirt-bike near Ellettsville, where Mark Freeman's uncle had a farm. Anyway, I wound up with two pins in my knee. No big deal, my knee worked fine. Still does, for the most part, although it doesn't like cold weather much.

Now, I can't say I wasn't warned. Brian Bussy's brother, a soldier himself, told Brian to tell me to lie about my knee when filling out the medical questionnaire. He said I should lie and then take a desk job...that way my little white lie, or gray lie, or whatever, it would never be discovered because, chances were, I'd never have an X-ray done for anything.

Well obviously I should've listened to Brian's brother. I told the truth about my knee and got rejected. The military was out. I broke the news after school, while driving Claudette home.

'The shit-sucking Army rejected me. Flat out.'
'What?'
'That's right. I'm not good enough to be shot at.'
'But I thought it was a sure thing. That's what you said,' she said, her voice filling up with alarm. I explained the knee.

'Wes, my God. I can't believe this is...My god, what are we—'
'I don't know.'
'But it's getting too late to, too late for—'
'I know.'
'But what are we going to do?'

WE went to school and graduated at the end of May. You should see our prom pictures, what with Claudette's basketball belly taking up the better half of a sapphire sequin dress. What a classic inner-city photo. West Side!

In June we married and I moved in with Claudette and Kandy, Claudette's mother, an unsavory guttersnipe with a raspy, pre-emphysema voice and a perpetual fake tan, which required no small effort, considering she was naturally a pale-skinned redhead. She was temperamental, uneducated, slutty, and hard to get along with. She could, however, provide more space than could my folks, with my sister still at home and nothing but the crowded basement to offer us.

I took a job at the Wal-Mart warehouse where Kandy worked, kicking boxes, loading trucks and shrink-wrapping pallets. Anyway, the plan was this... I'd put Claudette through school, then she'd put me through school right after...happy ending.

IN the wee hours of the morning, on July 29th, Claudette went into labor. I rushed her to the hospital. As you do. I was so worried for her, so helpless, so completely useless. And powerfully in love. I squeezed her hand until she yelped.

'Take it easy!'

'Sorry baby.'

'Wes, you look like you're about to pass out. Are you okay?'

'I'm fine I just I...'

'What's wrong?'

'I've just never seen you in pain like this before and it's, I don't know, it's...'

'Don't worry. I've had menstrual cramps worse than this.'

So strong!

Gretchen was born without complication. I'll go ahead and chalk this one up as the happiest moment in my life.

Throughout August, I worked nights at the warehouse and Claudette worked part-time at an Office Max. At the end of August, Claudette started school downtown at IUPUI (Indiana University/Purdue University of Indianapolis). She exhibited more than a fledgling passion for the arts and so she may've done something else with her life if not for the sense of desperate urgency that a child brings to a young couple. She wanted a sure thing. I don't blame her. She studied nursing, which explains C.J., her current husband.

One day, a shit day in February, we left Gretchen sleeping in her crib while we cooked dinner in that tiny kitchen. We heard something, it was Gretchen. She was screaming.

'Baba,' or perhaps 'Mamma!'

We argued, playfully I think, about her first word, if it had even been a word.

'Wes, give it up. She said Mamma.'

'Are you crazy? Get a Q-tip. She said Baba.'

'Tell yourself whatever you want, if it lets you sleep. Hey! Are you *trying* to overcook the pasta?'

I pulled the pot off the electric burner, 'Give me a kiss.'

'Hmmm, okay. I'll give you more than that if you do the dishes.'

The next day, we went to Mom's house for dinner. My sister was there with her brainiac boyfriend of the moment. The table could barely accommodate so many people. Between dinner and dessert, my stepdad excused himself and went to the bathroom. He never came out...or rather, he never came out alive.

When I was a boy, he and I were close. He went from being Mr. Vogel to being Daniel. He took me fishing...took me to Sunday school. Then I got older. We butted heads, and then we butted almost everything. But I really don't worry about that stuff anymore. The way I look at it, step kids have about a one percent chance of getting along with their stepparents. It's probably biological. Most other primate males, when they intend to mate with a female who already has children, will commit outright infanticide. The male will kill her children. And she, in turn, will begin to ovulate. A billion years of evolution from prokaryotes onward...you can't argue with it...you can't beat it...that's just the way it is. Sure, I have a lot of hang-ups. But my relationship with Dan isn't one of them. Our DNA had probably doomed us to failure…it was really no one's fault.

IN the fall of Claudette's sophomore year at college, we moved in with my mother and sister, who, following several rounds of negotiations, was forced into the basement. After my step-dad died, Mom needed people around her, I thought, at least through the first year of her grief, which was substantial and in no way repressed. Oddly enough, it really was one big happy family. Mom went on Prozac. We shared meals, shared moments. We all got along. At this point, my only nemesis was the warehouse.

'Jesus, I fucking hate that place,' I told Claudette as she rubbed the tenseness out of my neck and traps, 'It's been three days since I've seen the sun.'

'Baby, I can't stand to see you like this.'

'Like what? I'm happy, I just hate that place.'

'You need to quit. Honey, we've come this far. We'll figure it out. There's just no sense in you being miserable half the time.'

'And I'll…What? Wait tables?'

She pinned me to the bed, the damned thing wasn't much bigger than a day bed but I swear to God I can't imagine a better sensation…like on those Sunday mornings spent lying in that oversized cot with my wife jammed up against me and with my infant daughter sleeping and slobbering on my chest.

Well anyway. Claudette pinned me to the bed, her face up-side-down, engorged with blood, swelling at the temples.

'Go to school with me.'

I feigned a redneck sexist tone, 'Woman, quit yir crazy talk.'

'I mean it. I'm deadly serious. Deadly, shithead.'

'How?'

'Hello! Student loan. Ever heard of one of those things?'

'Ever heard of debt?'

'Ever heard of...you know, debt being in the best interests of our long-term financial future?'

'Nope,' I said, pretending to struggle against her grip.

'Not to mention your spiritual interests?'

'Spiritual, smearitsual. No debt.'

'Debt for the greater good!'

'No debt!'

She formed a tiny glob of spit, which dangled over my nose.

'You wouldn't.'

She did. Shortly after, we made love while Gretchen slept, and slept, and couldn't guess, I'd imagine, how very much in love her Mommy and Daddy were.

I noticed that, after the baby, the way in which we made love changed. Sure, we'd really go at it from time to time, using every prop and piece of furniture in the house. But most the time we did it slowly...adagio, if you like, with lots of eye contact and lots of kissing. It was great.

Well eventually, I did it. I went to college. Mostly because my Dad, whose marriage was on the rocks, had promised to support me before backing out once I had the bill from the Bursar's Office. Meanwhile my sister, two years my junior, started school at Boston College, having been awarded a scholarship because of her great big brain.

After one semester, I quit. We needed the money. Dad never came through. We were short all the time, begging loans from Mom and getting secondhand toddler cloths from church.

So, as much as I hated to, I went back to the warehouse, working primarily as a forklift operator. Professionally, things weren't looking up. But then again, at twenty, there was ample reason to expect a better future.

While at the warehouse, I got to know a guy we called The Marlboro Man because, well, he looked like one. Kandy had fucked him a few times. No surprise there.

Anyway, one night, while pretending to sweep the same corridor repeatedly, he told me he was changing jobs, that he was going to be a prison guard.

'How's the pay?'

'Better 'n here.'

'How's the, you know, how's the insurance and all that stuff?'

'Better 'n here.'

The Department of Corrections won't hire you until you're twenty-one, so I had to wait until the spring to submit my application. I could sign my name, and I had a pulse, so they hired me.

In July, I started working at the Greenborough Diagnostic Center, a maximum-security prison—a Level-5 institution, you'll recall. That's where I got my start...where I met Big Ed...and where later I would wind up in some pretty big trouble.

For a young kid, I made a decent wage, when you consider overtime and the various bouncer gigs that Big Ed lined up for me, from time to time. Claudette, because we'd been so broke for so long, was bringing down, say, another ten grand in student financial aid. Together, we made almost forty thousand dollars, back when that meant something. Not bad. Certainly not great. But above the poverty line for once.

We then made a bad though not terrible decision. We moved out of Mom's house and into a nondescript condo off of Crawfordsville Road, near the racetrack. Naturally Gretchen, who was three by then, wanted all the attention she could get and my mother had been a huge help. Still Gretchen remained, in relative terms, an enormously easy child to rear. Not daring, perhaps, but lovable beyond words and inherently obedient.

After we moved out, Mom pouted for a long time. She dropped guilt bombs left and right. We'd left her all alone, after all, so I guess she had a right to bitch.

Looking back, I think Claudette and I were reacting more than anything else to the occidental expectation that all young adults should move out ASAP and make it on their own. I understand the impulse, certainly I do. But I wonder if we're any happier, really, for being so damned eager to hit the door the first chance we get.

WORK at the prison went well.

I was young and eager to do my best, not yet cynical. Coop had talked me into law enforcement by this point, so my approach to work was that, even if the prison gig was temporary, I should do my best to strengthen my résumé...get some references...get as many qualifications as the State would pay for.

The new plan was to go to college in the fall, after Claudette graduated, then apply to the FBI. However, that plan was soon scrapped. While researching the FBI, I came across the Foreign Service...the State Department folks who staff our embassies overseas.

'Think about it baby,' I said one day, while we jogged along the canal, near Butler University, 'Travel. Good pay. We'd meet all kinds of fascinating people...'

'Like cannibals?'

'The kids, they'd grow up seeing the world instead of languishing in some redneck cesspool.'

'Wes. We can't just...What about our families?'

'I know but. Well, every third tour, we'd get back to the States. See, and if we decide to scrap it, I can take a federal job back here and all that time in service will still count.'

'Count for what?'

'More money, retirement. That sort of thing.'

'What about me? Sorry, but I don't plan on sitting around the house in curlers all day, waiting for you to come back and—'

'Are you kidding me? Have you heard of any country in the world that doesn't need nurses? So what do you say?'

She thought about it. Knowing her, maybe what she thought about, more than anything else, was about how hard I'd worked to put her through school. She probably felt that she owed me one, regardless of any specific thoughts, pro or con, on the Foreign Service. She always played it cool, but I knew her, and deep down she was a very sentient person. In the end, she gave the Foreign Service a green light, provided I could actually get through college and get accepted.

Granted I had, as they say, gotten the cart a tad before the horse. I mean, I hadn't even started school yet. That wasn't important. The important thing was, I had something to aim for...a goal, a beacon, whatever. I wasn't just floating anymore, professionally speaking.

Because it was temporary, I thought, working at the prison was enjoyable. Not cerebrally stimulating, I'll give you that. Just straight up fun. I joined E-squad, the Emergency Squad, the folks who respond to riots and so forth. I was also on the Cell Extraction Team.

Cell extraction? Well at least once a day, some nutcase would decide he wasn't coming out of his cell. I, along with four teammates, would suit-up in hockey gear and extract said nutcase from his cell. What a rush! Not particularly humane, in retrospect, but a rush nonetheless.

Now, in order to specialize, Claudette stayed in school an additional semester, which pushed my studies back until autumn of the next year. Just one year, that didn't matter. Remember, I had a goal. As long as the prison gig was temporary, it was really no big deal.

Somehow, after only being there two years, I was selected for Sergeant. Unheard of. I was flabbergasted. The quickest anyone had made it without a college degree was three years. This was in March.

Now I have to stop here and say that I don't believe in fate, certainly not in the sense that 'everything happens for a reason' and so on.

Complete dribble.

But what I do believe in is the uncanny ability of stupid, random, pointless Chance to forever change the course not only of History, with a capital H, but also the innumerable personal histories of you and me and everyone. Yes and it was Chance, that blundering idiot ogre who, bumbling, snatched the golden meadows of irreparable happiness from beneath my feet, who blow by blow obliterated all hope until at last my life, if I can call it that, has become nothing more than a pointless crawl toward a gray oblivion. It was Chance, that blind fuckhead nitwit, who by a series of senseless accidents channeled my life into nothingness.

And so. A lot of things had to line up just right to make the last day of July as interesting as it turned out to be…

Claudette had graduated and was working at the Methodist Hospital downtown. That was good, really good in fact. Dollar bills! Top shelf ice cream! New books! New underwear! More shelving! A toilet that works!

Gretchen was about to start kindergarten. I was a sergeant by then, which I believe I pointed out earlier. But in the fall, I was going to study political science.

Back then, I was working five eight-hour days per week. However, in July, we switched over to a rotating schedule, the same schedule I'm on today, whereby I work seven twelve-hour shifts out of every fourteen days. For example, I might work:
Friday/Saturday/Sunday
Off/Off
Wednesday/Thursday
Off/Off/Off
Monday/Tuesday

And so on. Confused? Well, whatever day I work one week, I don't work the next, unless I'm lucky enough to be granted some overtime. This system was designed to collapse three eight-hour shifts into two twelve-hour shifts while allowing us to have every other weekend off.

None of this matters.

What does matter, if anything does, is that on the first day we changed over to this new schedule, a lot of folks had screwed it up, had either not come into work when they should've or else arrived at work only to discover that they shouldn't have.

Because of the numerous avoidable screw-ups, we had a vacancy in Tower-3. And also because of the numerous avoidable screw-ups, we were undermanned but had a surplus of sergeants. The Captain, a different captain than the one I have now, a real piece of work, he made a seminal announcement at roll call that morning.

'Okay people,' he said, 'We need a shooter in Tower-3.'

Instinctively, my hand went up. 'Got it covered sir.'

I was a real 'team player' back then...a 'hard charger,' as you might recall. A great big ass-kisser.

Let me back up to the day before, which, as Chance would have it, had been Claudette's birthday, which, as Chance would also have it, is in the same month as my only daughter's birthday.

Because of the sudden cash influx into our lives, I had splurged on Claudette's birthday. I treated her to dinner at Saint Elmo's, gave her two tickets to The Symphony on the Prairie, which I'd recommend to anyone, and I took her on a late-night carriage ride around the Monument Circle and its environs. That took place after work.

Work, however, had not been so pleasant. As the head of the Cell Extraction Team, I was called to the cell of one José Sanchez, if that indeed had been his name—he never did provide any papers.

We call them ghosts. They come here with fake IDs, or no ID at all. They get busted selling dope. They make bail or they do a short bit in jail, and then they go back to Mexico or South America. In the future, when they come back to America, which they always do, they do so under a different name, and so they never get slammed with the Three Strikes Rule, or with any of the harsher measures aimed at repeat offenders. It's basically a revolving door.

Mr. Sanchez, or whatever his real name was, presumably cursed at us when we showed up in front of his cell, though he did so in rapid, machine-gun Spanish. And so I didn't catch everything that he screamed at us. He was a short wiry man, reportedly twenty-nine years of age, with long black hair.

I took three years of high school Spanish and, while I can't spell shitt, I can speak the language pretty well, all things—like my school—considered.

Now then. I removed my mouth guard and my hockey mask and tried to talk him down, which I never should've done. By the time the Cell Extraction Team shows up, negotiations are finished (or should be). He held in his hand a bloody razor, which he had used, apparently, to carve sizable chunks out of his arm. He was ready for us...had a box of books jammed in front of the cell door...covered himself in baby oil so we couldn't get a hold of him.

From what I gathered, slowly, through much effort, Mr. Sanchez had promised his daughter that he'd be home in time to take her to some annual carnival in their podunk village down in Mexico. He had broken his promise and missed it, this carnival, so he decided to croak himself. Being an imperfect speaker of any language tends to make you either unclear or direct.

I said, or I think I said, 'José. Your daughter wants you home late, or your daughter wants you dead?'

He pondered this a while, or seemed to. He threw down the razor, balled himself up against the stainless steel toilet and sobbed himself into state of tranquility.

As he did so, the Captain showed up and chewed my ass for not barging into the cell, so we promptly dragged José out of there, no longer tranquil, and hauled him to our medical staff for treatment.

Then I did something else you should never do. I pulled his file. Mr. Sanchez, so said his dossier, was not a child molester, or a killer, or a cooker of methamphetamine. He had smuggled, or tried to smuggle, thirty pounds of marijuana into the United States. A human error, I thought.

I'm not saying he should've been a free man. Granted, he broke the law and civilizations need to uphold their laws, even the stupid ones, or else the rule of law goes south and you're in big trouble. I'm only saying that it's impossible to view all criminals in the same light. As a father and a son and a brother and a former husband, for instance, I have always found it difficult to be entirely fair to sex offenders. I realize this bias constitutes a professional faux pas in the same way, for example, that a male heterosexual gynecologist should be able to examine a swimsuit model with no more arousal than if she were a pet rock. But get real.

My only point, and I really do have one, is that I viewed José Sanchez as being completely human without qualifiers. He was a guilt-ridden father, not a murderer, not some child-raping monster. It was easy to empathize with the man. Over dinner and during my carriage ride with Claudette, I thought of him a great deal.

Where was I? Ah, yes. The next day, because of typically poor execution on the part of the State, everything was screwed up and I found myself alone in Tower-3, where I listened to National Public Radio and considered masturbating to stave off boredom, which I would've done if Claudette hadn't been such a gracious and I dare say acrobatic lover the night before.

Now, working in a guard tower doesn't have to be dull. My mother, as I think I mentioned, receives audio books from the library, free of charge, because she's blind or nearly so.

When I first came to the Department of Corrections, they stuck me in Tower-1 for two months. Per the standing orders, you're not allowed to read up there, which makes sense I guess. But you are allowed to listen to the radio. I must've listened to at least twenty books up there in Tower-1.

But on this day, coming as my assignment had, that is, as a surprise, I was unarmed in the way of audio books. While trapped up there, I made a prioritized mental list, regarding my professional future. It went something like this.

A. Foreign Service.
B. FBI.
C. Federal Marshal.
D. IPD, and then work my way up.
E. Law school?

Suddenly my radio, not the AM/FM cassette-playing radio, but the one that means business, came alive with activity.

'Nineteen-O-one,' it said, 'twenty-two.'

'Nineteen-O-one,' the Captain responded.
'Sir, we have a possible signal 2000.'
'Ten-nine?'
'We have a possible signal 2000.'
'Possible? We do or we don't. So, which is it?'
'Sir, we have a signal 2000!'
'Where the hell is he?'
'We don't know, sir...we think. Hold on. He's headed toward Gate-3.'
'Gate-3? Forty-three, you copy? Forty-three?'
'Clear,' I said, shitting my pants.
'All units, this is the Captain speaking...ten-three until further notice. Hold all traffic.'

Random goddamn Chance. I looked down and, sure enough, there was José Sanchez, in broad fucking daylight, halfway up the first fence, mangling his hands on razor wire. I would later discover that, due to the findings of a psychological evaluation, our Mr. Sanchez had been scheduled for a transfer to the mental ward in New Castle.

Though I have no memory of breaking the damned thing out of its box, I realized, almost in third-person, that I held in my hands a Ruger Mini-14. At this distance, which wasn't much, I should've grabbed the shotgun, not the rifle. But it was too late. I had to react. I knew that much. I was supposed to say, 'Halt, or I'll shoot!' just like in the movies.

But instead I said 'José, what the hell are you doing?'

Either José didn't hear what I said, or he chose to ignore me. He landed in the space we call no-man's land, the space between the two fences. At this point, I did what I was trained to do, which was to take aim and say,

'Halt or I'll shoot!'

I never could get a proper site-picture with that damned Mini-14. I was a marksman with an SKS or an AR-15. But the rear site and the front site on a Mini-14 are so close to one another, and the rear site is such a tiny pinhole of an excuse for a site, that I simply could not get a site-picture half the time; meaning, all I could see that sunny afternoon was a brownish blur.

So I did what they tell you never to do, which is to look directly down the barrel, using only the front sight. He was close enough, as he reached the top of the second fence, that I could make out his face. And if I had to say what expression it wore, I wouldn't say crazed desperation. Not at all. I would have to say raw determination.

At all costs, he was going home.

My hands started shaking. He had one leg over the second fence and somewhere toward the end of my plea…

'José, come the fuck on!' my rifle went off and, with seeming simultaneity, José's face exploded and he dropped on the free man's side of the fence.

Was he dead? He was not. The bullet, as I later learned, had entered his mouth and, after removing the better part of his tongue, exited, lodging itself in the parking lot where it remains until today. With horror I came to realize that the poor bastard was not only alive but awake!

He moaned and simpered, his face a plate of twisted meat, while the medical staff arrived with—what? What were they doing? What could they possibly do, aside from get the man to a hospital? They got an IV going. The stuff in the bag was clear, so it couldn't have been blood. Pain reliever, one could hope.

Later, I was told, an ambulance arrived.

I wouldn't know. I had passed out with a loaded rifle in my hands and I'm damned lucky, or at least my son is, that it didn't go off.

José Sanchez, or whoever he had been, died of a heart attack on the way to the hospital.

RETURNING to Christmas last year.

We peered through my filthy windshield at a moonlit hummock of sand on the other side of which the Indiana Dunes gave way to Lake Michigan.

'What I mean,' Claudette said, choking on snotty confessional tears, 'is that I'll always love you...I'm always going to love you...I can't help it. I can't, it's...under my skin. I know soul-mate is such a corny word, but...tell me you understand.'

'I uh...'

'You haunt me, Wes...And why?? Why can't I get over you?'

'Good question. But ditto,' I said, trying to joke my way out of a serious situation, 'Hey, you can be my mistress if you want. God knows I could use a sugarmama.'

I was only partially jesting. Who am I kidding? It wasn't a jest. Anyway, she turned to me, snot hanging off her upper lip.

'Do I really seem the type who'd be somebody's mistress?'

'Honestly?'

'But I'm not, I'm really not. I'm totally reformed in that department.'

'Oh,' I said. 'Worth a shot, at least. Forget it. It's probably just as well. I've never had a mistress, I wouldn't be much good at it.'

I took a piss into Lake Michigan, then came back to the car. When I got back, I cracked a beer and let Claudette thump me with more questions.

'So tell me Wes...tell me, then maybe I'll understand it myself.'

'Tell you what, exactly, how I came off the rails?'

'No. Tell me why it is that you still love me...'

'Simple. I've thought about it way too much. Part of it is this. You have a woman's body but an androgynous mind. You can understand me like no one else. And plus...I don't know. A bunch of other stuff. Shared history...the rest of it I can't explain. I don't know...'

'So then...I'm like your Vitruvian Woman?'

I didn't know what that meant, actually.

'Yeah,' I said, 'More or less. And why, pray tell, do you love me?'

'I can't put it into words. It's hopeless. All I can say is that I'll never forget your potential greatness. There was a time when...you really did carry an aura of greatness. Not goodness. Actual, proper, greatness.'

'Greatness? Really?? Sounds like a bit of stretch.'

'Greatness, really. But also goodness. Usually you only get one or the other. Maybe that's why...'

'And now? What about now?'

'Goodness, yes. Very much so.'

'I know. Yeah. Any vestige of greatness is gone, if it was ever there in the first place. Long gone. So you don't have to say it.'

'No, I'd say the residue remains. The patina ,or whatever. Does that make sense? You look hurt. I'm sorry. I didn't mean to...'

'That's fine. I'm glad you told me. I mean, I thought I was crazy for a long time. I thought it was just me who couldn't let go.'

She squinted her eyes at me through the moonlit semi-darkness. 'One thing still bothers me.'

'What's that?'

'Why'd you isolate us? Why did you...well, why'd you give up on us?'

'Funny, I was going to ask you the same thing...You know, if only you would've followed the pattern, the logical steps. I mean, as soon as you left me, I woke up. All you had to do was leave, I would've snapped right out of it. I did snap out of it, you know. So why didn't you just move in with your mom for a while, like you were supposed to, like every other disgruntled wife, like how the script is written...frustrated wife leaves; penitent husband makes amends. But fuck's sake Claudette, why'd you have to leave me for another man? You ruined any chance we had. Don't you see that?'

'I've, yes, I've thought about all that. What can I say, except you're right. Not about everything. Just about that part. Still...'

'Still what?'

'I don't know,' she said, sounding a bit choked up. 'I suppose you better take me home.'

Merry Fucking Christmas.

Were her professions of undying love followed by anything tangible that could help me out of my hole? Fuck no. Not by a long shot.

Admittedly, I used this sentimental tête-à-tête to leverage a new deal, an arrangement whereby I wouldn't pay child support for three years so I could finally go to college. She went for it. Her husband, the breadwinner, as it were, he balked. Although a cardiologist, what C.J. brought to their marriage, in addition to a well-trimmed beard and a high earning potential, was a mind-altering amount of student debt.

So if it's not too much of an abstraction, I'd like to say that the monthly child support I pay, at least in part, gets applied to the debt of a man who's fucking the only woman I've ever loved. At least that's how I tend to view things.

AFTER I killed José Sanchez, as you've probably guessed by now, I completely disintegrated.

I came to regard human beings as nothing more than talented insects...just as brutal and morally blind, with a system of applied ethics no more advanced, however elaborate, than those of the blue-green algae plumes from which we slithered a billion fruitless years ago.

So I gave up on my amorophic, wishy-washy, enigmatic version of a Judeo-Christian God, the one who'd been receiving my thanks and unassuming prayers since I could remember. Granted, I didn't completely discount the notion of a prime-mover, of a creator, or whatever, as such. What I gave up on, when considering Bosnia, and the Third Reich, and Pol Pot, and José Sanchez and so on, was the conviction or even the hope that if there is a God, He or She or Thou or It is anything more than a sadist, a cruel prankster, or a negligent bureaucrat with no idea about what's really going on inside his organization beneath the upper echelon of detached management. Either God doesn't exist or else he's completely out of touch with his constituents.   If there's a God, I decided, he's completely out to lunch.

Oddly enough, I still pray. It's a hard habit to break. But when I do pray, I snub the God of Earth—invariably. I go around him. Over his head. I pray to his boss...God of All, perhaps. And each prayer includes this humble request, please, please, please God of All...get rid of our direct superior, that incompetent charlatan, that so-called God of Earth. Give him the heave-ho, the pink slip, the axe. He's fucking nuts.

I never wept after killing José Sanchez. I am, by nature and by training, not a crier...and I cannot help but feel disdain toward men who weep too freely. Trapped forever, the words 'if only' kept rattling around my head.

If only I had stayed in college.

If only I'd been in a different tower, or no tower at all.

If only I hadn't talked to José the day before.

If only I would've shot him from a distance, if only I could've avoided seeing his face.

If only he'd been maimed...why'd he have to die?

Chance, Chance...that drunken brute.

The problem, I have seen only recently, is that I was never who I pretended to be. I wasn't tough, as I had believed and made others believe through futile posturing. There's no correlation, for example, between catching a football and shooting a man through the jaw, thereby leaving most of his tongue on the sidewalk.

But I wasn't able to see things for what they were. Not yet. So, in addition to the constant gnawing of low-grade guilt, I came to consider myself a weakling, to use my father's terminology. Or a pussy, if you will. Thin-skinned. Now circling back to themes of divinity...on one hand, I mourned my sin against humanity and, on the other hand, I mourned my sin against my masculinity, which the former sort of mourning implied.

'Just doing my job,' I would say, stoically, mystically, to anyone at work who brought up that little shooting incident. What a farce.

The whole act finally caught up with me. For one, I couldn't sleep. At least not at night. I found myself sleeping at work—a real no-no, as you might imagine. I found myself calling in sick, even when I had no sick days left on the books. Soon enough, on the topic of finding myself, I found myself demoted from sergeant to plain old officer. Rank and file once again. Circle of life.

I gave my wife and child what you might call an adult version of the silent treatment. I didn't scream, I didn't weep; I neither berated them nor broke things on more than a few occasions. I just wouldn't talk to them. I was almost not there. They were living with a zombie.

Claudette tried to get me into counseling. Big Ed tried to get me into counseling. Cooper got me drunk. Strangely enough, my mother sent me flowers, as if I were a patient in a hospital. It became obvious to everyone that I was all fucked up inside.

Naturally, I started drinking. It was a phase in my life during which reading Bukowski was a bit like puking over a mirror. Well, one day I looked up from the couch and Claudette was standing by the door, bags all nice and packed...perfume...hair done up...the kid on one side...the dog on the other. I staggered to my feet and launched my glass of drugstore bourbon against the wall. Gretchen started crying.

'Hey,' I yelled. 'Hey! Wait one fucking minute, lady. You're not taking my kid *and* the dog.'

Hence I repeated a cycle that I had vowed never to repeat, thereby giving my child some nice new psychological scars of her own. Well done, sir, well played.

After that, getting off the couch was an even bigger chore. An apartment couldn't feel any emptier. I never wept but my hair turned gray and fell out in clumps. I lost forty, maybe fifty pounds. But at least I kept the dog.

LAST year, after dropping Claudette off in front of her treeless new McMansion, I thought about my little meltdown, my crying fit, which was humiliating, of course, and awkward to boot, because Claudette couldn't decide if we were allowed to touch. She'd reach for my hand, withdraw, reach, withdraw. And so on.

Well the way I viewed it, I'd already broken the contract that I'd made with myself never to weep. So I figured, if I just kept weeping, it could later be justified as being part of one long but discrete session. So I wept all the way back to Indy. Four hours. I stopped for a while but then an old Cat Stevens song came on the radio and the water works started right up again. I felt better for a day or two and then I felt much worse.

DURING my trips to Portage, I normally stay at the dumpy Days Inn downtown.

Not this time. It's Christmas, so I splurged. I just checked into the Ramada and I have to admit, it feels nice to be staying in a roach-free hotel, one in which you can almost trust the sheets.

But it's not cheap, not in relative terms. What I really find amusing is that, in addition to the child support I pay, twice a month I get to shell out dough on hotel rooms and gas because Claudette's husband, having completed his residency, suddenly had to move away from Indy so he could be near his ailing mother...okay, a nice enough sentiment if he hadn't ripped my daughter away from me. I can't believe the shit that the State of Indiana let's people get away with.

His mother is still ambulatory and what not, so I don't see how tearing my daughter away is justifiable, but it doesn't matter because it's legal, especially if you have more money and can therefore purchase a better attorney.

My ex-wives, they can move anywhere in the world. I can stay and pay or follow and pay. Either way, I pay. That's guaranteed.

ALONE in a new place—one with cable TV, no less—I flop down on the freshly made bed and take this opportunity to borrow and assemble visual elements from MTV in order to jerk off, quite listlessly, with very little conviction or enthusiasm. Even though my dick itself cooperates, my fantasies do not. Claudette creeps in there...waits in the wings at first, then takes center stage...wearing this glossy lipstick that makes her juicy lips look so gluey, so inviting.

No. She doesn't get to have me. Not even in my fantasies. It signals another defeat. I won't allow it. So I jump in the shower and stay there for an hour, with the water coming down as hard and as hot as I can get it. I sit down, bring my knees to my chest, and let the water slap my back. If I didn't have to meet the kid, I could stay in here forever.

I dry off, stare at my scrawny body in the mirror for a while, and then pick up the phone.
 'Claudette? Wes here.'
 'Hi ya Wes. Merry Christmas.'
 'Yeah.'
 'You in town already?'
 'Yep. I'm staying at the Ramada.'
 'The Ramada? Look at you. Wesley Warbucks.'
 'Right. That's me. Could you uh, have Gretchen at the hotel restaurant by five?'
 'Sure, sure thing.'
 'I know that's a little earlier than we'd—'
 'Not a problem.'
 'Good.'
 'Actually Wes, I'll need to pop in for a sec. I have to hand you some, um, paper work.'
 'Regarding?'
 'Gretchen's braces.'
 'Right. That's okay...just hand that stuff off to Gretchen. She's a big girl.'
 'Oh, I don't mind running in for a sec.'
 'That's okay.'
 'Oh.'
 'Thanks.'
 'Then...bye, I guess?'
 'Yep. Bye.'

GRETCHEN walks in late, at twenty-after, swinging a blue gift bag and wearing natty jeans, a new olive-green Kashmir sweater and brown boots with heels redolent of circus stilts because, I believe, she thinks that making herself look taller also makes her look slimmer. She's said some really hateful sad things about her body.

She's fourteen, and already headed to a dark place, even though she's beautiful. Darkish skin, wavy black hair, shiny blue eyes. Perky nose. To me, she looks like an Afghani princess. To her, she looks like a big fat pig.

She sees me from a distance and smiles. It's good to see her. Painful, but good.

'Daddy!' she runs for me and, in so doing, nearly snaps off a stilt-like heel.

'Hey Miss Gretchen, you look nice. I like your sweater.'

'Thanks. Mom gave it to me for Christmas.'

'It's nice. Compliments your eyes. So you did the Christmas thing already?'

'Yeah because we're flying to some island for a couple days.'

'What island?'

'I don't know. The Caribbean? You know where that's at?'

'Saint Thomas or...?'

'Maybe. That might be it.'

'Saint Martin?'

'I don't know. But yeah I think there's a saint in the name.'

'That...that should be great. Take a seat.'

'Daddy you look sad.'

'A little tired from the road, maybe. Have a seat, sit down. Tell me about your holiday break so far. What've you been up to?'

Just like me at her age, she's one loquacious teenager. She knows it all. Yak yak yak. And thank God for that. It would kill me if I had to do the talking. I've known fathers who complain, saying they never know what to say to their teenage children. I don't see what the big deal is. They don't care what you have to say anymore. Just listen or at least pretend...that's about all that's left.

Gretchen's awfully good at hiding the fact that she doesn't have many friends, that while she's adored by teachers, she's too adult-like in many ways for the other girls, and she's not had much luck with boys, either.

AFTER we've eaten, I order a scotch on the rocks and Gretchen hands me a gift bag. I wish she would've wrapped my present. After all, I went through the bother of wrapping hers and I loathe wrapping gifts. Well, whatever. I hand her a gift, the first of three.

'Go ahead, open it,' I tell her.

Right away, her face tells me that she doesn't like it. It's Salinger's *Catcher and the Rye*.

Regardless, I go ahead and plug the book. 'It's a classic. It's, I don't know, about coming of age, about not wanting grow up and turn into a phony adult. I thought you might like it.'

'Thank you, Daddy.'

'That's not all. You've got two more. Here...'

'Open yours first.'

'Open it? It' not wrapped. You mean, reach into the bag??'

'Yeah, basically. Are you like...mad I didn't wrap it?'

'Of course not. I'm just giving you a hard time.'

'I totally would've wrapped it, only I picked it up two minutes ago...so I didn't have time.'

'Advanced planning. Glad to see you're all grown up.'

'Daddy.'

'What?'

'I totally knew what I was going to get you, just I didn't have the money till I cashed my Christmas checks.'

Now I feel like shit. I look around at everyone watching us and wonder if they've ever seen a gift exchange in a hotel restaurant. I look in the bag but can't tell what it is. I pull it out. It's a CD player for my car, the portable kind you plop on the passenger-side seat and plug into the tape deck with a faux cassette. It's a nice model. Must've cost at least eighty bucks. Jesus. That must be around three hundred dollars, when you factor in the teenage exchange rate, I mean the average teenaged buying power. I kiss the dimple in her dimpled cheek.

'Sweetheart, it's *perfect*. How' d you know I wanted a CD player?'

'You complained enough...it didn't take a Sherlock to know what to get you.'

Wow, sarcasm. Is that from me? Maybe. Could be from her mother. Claudette's no slouch.

What I start to say isn't that funny so I skip it and tell Gretchen to open up her other gifts.

Gretchen's face tells me that this present is slightly more impressive than the first, a pocket-sized digital camera. A nice one. A Sony. She lost her last camera at the mall, and she loves taking pictures (of other things and people, not herself).

'Did Mom tell you to buy this for me?'

'Thanks a lot.'

'No silly head, just I was telling her last week I really wanted a new camera.'

'Yeah? What'd she say?'

'Said she'd think about it. Money's tight, blah blah.'

Yes! I beat her mother to the punch! Victory!

'Guess you won't have to wait,' I say, inwardly glowing for a moment.

'Thank you Daddy.'

'*De nada.*'

I wonder why Gretchen calls her mother Mom and her father Daddy. We were separated when she was five years old, which may've left her conception of me in a state of arrested development, as it were. Perhaps I really am her Daddy, not her Dad.

Gretchen goes absolutely apeshit over the last gift, the dead ringer. It's a cell phone. A mid-range Ericsson with Internet access. Claudette had forbidden her to have a phone until next year, when she starts high school. And if I happened to be a full-time father, I wouldn't contradict her mother, but, well, here we are.

Non-custodial fathers must purchase the love of their children.

'Thank you so, so much,' she tries to say, rising from her seat to give me a hug.

'No sweat. That's what dads are for.'

'Think Mom's gonna spaz?'

'I don't give a fraction of a damn,' I blurt out, 'She's not paying the bill, I am. Anyway, just leave it on silent when you're in the house.'

Call me Machiavellian, that's fine. But the main reason I got this phone was so I wouldn't have to go through some mediator, like my ex-wife or the guy who's screwing her. When I want to talk to my daughter, I shouldn't have to go through someone's chain of command.

Against my better judgment, I ask Gretchen if she wants dessert. She looks all conflicted and changes the subject.

'What time's the movie?'

'Eight-something.'

'Should we hurry?'

'No rush. We don't need to see the first hour's worth of pre-view commercials. So, is Melissa coming with us tomorrow?'

Melissa, her best friend, and the only one Gretchen speaks of regularly, seems to be a good influence. Plays a few instruments. Studies a lot. You never know, but it seems like Gretchen could do a lot worse.

'Mom didn't tell you?'

'Tell me what?'

'I can't go to Chicago.'

'No,' I say, my voice and upper lip tightening, 'She overlooked that one. Why can't you go?'

'Just because.'

'Right. Because why?'

After a while, I drag it out of her. She's going to see a counselor tomorrow at one-thirty in the afternoon. This isn't a first. About four years ago she was going to counseling because, like me, she couldn't get it through her head that her mother and father would never again live under the same roof, that it was over. Finis. Wrecked. Kaput.

'Why are you seeing a psychologist? And why is this the first I've heard of it?'

'She's not a psychologist. That's not what they call them.'

'Why are you going to tell some stranger a bunch of stuff you can't tell me? Can't I help?' Irrational reaction...Unchecked emotion...Stupid response...I'm kicking myself (again).

She makes some learned, practiced, adult-like facial expression and says 'I don't feel like talking about it.'

What do you know, like father, like daughter. I press the issue, though not much. She becomes sullen and withdrawn as she separates and organizes the packs of sugar from the packs of imitation sugar.

Frankly, I can't solve much over a weekend...so I always do my best to keep things light, cheery. Resigned, I change the subject to her studies and we talk about Steinbeck's novella, *Of Mice and Men*, which she recently read in her English Lit class, and I'm so impressed with what she has to say that it makes my hair stand up because I realize that the mental life of my daughter is transitioning into adulthood.

AT last, we're in the palliating womb of a darkened movie theater with Jim Carey on the screen and between us a mammoth bucket of popcorn.

This is pretty typical, movies and museums. It's always some form of entertainment with us. See, a 'normal' full-time dad might do very little with his teenaged child in the way of entertainment. He, this hypothetical father, could enjoy a typical domestic routine to include meals at home, card games, grocery shopping, the nightly news, arguments, school functions, dreaded trips to the mall...conversations in passing.

In my case, I show up after a two-week absence and have nowhere to relax with my daughter except in a hotel room, usually a cheap one. No thanks.

So. We take the train into Chicago where we go to the Field Museum, or the Aquarium, or the Art Museum, or The Old Navy Pier, perhaps, or to the observatory, when the sky looks clear.

Otherwise, when I'm totally broke, we remain in Portage and take in a movie or else, on warm sunny days, we go to the dunes. On the rare occasions that Claudette brings Gretchen down to Indy, we typically find ourselves at the zoo, or the State Museum or maybe the IMAX. Once in a while, though it's not cheap, I take Gretchen to a play. It's always Go Go Go.

How does all this add up?

Gas - $210/month

Hotel - $290/month
Food and Entertainment - $190/month
TOTAL: $690/month

And these are pretty conservative figures; they fail to capture the intangibles...the wear and tear on the car and so forth, the missed opportunities to work side jobs with Big Ed. Actually, eight or even nine hundred bucks a month is probably closer to the truth when you factor in that, like most over-compensating fathers, I buy her lots of stuff she doesn't need. Between both kids, I fork out at least half my pay. Easily. That's fine, except I hardly see them...so the cost per visitation hour is extravagant.

I'M not even watching the movie. I am but I'm not. I keep spacing out.

As I look at Gretchen's profile it occurs to me that I honestly don't feel like her father. Nope, I just don't feel like her father.

And she just doesn't feel like my daughter. I feel like an uncle, maybe a really good uncle, more involved than most. Nothing more, nothing less.

Uncle Daddy, that's me.

◎

THE oaken pews inside the sanctuary of the West Olive Branch Church squeak with every adjustment, however subtle. Two congregations have jammed themselves into this church tonight.

The English-speaking congregation, so I'm told, meets on Sunday mornings. The Spanish-speaking congregation meets on Sunday afternoons. These two congregations, neither one large enough to fill up even half of the sanctuary, share the oversized redbrick building as a cost-saving measure. But because each congregation wanted to hold a midnight Christmas Eve service, they've teamed up tonight and so every other speech and hymn is given or sung in Spanish.

Both the Latin minister and the Anglo minister are wearing roughhewn robes, as in Holy Lands in days of yore. Everyone else is dressed up. I'm wearing my only long-sleeved collared shirt. Mom's wearing a cheap, blue-and-white pattern dress from Target. I told her it looked nice.

'It was on sale,' she said, 'I can hardly see. What do I care?'

On her knee she's dandling Shane, my son, who won't sit still. He keeps toying with his braids. The braids are too tight...Cassandra over did it. Mom unties them slowly, carefully. This, her fingertips on his scalp, makes him sleepy.

Shane quits squirming, his eyelids droop. Shane doesn't resemble me much. Looks more like his mother whom years ago I met at work...

TWO months after Claudette left me, I nearly got fired. The Major, who had emigrated from Poland and still had a strong accent, he called me into his office. I found myself at parade rest, involuntarily. He had a very imposing presence.

'Good afternoon, Major.'

'Take a seat,' he commanded.

'What's up?'

'Weimer, we make you deal. You go work next door. You need fresh start, no?'

And that's how I ended up at the GCF where, as you'll recall, I had my ass mightily beaten by Big H, that crazy bastard.

So. Disgraced, I left the diagnostic center. Disgraced again, I left the day shift for the night shift. Not that word didn't get around, but at least I wasn't working with anybody who had saved my neck. Big Ed eventually followed me; I think he was looking after me. We ended up in the same dorm. But that came later.

Anyway. Part of me refused to quit the prison racquet because of what folks commonly refer to as male pride, though I'm not certain how male pride varies in its fundamental essence from female pride. How about, plain old pride. And let's not forget money, believe it or not. And the retirement fund. Cheap insurance. I had no skills to speak of and while a couple grand a month isn't much, it's better than Burger King.

Besides, I was simply floating...rudderless...because it was easier than thinking my way out of it, because I couldn't see a viable escape and, more than anything else, because there are times in our lives when we simply succumb to momentum, when we're no longer driving the train, so to speak, when in fact the train seems to be driving itself (God knows where).

Granted, I've had a hand in my own demise. I know that much. I won't deny it. You screw yourself...then in walks Chance; he bends you over the love-seat with a gruesome smile and a litany of sick ambitions. Or vice versa. It's a combination. I can't go around absolving myself completely. But rationally, I can't take all the blame either.

It's foolish to think you have no control over your life and equally foolish to think you have complete control. Finding the balance, the proportionality, the degree to which one should affix blame to oneself and how much we should pin on Chance, now that's the trick. Shooting from the hip, I'd give myself a solid 50/50 breakdown.

So anyway. When I first came to the night shift, I was floating from job to job to job...from the kitchen to the lobby...the towers, then the parking lot. And so on.

Mostly, however, I served as a Yard Officer. Meaning, I worked outside, supervising the movements of all the prisoners. Caught a lot of colds. And saw a bunch of fights, which were usually broken up by the time I got there; the anonymity of mass movements makes it much easier to punch or shank somebody without being identified.

Well eventually, about a year in, I was able to bid on a permanent post, which I did. I bid on the Control Room, a glass box from which four sets of glass doors are controlled electronically. More or less, it's the last barrier between the prison and freedom. Hence, the door to the lobby should never be open while the door to the lounge—or to the admin wing, or the door to the yard—is open.

So for the most part, I closed and opened doors and read a bunch of books...I went through a serious Kundera phase, as I recall. I was twenty-five by then, and obviously going nowhere fast.

At first, I worked with a wizened hag of a character named Sylvia Watkins who rarely spoke but, when she did, tended to curse with unrepentant gusto. She liked making ceramics and would on occasion haul in something tacky for me to admire.

Looking back, she was a nice enough lady. And we had something in common. She was, in fact, the only other currently living employee at the prison to have shot a man off the fence. I asked her once—back when I used to drink a little on the job, before I received written counseling and got placed on probation for a week—if she ever felt guilty.

'What for?' she said. 'I made that stupid dumb-ass run for the fucking fence?'

Fair enough.

With thirty plus years in service, Sylvia found herself at the center of a relatively elaborate retirement ceremony in February, eight years ago. In walked Cassandra Footman, soon to be mother of Shane Andrew Weimer.

We laughed a good amount, up there in the control room. Mostly we made fun of fellow employees and speculated on their private lives. Cassandra had a sharp tongue...she knew how to cut people to the bone. She had a deep, mannish, contagious laugh and her body language was snaky in a winsome sort of way. Oh, and that woman could really sing.

She had dark flawless skin, kind of shiny, like she oozed coconut butter instead of sweat...Big brown eyes, invariably framed by silvery eyeliner and silvery eye shadow...

Her narrow waist accentuated the noticeable verbosity of her derriere. Her breasts were ample, though not unwieldy. By unspoken though mutual agreement, we usually did it from behind, so we could avoid eye-contact...doggy style, if you like. This whole thing started on the job, right there in the control room.

My reasons for proposing marriage to Cassandra Footman seem simple enough, with the benefit of hindsight.

1. Proximity. Always a factor, especially in this case. I wasn't getting out much.

2. Loneliness. Like I said, I wasn't getting out much.

3. Horniness. She was damned sexy. Our relationship was physical, very. Luckily, in recent years, her once perfect ass has ballooned into something that would make flying on a coach class ticket a real challenge.

So there it is. That's why I tied the knot again, laziness, lust, and loneliness. A lot of times, I'm sure, any given structure might endure one or even several blows, but not in unison. That's what happened, several blows at once.

First of all, Cassandra had two adolescent daughters, Lashanda and Cassandra, each from a different father. Who am I to talk? That's not my point. I mean we had two mouths to feed and the fathers of said mouths never paid a nickel of child support, unlike yours truly. So we had some extra money going out, but not coming in.

When we were dating, it was fine, but when I moved in, her girls resented me, especially when I actually tried to assume the role of a parent...the way I checked up on their homework, the way I insisted on knowing their whereabouts, the way I corrected their grammar and so on. Not many folks voluntarily give up freedoms. That's what it was about. I show up out of nowhere and start laying down rules. It was doomed to failure. I understand that now.

I remember one night Lashanda, while continuing to chew with her mouth wide open in direct defiance, she told me, 'I'll chew however I want. You a prison guard. You ain't nobody.'

Wow, do kids know how to lay it on you.

Two prison guards with all these mouths to feed can't afford much in the way of accommodation. We bought a slapdash box over on Tenth Street, near the High Neighbor Tavern. Cassandra still lives there with my kid as well as her other kids and that useless thug boyfriend of hers. Her dump is only slightly better than the dubious shack in which I currently reside.

Back then, when we were living together, that house was a regular pressure cooker with two minuscule, thin-walled bedrooms through which one could hear the lightest cough or the least intentional fart.

Right away we ran into trouble. Cassandra duped me into taking on her credit card debt...twelve thousand smackers worth. She drove a slab of shit Delta '88 but at least she had her Gucci bag.

It wasn't just the money problems that got us. Cassandra was completely mono-cultural. She was simple, useful, fun-loving, uncomplicated and anti-intellectual. I was basically useless, morose, complex and intellectually curious, at least relative to my spouse. She was smart but willfully ignorant and utterly disinterested in the world outside her narrow band of experience. She disdained my taste in just about everything. I thought she would change over time but it would've been easier to move the Himalayas to Kansas with a pair of chopsticks. After a certain age, people don't change. Their borders are defined. Of all my life's derailments, clearly my marriage to Cassandra is the one that sticks out, I mean the one for which I am wholly to blame.

After a while, I started drinking again and I stopped trying to be a father to Cassandra's daughters. They didn't want a father, apparently, and I didn't have the energy to force the issue. We carefully made our way around each other, me in my silence and they with their ready claws.

Then, after her mother had a stroke, Cassandra turned Pentecostal on me and we started fighting constantly. She beat me a few times. She hit me with a dish rack. We fought so much that we couldn't work together anymore. Cassandra took a job at Lake Land, a minimum-security prison fifty minutes south of town. Things got a little better after that, but not much. We would've split before our first year anniversary but one afternoon, when I was still sleeping off the night shift, Cassandra rolled over and whispered, 'Wesley.'

'Shhhh.'

'Wesley.'
'Huh-uh.'
'WESLEY...wake your ass up.'
'For fuck's sake, what do you want?'
'I'm late.'
'For what?'
'It's late.'
'What?...Ah, Jesus Christ. Are you serious?'

Despite our growing bitterness and complete lack of interest in one another, we still screwed once in a while, whenever we were both drunk enough. Well, there were consequences.

By the time we hit the second trimester, I had made one hell of a turnaround. I mean, life is life and all. I wasn't joking around. I rubbed feet, paid compliments, bought flowers...bit my goddamn tongue to no end. I bribed my stepdaughters with whatever I could afford, usually cheap shit from Value City...sequined handbags, sunglasses, scented soap.

The way I looked at it, I wasn't married to Cassandra so much as married to the family. That's what mattered. I couldn't fail twice.

WELL, I did fail twice. And yes, even with one divorce, for some folks, I'm sure there's an extreme feeling of failure. But when the second one starts to unfold? There's this feeling of...Wake me up! Somebody wake me up...No, no...this can't be happening again...WAKE ME UP.

Shane wasn't even walking before Cassandra threw me out on my ass. In retrospect, I think she'd already started messing around with Yellow. So much for newfound piety. He moved in with Cassandra a few days after I moved back in with Mom.

Yellow had at least one thing I didn't...a gigantic Y-chromosome. He's a certifiable fuck-up...a convicted felon...an ex-con twice busted for selling crack...can't hold down a job...can't shut his mouth, and can't stay out of trouble. But he truly is a badass...passionate, stupid, quick-tempered and merciless...the kind of guy that would've thrived throughout every period in history except maybe the last one hundred years.

Cassandra, or so the rumors go, became involved with Yellow back when he was still locked up at Lake Land...'transitioning,' they call it, having been transferred to minimum security for his last ninety days.

Now he's a bagboy—bag man?—over at the Meijer's on 38th Street. What a joke. A joke on me, of course. It didn't take long for the word-of-mouth prison telegraph to spread my business...along with embellishments, I'd imagine. The prisoners at work think Yellow 'stole' Cassandra from me. They think those two were screwing in the staff bathroom, which might be true, while she and I were still married. He's probably the only guy I've ever truly hated. Which brings me back to the present. Or actually, to earlier this evening.

I picked up Shane at their dump over on Tenth Street. After knocking endlessly, the door finally swung inward and I was greeted by gilt teeth and gold chains...Yellow, that nitwit, was dressed like a teenaged gangster instead of a parent nearing middle age. The smell of a recently consumed meal mixed with marijuana and together it all poured from the house along with the low, steady bumping of gangster rap in the background. Here's a guy who tortured me as a boy, slept with my wife, and later took my son. There's not a bridge big enough for all that water to go under.

'Merry Christmas, André,' I said to him in a measured, controlled voice. I didn't want to acknowledge our shared past anymore than I had to, and using his old moniker might've done just that.

'Whatchyou want?' he said, scowling with his arms folded on the beginnings of a beer-belly.

Such bitterness. I'm the one who got massively dicked here, so I can't comprehend his animosity.

I'm afraid of Yellow, I admit, so I didn't say what first came to mind. I just said, 'Is Shane ready?'

'He in the bathroom.'

Cassandra appeared, looking high as a kite, her eyes half-closed.

'You can't get him,' she said over Yellow's shoulder.

'What?'

'You said you'd give us money for school books.'

This was all taking place on their rickety-ass porch; they never invited me in.

'No,' I said, 'No. What I said was, I'll buy the books for next semester.'

Yellow spoke up, 'Same difference.'

'Well, not exactly.'

'Quit playin, and just write the check,' Cassandra said, scratching at one of her deepening neck wrinkles. 'Don't you know it's Christmas?'

Yellow chimed in, 'That boy ain't goin no place till we see the cash.'

'Actually, André. That's not legal. You can't do that.'

He gave me a fuck-off smile, full of gold. I pulled out my cell phone. 'This is me, André, dialing the police. Is this *really* what you want?'

GETTING back to the bilingual midnight service at the West Olive Branch Church...

My son's asleep now, with his head in my lap, which is nice but far too rare an occurrence for it to feel completely natural.

Because I was never with him during what the Disciples of Oprah might call 'the crucial bonding phase,' Shane feels even less like my child than does Gretchen. If I feel like Gretchen's uncle, then I must feel like Shane's next-door-neighbor. To top things off, he really pissed me off earlier on the way to Mom's. We were driving when he said it; shocked, I asked him to repeat what he had said.

'Daddy says you a honkey.' His exact words.

I laughed, bitterly. 'First of all, André is not your daddy. I am. Second of all, he's an idiot. Don't...don't tell him I said that, it might upset your mother.'

Yellow's half white, so I don't know where he gets off telling my boy that I'm a honkey, as if...well, and anyway, that term seems so antiquated it's absurd. If I had experienced this in third-person instead of first, I would've laughed out loud. Anything else? A cracker? Sissy? Polar bear? The devil, maybe? Nice. Again, Merry Fucking Christmas. If I had any balls, I'd fucking kill that guy. Or at least have him killed.

And I seriously doubt that my four afternoons a month can do much to counter the mind-rotting effects of Yellow's presence combined with the inner-city school experience, not to mention the peer group that usually comes with it. I know all about it. Firsthand experience. Fucking tragic, but there's not much I can do. As a noncustodial parent, I'm basically participating in a really expensive version of the Big Brother program.

IF I was this broken, and I didn't have kids, I would've snuffed it long ago. On the other hand, if I didn't have kids, I wouldn't be this broken in the first place. Chicken or the egg. Take your pick. It's one of them there catch-22s.

I often wonder what I would've done with my life if I hadn't had kids. In fact, I was just mulling that over. Naturally there's no quick answer. Counterfactual history is always problematic. I mean, it would depend on what period we were talking about. I bet I would've married Claudette no matter what. Only we'd be someplace completely different.

I think regardless of the many possibilities, we would've wound up overseas for a good stint. Even if we didn't end up married, same deal. Overseas. I couldn't have ignored the lure of foreign lands. It had too great a pull on me. I may've done the Foreign

Service thing, which seems likely. Or perhaps I would've found my niche in some journalism class, done a bit with the AP overseas and back-doored into something that way. Politics or journalism, most likely. Those had been my primary fascinations, when I still had fascinations. Even today... if suddenly somehow I didn't have kids, I'd be on a plane the next day...to anywhere. Anything different. I'm so tired of strip malls and Applebee's and Wal-Mart that I'd rather be in Kabul at this point.

BEFORE I knocked up Cassandra, who was religious in general but not so religious about taking her pill, I had taken two courses toward a degree in finance.

I wanted to know all about money. It might not buy happiness, I thought, but poverty buys jack shit. I was going to be a banker, or a financial consultant—something where I managed money. In fact, I had sold Cassandra on this big bright shinny future, which is probably why she agreed to marry me in the first place.

She bought futures in my stock and lost a bundle. Granted, there's always a gap between the marketing material and the product itself, especially when it comes to dating, but in my case I had promised a Bentley and delivered a Hyundai. Cassandra had promised and delivered a no-frills domestic sedan, with no deceit about the vehicle itself, though the trunk was full of skeletons.

FOLLOWING my second divorce, I tried once again to get off my dead ass and do something. Anything. I applied to the police department...IPD and the Marion County Sheriff's Department. This was back before the merger. As a backup, I tossed in a package with the Speedway Fire Department, which was hiring at the time. But here, Chance and stupidity collided once again.

As for negotiating a reasonable divorce, Cassandra wanted to keep everything but my clothes. She even wanted CDs that she never listened too. Books she never read. She threw all my stuff in her bedroom and locked the door. I got all pissed off and started kicking the door. She called the cops and said that I had shoved her, which was true, only she left out the fact that she had shoved me first, and then bitch-slapped me into yesterday. I split before the cops got there...But they found me at the gym.

Luckily, avarice won out. I basically told her 'Hey, if you get me locked up, you won't see any child support money because I can't make any dough behind bars.' That woke her ass right up. She dropped the charges.

Regardless. Every time I apply for a job, now, they ask me...So, ever been arrested? And I have to say yes. They say, what for? I say, domestic battery. Not surprisingly, I was never able to convince any police departments or fire departments to hire me. I was lucky just to keep my job at the joint.

This little shoving match, and my subsequent arrest, made me reflect on the core of my predicament. For thousands of years, literally *thousands*, women were screwed over by men. I mean they really had the short end of the gender stick. But pendulums, once in motion, rarely stop dead-center. Today, one vindictive phone call to the cops can ruin you with a lie... Meanwhile, you're forking over your hard earned cash so she can cook a little pasta for your kid and pocket the excess or else spend it on booze or weed or lottery tickets.

AS I pore over the happy faces of this church congregation, I envy everybody here. Every single one of them. How nice, how salutary to believe in something. My God, I wish I could. I really do. I'm not one of those bilious atheists with an upturned nose, thinking I found all the answers by smoking dope and reading Sartre.

In fact, I often look back, nostalgically, to the days when I thought there might be a point to all this suffering and ceaseless making of turds and carbon dioxide.

Suddenly, while flipping through a fusty rouge hymnal, I realize that nothing matters. I'm not the first person to have this thought, I know. You hear it in songs, sometimes, and you read it in books... but to embrace it, to make it your own...well that's another matter. I'd been holding on, in vain, to a shred of hope that just went fluttering into a gutter. Not a goddamn thing matters. To anyone or anything.

With no God to judge us, and with no possibility of an afterlife, then in the long run nothing that happens here on Earth could possibly matter. Not in the long run. Mother Earth is waiting for your coffin...and, sooner or later, she'll have it. Sure, make a case for 'the moment' if you feel like bothering. But the future is ultimately meaningless. We won't be here for it. Neither will our kids. Eventually, the future pushes everyone aside. Just give it time. Anything divided by infinity is zero.

Who cares about all those misbegotten fools slain on battlefields for some cause remembered today by only a handful of historians who quaver over the pointless details of Culloden or Zama, or any of the great forgotten killing fields. They're dead! We didn't know them. We don't give a fuck! Nor do they...they're dead! Who in a hundred years will care about Darfur or the breathing skeletons who hopeless lie like zombies in the dust of Somalia to rest their eyes forever? Nobody. Zero. Such massacres are footnotes, if anything. Not even Auschwitz will matter in ten thousand years, which is nothing, compared to the age of the earth, let alone the age of the universe.

We are flesh-covered computers, meat machines with hard-drives we call brains. And onto these brains—these green, slimy, squishy, convoluted hard-drives—resilient programs and insidious operating systems were installed without our consent; out of all these programs, Survival and Procreation remain the most formidable, the least escapable. There it is, all laid out for you from the outset. The basic formula of life...

SURVIVE. EAT. SHIT. FUCK. BUY A HOUSE and DIE.

It's all been scripted. But there's no need to see the second act. You already know how the play ends, don't you? Even worse...to find yourself shackled to this prosaic formula of life without reaping any of its benefits; you pay and pay and only see your kids a couple days each month. $29/hour, that's what it costs you to see them. More than you make.

What the fuck's the point? I need to stop this bitching and moaning, this hemming and hawing...need to figure out a way to override this Survival program. It tells you to keep on breathing long after you've lost the taste for it, after you're spiritually dead and you're just a walking carcass anyway, long after you're so cut off and broken that you couldn't possibly enjoy another year. I'll tell you how it happens. You reflect...you contemplate...you *think*...that's your first mistake, the first step toward the big downfall, toward erasing all those crucial illusions without which we go nuts.

You come to care only about the metaphysical—man's search for meaning and all that horseshit. Everything else falls away from you. You give up on sports. You stop playing the guitar and stop watching lighthearted films and so on. The people who matter most to you have left and you've left the others, the ones who never mattered in the first place. You're serious now. At first, you may consider yourself oddly emancipated. Everything but the pursuit of meaning seems, well, meaningless. You stop following your favorite teams; you quit doing things that others do. You can't talk to anyone because you've lost the common language of trivialities, the piety of pop culture.

Eventually, you'll become something other than what everyone else is. If they're human, then you're not. And vice versa. You're not the same. For all you know, one day, you might look down and see your hand covered in reptile skin. You might gaze into a mirror to find the eyes of an insect staring back at you...a forked tongue, horns...you might start eating rocks and shitting out stamped envelopes, who knows. You're an alien.

You thought you were heading somewhere, nearing a destination. Ah, but you were only moving in a loop. You're back to where you started, only this time you're impoverished in every way. Deflated. Defeated. It was all a waste.

The books you read no longer teach you anything...they only confirm what you already knew at bottom...that life is meaningless, of course. But now you've lost your hold on all those important distractions like the nightly news and your pointless hobbies. You've nothing left to obsess your mind but that one thought, the thought of nothingness. You're stuck with a twenty, a thirty, maybe a forty-year sentence to serve on Earth. Welcome to the big house.

Here's the deal. You're in the bottom tier. That's the problem. See, four common states of being exist in the world today. You have the religious winners. They're the happiest of course. Next, you have the religious losers, who can justify their shortcomings and compensate themselves with sweet lies like eternity and redemption and so on. They're not too bad off. Don't forget about the non-believing winners. They know there's no real point to anything but they don't care because they're getting what they want, they're having fun. They're having a ball!

Then we have the spiritual underclass...The non-believing losers. They know they suck, they know there's no escape, no hope of redemption. They've been programmed for Survival, beyond logic. And they know it. They live as marionettes, jerked and prodded and made to dance by an antediluvian biological drive. The strings are visible enough, but most can't break them. They can feel the full weight and implications of their irredeemable failures but only the elite can override the program, quit the game and get out. Logically, a case could be made for living on the condition that life is enjoyable or at least, at minimum, it has the hope of being so within a reasonable time frame. Otherwise, good-bye. It's only logical. People come. People go. As they do. As they do. Nothing matters in the long run. Time washes all...it makes blank slates of everything.

For losers like us, we may as well be sheep. Or a bunch of cows, being fattened up by the hungry winners...One day you wake up from your nap and find yourself in rather unfamiliar surroundings. Moo, you say Moo. You're not a calf anymore, are you? You're not on that nice quiet farm any more, are you? No! You're huddled on the ground with other members of your species, next to a tall chain link fence capped with concertina wire. There's your buddy, slumped across your hindquarters, still snoozing away.

That was one heck of a trip; freeway travel did not agree with you. But it all seems worth it now. You've been invited to the biggest party of the year...just look at all your brethren out there gathered in the field! Now what's that sound, Mr. Cow? Loud voices. Human voices. So who are these guys? New friends? No! They come over and poke you with a stick. Stand up! Up!...Up on all fours, you stupid cow! A river of cattle forms. Get moving! Go with the flow!

Go!

Go!

Go!

The meat river flows toward a smelly brick building in the distance. Your jovial little tail swishes back and forth. Welcome to your destiny! Some of your buddies refuse to fall in line...they have other ideas. Don't worry, they'll be redirected with long metal poles that deliver one hell of a shock when they go *zap* against your ribcage. Better just get in line, stay in step. ClapClapClap up a stainless steel ramp. Amid the excitement, a massive misguided bull tries to mount you. Is mounting you. But the flow of traffic throws him clear of his ambition.

Everyone seems to be in such a hurry! Must be feeding time, or a sale on somewhere. Shoves, moos, and human screaming. What's the big idea??? Heads and bodies thump against your ears and shoulders. Inside, everything is steamy. Hot fog. Can't see much. Just go with flow, my furry friend, we call it blind faith. Don't make waves. Well all right, if you say so. Faceless loud men in tall rubber boots. Around the corner, you see a hot vat of some damn thing or other, and a tall pile of cow's feet. That ain't good. No, it's not. But shut up and go with the flow! Well all right but...all along the steamy corridor, parts of animals hang from pegs like Calvary taken one step further.

Welcome to the slaughterhouse you idiot, you stupid cow! Ta-dah! A motion picture brought to you by the hallowed one-percenters...

Next scene?? A clattering, rattling mixture of noise. That sounds familiar. Is that...? Yes, that's a chainsaw, dummy, you've heard it used to cut down trees. Now a violent shove comes from behind. What the...?

Something unforgiving claps shut against your rump. Why, you seem to be boxed in! Moo, you say, Moo. So what. Fuck you, dumbass, you stupid cow, now get in line! And stop that mindless bleating!!! It's much too late to panic, much too late for that. Better savor these final moments, dummy, as a dying member of the Loser Class...

You look left and see a wall of steam. You look right and see your old pal from the farm. You look at him and say, 'thought I lost you buddy!' He stares blankly and gives you a great big smile. Wait. That's not a smile...it's way too low. That's right, stupid-ass...that's no smile...that's what a cow's throat looks like after it's been slit! Naturally, you piss and shit yourself, overwhelmed with fear. Never have you felt so all alone in all your life. So tell me, dummy, do animals pray???

Something crashes down against your skull...you go blind for a second. That's the feel of mercy in the slaughterhouse! So there's your anesthesia, a great big whack to the head. And friend, it's the only brand of kindness you're gonna get.

A stout young man leans over you...bulging biceps, a fat set of nuts popping out of his tight blue jeans. He's got this oily hair and a thin sweaty mustache, strawberry blond. Now he sharpens something big enough to be a sword, while sucking on a piece of candy, or maybe a throat lozenge. You follow his movements with your big brown begging eyes. Is that a fucking machete?? He tenderly caresses that sensitive lump of meat behind your ear. His molars crash down on the lozenge, shattering it to bits.

'Goodnight sweetheart,' he says, with a just-following-orders gaze.

As he embraces you, his menthol breath tingles the clammy surface of your moist cow nose. Oh look...now you, too, have a smiling throat!

You wheeze and kick. So he breaks your hind legs with an aluminum baseball bat. Your heart pumps a red waterfall down your chest. You wonder...of course you do!...You wonder, 'What'd I ever do to deserve such treatment?' You crash to the floor, struggle back up, and collapse again with a thud...there's some backsplash from a puddle of your own blood. Something is twitching underneath you...it almost tickles. 'Oh my legs! My legs!!'

Your big fat belly is blocking the drain, so blood pools up around you. Our sweaty young friend with the menthol breath, he grabs a hose and irrigates the stall while yawning with a set of watery bored eyes. A rosy red liquid rises up toward your face. Your mind rushes back to the farm...to your comfortable stall, the feeding trough, the salt-lick, your old fury buddies and that comfy bed of straw you grew up in. Your mind tries to flee, tries to seek out Yesterday. But surely, you know it's over, right? By tomorrow night, a bunch of Winners will be eating your shoulders, your tummy, your chest...your ass...maybe your tongue. You've got time for one last thought. *Do animals pray*???

NOW the three of us—Mom, Shane and I—we step into the earliest hour of Christmas Day...snow like white dust coats the cars and the curbs and the serried rooftops of hovels, leaning wearily against one another.

Snow continues to fall from a moonless sky as Mom bangs her cane into divots along the pockmarked sidewalk, into NO PARKING signs, and the ankles of churchgoers as she mole-like navigates her way to my Japanese jalopy.

My son, still sleeping and smelling of childlike farts, has clapped his arms limply about my neck and nuzzled his afro under my chin. I can feel, through the V-shaped opening of my doughty black leather coat, the pulse of his sleep-warmed body. And that alone, for a moment, is enough to make me question my conviction that nothing could possibly matter. But it's only a moment, after all. It'll pass. That's what moments do best.

◎

MY circadian rhythms are all fucked up from working the night shift, so there's no way I can fall asleep when we get back to Mom's.

The spare bedroom is no longer spare...it's stuffed with bits and pieces that belonged to my stepfather before he threw a shoe. Hence, we are resigned to the futon in the basement, where I wedge myself between Cleo and Shane. They fall asleep instantly, the dog and the child. Must be nice. Cleo fidgets and yowls her way through a nightmare. Giant cat? Abandonment? What's a doggy nightmare like?

Shane seems to have fallen through the first fidgety minutes of sleep, into a deeper sleep, so I creek upstairs. At the kitchen table, I open up an Iris Murdock novel that Mom had given me years ago. I re-read underlined passages by the tangerine light of a kerosene lamp that had originally belonged to my mother's father, a drunk from Missouri who became a notorious land speculator in Zephyrhills and on weekends got his kicks by staring in local minstrel shows. Boy would he be thrilled to see his grandchildren.

I can't seem to read...can't focus for shit. So I sit back in Mom's broken love seat, submerged in darkness, gazing vacantly into the kerosene lamp. My mind strains to conjure up a memory that's just out of reach. What is it? I don't know. But this memory, however murky, exudes a visceral response. Finally the memory takes form...it's the smell of Claudette's hair conditioner; it bubbles up to the surface, pops, and disappears, leaving a weightless nothingness in its absence.

Minutes or hours later, my mother, bumbling for the restroom, rips me from my nothingness. All of a sudden, I have to be something again. I sit quietly still, hoping to avoid detection. It doesn't work. She sits down next to me and holds my hand.

'Darling,' she says, 'I know it's a tough time of year for you. But it'll be okay, I promise...Shane's cute as a bug's ear, isn't he?...I remember one Christmas, when you were his age...you had a red towel, safety-pinned to your collar...You pretended it was a cape. You wanted to be Superman remember?...And you kept saying "When I grow up I'm going to be a doctor, and a fireman, and a soldier, and Mayor of Indianapolis," on and on you went, like a bat outta hell...But you couldn't say the word Indianapolis correctly...you'd say Indianapodis...you were so cute, you can't imagine...do you remember?'

'Yeah. That was right before Dad split. I remember. He bitched at me for poking a hole in his favorite towel.'

'Wesley. Son, please. Can't you make the slightest attempt to look at the bright side of *anything* for a moment? You always harken back to, to...It's like you have to find some darkness at the center of everything, no matter what it is. And it never occurs to you that some of what I'm telling you...some of the things I'm bringing up, these memories from when you and Wendy were children...These were the best days in my life, and you seem to want to...Son, it's *Christmas*.'

'So it is, Ma. So it is. I'm sorry. I am. I wish…'

'What? Tell me. I want to know. What is it you wish?'

'I don't know. Things really got all messed up, didn't they?'

'If that's the way you want to look at it. You have your health. You'll come to appreciate good health someday. Believe you me. Two beautiful children. If you'll excuse me, I wouldn't say the situation is quite as dreadful as you make it. It could be worse. Much much worse, wouldn't you agree?'

She bludgeons me with platitudes…there's a silver lining, all that shit…and some naïve well-wishing too, along with a desperate stanza of motherly hugs. She must feel like a total failure when she looks at me. Bet she feels like shit, holding in her arms an albatross like me. If only I could give this kind woman a believable smile. That's the lie she needs.

My mother is right of course. It could always be worse. Certainly. I could be in Thailand, watching some overfed tsunami gorging itself on property and human life, on wooden bridges and my children. Could be a political prisoner in some third world cellar that reeks of rat piss and my own rotting teeth. Could be paralyzed from the waist down, or even the neck down…dickless, essentially. Could be. Could be a potbellied Congolese orphan, I guess.

But first of all, why should someone else's pain alleviate my own? Wouldn't that be sick, warped, grotesque, inhuman?

And anyway, everyone has a different threshold below which life is simply not worth living. It's individual, not standardized, not universal. I saw a prisoner once in the cafeteria. He was bleeding out of his ass through his khaki pants. He'd been raped and then some. How'd he keep going? Courage? Fear? I guess I'm not that guy.

AROUND five in the morning I wake up Shane, who cries for fifteen minutes straight because it's so early and because, he says, he wants his Mama.

'Wait little buddy,' I say, in the cheeriest voice I can manage, 'you'll be happy when you see what Daddy got you.'

'What is it?'

Instantly, his tears dry up.

I, with the help of my addled mother, attempt to feed him some oatmeal. Not a chance. He wants his presents now.

I'm disgusted by what I bought my kid for Christmas. I bought him the newest Play Station because that's all he seems to enjoy; he already has the same system at his mother's house, and I despise all of this wasteful duplication, but that's not the part that appalls me, really. It's the game that goes with the Play Station, that's what appalls me.

Now Gretchen, she likes museums and, provided we move at a cadaver's pace, she seems to enjoy nature. Not my son. He likes air conditioning in the summer and heating in the winter. He'd rather play a video basketball game than step onto a court. In fact, a few weeks ago, I took him down to the White River Parkway but he cried his little ass off because it was colder than room temperature outside.

Frankly, and this is terrible, I don't like my son. Maybe I love him, maybe I don't. Regardless, I don't like him. I just don't like him. What of it? I know, I know...what a socially repugnant confession. But there it is. I don't like my son. Is that really such a horrible thing to say? After all, if you don't like your own kid, then it follows that, at least somewhere along the line, it's probably your own fault, right? Makes sense, in most scenarios. But in my case, Shane spends a lot less time with me than he does with his mother or with that moronic boyfriend of hers. I see my son less than his teachers or his friends...I see him less than anyone else who's a part of Shane's young life. So really, why should we share any interests, however seminal at this age, or be bonded by any commonality? Maybe there's an argument for love and obligation. But as far as me liking my son, forget it. I came to terms with this about a year ago.

SHANE opens the first video game I bought him, Nemo. He regards the game with a young boy's version of vile contempt, then he moves onto the next, the latest version of Grand Theft Auto. I've never seen the game before, but he mentioned, repeatedly, that it's his favorite game. He already has a copy at Cassandra's; but hey, Daddy should probably have his favorite game as well. Oh this game is sick, really sick, but I figure the damage is done and I'm tired of never having what he wants.

As soon as Shane realizes—not by words but by the artwork—that in his hands he holds his favorite game, he jumps the chain of command and goes straight for Grandma.

'Can I play now?'

I correct his grammar 'May I play.'

'Can I?'

'No,' I say, annoyed by his willful disobedience.

'But why?' He kicks up the tears, just that quick. He's a moaner, a first-prize moaner, which is why I enjoy his company so much.

'Because I said so,' I say, trying to put my foot down, trying to establish myself as a disciplinary figure. We both know it's a farce. Who am I kidding? What can thirty-two hours a month possibly contribute to the realm of good manners, to respect for one's elders? I change my tact, injecting into my voice a placating, infantile quality.

'The Play Station needs to go to Daddy's house so you can play when you come over.'

'But how come I can't play now?'

Mom chimes in, completely undermining me, 'What the heck, let him play. How's this thing work?'

'I would,' I say to Mom, then turn to Shane. 'But we need to get you to your mother's house, little buddy. You have people and more presents waiting on you.'

WE don't talk much in the Civic. Shane runs from my car to Cassandra's wobbly porch without saying goodbye.

I watch him knock on the storm door. Suddenly he turns around and, smiling all the way, runs back to my car with his tiny bundled arms flapping like a penguin. He raps on the driver's side window. With some effort, I roll it down.

'Love you Daddy,' he says. Then he kisses me on the lips and runs back to the porch. It kills me. I'm floored. I'm reeling all the way back to my shack. Maybe...I don't know, maybe somehow he does actually love me.

FOUR hours later, I wake up for work. Had the same nightmare again. About the prisoner whose face I shot off, José Sanchez. In the dream, I'm standing in the kitchen when the microwave beeps. I walk over and open the microwave. José's head is in there. Just his head. Sometimes it's covered with tinfoil and I have to open it up.

In the shower, I try to jerk-off but I'm just too tired. Besides, I can't wank effectively without pornography. I don't have much to work with...I don't have much of a highlights reel. The only time I spent philandering was back in the high school, and just the first three years at that. Well, I'm not going to conjure up sexual conquests involving teenage girls, so that period in my life is of no use to me in the shower. I likewise refuse to fantasize about either of my ex-wives, though for completely different reasons. And I don't even want to talk about the meager handful of other women I've slept with.

Moreover, the few females I work with are either battered-looking or else two decades older than me. Or married to someone I know, which kills it right away. If I like a guy, I refuse to wank while thinking of his wife. Call me old fashioned. So I suffer from a dearth of imaginative possibilities with regard to tugging my meat. Hence I need pornography to relieve the periodic pressure that builds up in my prostrate and, through the miracle of biochemistry, affects my brain.

Having failed to masturbate, I boil a pot of water and, while that's going, slug a jug of bottom-shelf coffee to counteract the bottle of cheap bourbon I quaffed after dropping off Shane.

Cleo paces the floor excitedly. I open a can of tuna using a decrepit can-opener that barely opens cans...Now I whip up a batch of Kroger brand Mac & Cheese, a faithful staple, then chuck the tuna in with some butter, some powdered milk, and a packet of orange powder that came in the box. The last squirt of my watery-ass ketchup serves as my vegetation for the day. Running late, I place half of this slop in a Tupperware container and then scarf the rest while standing. Meanwhile, Cleo licks my plate as well as the green plastic bowl in which I mixed that garbage.

As she delightedly sets to work without once looking up, I'm seized with guilt because I don't have time to take her for a walk. She'll be stuck in this dungeon for thirteen hours straight. By herself. How can she hold it that long? I should give her up. Drop her off on a farm. I should give her to Mom. Tomorrow. But I *need* to see that wagging tail when I come home.

MY raggedy tin can wheezes and farts and vibrates like Katherine Hepburn's voice toward the end of her career. Well, at least I have a CD player now.

Heading down the alley in front of my house, I pop in Pink Floyd's "The Wall." Granted, it's been clichéd all to hell. But I must confess that recently my taste in music has digressed, shifted backwards...I think of it as 'comfort music' in the same way that some people call comfort food comfort food. Until recently, I stayed up on music. But now I'm listening to "The Wall" and gazing with disgusted sadness at the strip-malled architectural crime scene called Indianapolis. It didn't used to be like this. Not when I was a boy. And it's important to blame someone. Twelve years of lower-rung law enforcement has taught me that.

Me, I blame the upper class. I blame the snobs; I blame them for not being snobs, for not giving us any aspirations. They're just like us only with bigger houses, safer neighborhoods. Seabrook was wrong about her Nobrow culture. Lowbrow trickles up, sure, but there's no highbrow trickling down, no throngs of enlightened proletariat lined up for some celebrated ballet or even the latest art house flick. Give me a break. We are bombarded daily with non-art that's cranked out by automatons for people trained by television to have bad though consistent taste in everything so that marketing is that much easier.

This whole city, and every city like it, is a strip-malled ghetto as far as I'm concerned. In fact, I sometimes wonder if aliens—aliens without radiometric carbon dating and so forth—were to come down to earth, say, two thousand years from now...and let's say they did some archeological digs...well, I wonder if they'd get it wrong. I wonder if they'd view the crap we're slapping up today as obviously pre-dating the buildings that, in reality, had been erected tens or hundreds of years beforehand. If they assumed our culture had been progressing in a somewhat linear fashion, I wonder if they'd think the older buildings downtown came much later than the North Side strip-malls. I wonder if they'd read our books and watch our movies and get the timeline completely wrong.

SAME shit at work. I count the convicts and start the coffee.

Christman approaches me with jailhouse keys jangling and bouncing off his prosthetic hip...his yellowish, myopic eyes are magnified a hundred times by quadro-focal lenses so thick I find it amazing that they've never once fallen off his face. God, I miss Big Ed. I mean, is this guy really supposed to get my back?

Christman is smiling like a pervert on a playground, showing me his straight white dentures. I ask him what he's cheesing about and so he shows me a wallet photo that nearly shocks me out of my boots. He chortles, 'Her name's Cathleen.'

'Oh?'

'She's the one I was telling you about. Finally met her, after all that email.'

'She's a beauty.'

'Use to teach grade school. History. Taught for thirty years, see where I'm coming from? We're on the same educational level. She don't want me to be nobody else but me. Says I'm real nice...but she don't wanna put all her eggs in one basket...So I said, I said, give me a couple eggs by golly. Just a couple, hear? And she said I'm thoughtful, and that's a real big egg in her book. I brought her a rose last night. I'll bring her two more in the morning, soon as we hit that gate.'

'Have you uh...considered a dozen?'

'What's that?'

'Roses. A dozen or even half a dozen, I guess. I don't think people really hand out two roses at a time.'

'That right?'

'I don't know. How was the first date?'

'She cooked me diner. Spaghetti. She can cook. Keeps a real clean house too.'

'That stuff's underrated.'

'I'm telling you. She'll have to work real hard to get rid of me. I told her so...D'I tell you she's got a hot tub?'

'You old dog. On the first date?'

'Say, we've both been married once before. Understand?'

I let him yammer on for a while. With my son's unprovoked kiss still lingering on my lips, I really don't feel like thrashing anyone's triumphs. Christman's a good guy. I can't say he's a good man because that phrase, to me at least, seems to carry a different connotation, a higher endorsement. I'll include myself in this pointless digression. I think that, soon enough, Cooper will stand over my casket and say to himself...What a *good guy*. And that will that.

CHRISTMAN rambles on, does he ever. I look at his face and not for the first time does it strike me that, in his day, he must've been a handsome man. His thick glasses, wiry mustache and nearly hairless pate do little to support this theory but his strong jaw and symmetrical features do. Yep. It wasn't bad genes that ruined him, just old age.

He frightens me, frankly. I can see so many similarities, not between Christman and me, strictly speaking, but between the far off destiny of emotional desperation that finally swooped down on this old man, and the destiny that, if I don't croak it soon, certainly awaits me. I too would find myself living alone far beyond my tolerance for it, searching for aged love on the Internet and wondering if my grownup kids will ever call me back. Oh yeah, I can see that.

B-Ray appears from nowhere and waves a hand in front of my face, having apparently left the Protective Custody Unit without first being properly relieved (never authorized, frequently done) in order to replenish her stainless steel, wide-based coffee mug. From her shoulder she flicks a curly tress of rusty hair made crunchy and darker by hairspray. My eyes follow a greenish blue vein that courses through the warm white marble of her neck. She coughs, intentionally, thus interrupting Christman's never-ending saga of romance and hot tubs.

'How do, Weimaraner?' she says, mocking my last name. 'How'd Christmas treat ya?'

'Good, good. You?'

'Super. Ronny was askin bout ya, wantin to know why you ain't been over.'

'Yeah. Tell him I'm sorry, tell him I've been busy. How's he doing?'

'That busted back of his, it's still hurtin him somethin fierce.'

'That's too bad. I hope he...'

'Anyhow. I need to slip off to the lady's.'

'Uh-huh,' I say, knowingly...she's going to smoke a cigarette in the bathroom. Not her first. I can smell it on her, even though she tries to cover it up with gallons of perfume. Hey, whatever it takes to make it through a shift. As long as she's not trafficking with an inmate, I hardly see where it makes a difference.

IT'S rush hour in the day room of my unit. Through the glass I watch the bustle.

A young black man hunkers over a chessboard across from an old white man, who appears to study the game, staring through the long shaggy bangs of his fading blond hair. The white geezer's queen looks mated if the black kid brings up his rook. Two chumps, looks like. Can't play for shit.

A game of spades grows louder and louder in the corner but it's no competition for a trio of rappers who have come up with some song about prison blues, about missing all the bling-bling, and so forth. Their accompanist is White Boy John, a pale young kid with braids; he drums a blue plastic ice container with the heels of his tattooed hands...almost sounds like a real bass drum. He's talented. They call him White Boy John because his name is John, and indeed he is white, but his cultural allegiance is to hip-hop America. He's like a younger, less spooky version of that pimp who gets killed in the first Tarantino film I ever saw, True Romance.

As for the rest of the fifty or so prisoners, they watch one of the two wall-mounted TV's, a playoff game on one, *Fear Factor* on the other. Unlike me, they have access to cable television. And, just as many parents have outsourced parenting to television, we rely on TV to keep these guys distracted, not caring much about reforming anyone's character.

With my face one inch from the glass, it dawns on me that not a single prisoner in here looks the slightest bit depressed. Not one. And rarely do they. Angry or frustrated, sure. Depressed? Almost never. Why should they be? They only have one worry, which is getting out of course. 'Three hots and a cot,' they like to say...or 'three squares and a chair.'

Yep. Three hot meals a day with no job to dread. No insurance to worry about. No bills. No taxes. No pressure, really...Access to three libraries. Cards and board games. Cable TV. Basketball, weights, the whole bit.

I watch it all and can't help thinking that prison life seems like some kind of a...I don't know, a return to the tribal, to the community (in the strictest since of the word). In fact, I'd venture to say that while every purported communist nation to have ever existed will be considered a total failure by history, you have to wonder how many Marxist aims have been and are being met successfully in prisons around the world.

Of course, this has to vary from nation to nation...different resources, different values...it all has an impact. For example, I read a book by Warren Fellows about this Thai Prison—no thanks. Nor would you want to be locked up in some American 'Super Max' prison, where inmates remain isolated in one-man cells for twenty-three hours a day. Doesn't sound like a carnival by the sea. A minimum security American prison, now that would be ideal. But the GCF would do. It's probably representative of the average American prison, despite what sells on television.

Yep. I'm looking at their faces and each one either says 'I'm bored' or 'I'm happy.' A lot of them are laughing. It reminds me of Cooper's fraternity.

Sure, that first year behind bars must really suck...it must be tough...it must hurt, at first, as you futilely cling to the world you left behind like the dead in *Our Town*. That's the true pain, the true punishment, separation from the people you love. That, and, if you'll excuse me, the inability to get laid—well, by the opposite sex, at any rate.

Otherwise, the conditions here aren't that bad. It's about like a sailor's life, I'd imagine. It's the separation that hurts them. But that kind of pain remains contingent on the will to hold on, and once that's gone it's gone, and you're free to move on. For many, home was never a picnic in the first place and half their friends are locked up anyway.

Yes, I think institutionalization, in more ways than the institutionalized would like to admit, must be a great relief, a great release from modernity. To be free from the mechanized grind...to be liberated from the isolated lonesomeness that so many of us are imprisoned by...and yet they still have access to the pleasurable and even life-extending accouterments of the modern age, such as free modern medicine as well as heating and lighting. And cable TV, as I've noted. It's a bizarre form of utopia.

Then again, I could be bullshitting myself. I wouldn't like being locked up one damn bit. But my objection to such an arrangement wouldn't have much to do with the lifestyle, which doesn't look that bad. Again, I bet the field conditions for the average solider—sleeping outside or in tents, shitting in holes and so forth—must be a lot worse, all things considered, except for one fundamental difference, choice. Free will, if you like. Still, even a soldier doesn't choose when to quit his assignment. He serves his time like any other prisoner. The difference between the two is the soldier's initial decision to sign up, a choice that's typically absent for inmates.

But is that true? I don't know. At the GCF, according to the most recent report I've read, we have a seventy-six percent recidivism rate. Meaning, three quarters of the inmates here, once released, shall eventually return.

Johnson likes to say 'They're all doing life on the installment plan.' So it would appear. On some level, it's a choice.

Okay, three out of four prisoners will be back and you can chalk a lot of that up to economic deprivation, patterns of interaction and plain old stupidity. Rightly so. Yet you also have to wonder how many inmates, whether consciously or subconsciously, catch one whiff of the real world and say TO HELL WITH THAT. Back to the State! No more of these worries…No more of this howling loneliness! Back to that utopian commune, back to the GCF! Sure. Why not?

I'll say this. Most the prisoners I've met—no small number—have enough inner dignity to stop themselves from answering 'Yes,' if asked 'Are you happy here?' However, I have my own two-cent theory. If you could test for happiness—biochemically, say, using endorphins or whatever—I bet the average prisoner in America is happier than the average single, divorced, non-custodial father. That's just a guess. Richard Lovelace was right. Stone walls, that whole bit.

Thinking all of this through, I take a stroll through the day room. It's important to know your offenders but they shouldn't know much about you. Well, that's my opinion. If you get too buddy-buddy, then it'll be hard to write them up for misconduct. It'll be hard to put them in the hole and say NO when you need to. On the flipside, if you know nothing about them, you'll be blindsided by every little skirmish and personal problem that comes up.

I first approach Anderson, who's standing in the back, unenthusiastically watching the game on TV. He's the color of café au lait...like my son, he is 'mixed.' With only one side of his hair braided, it appears that the other side has exploded from his head. He's a soft-spoken man appearing somewhere in his mid-thirties.

As I enter his peripheral field of vision, Anderson looks away from the game, looks at me, turns back to the game. 'What's going on CO?'

The inmates call us CO, short for Corrections Officer.

'Not much,' I say. 'Any New Year's resolutions?'

'Stop selling drugs.' He gives me a crumpled smile.

'Sounds like a start. How much time you have left?'

'Fourteen months.'

'Short-timer.'

'Mmm-hmm. Ready to go. Twenty-four years is long enough.'

'Twenty-Four? Jesus. You look younger.'

'All that clean prison living.'

'Plan on settling in Indy?'

'Sure do. Got me a girl up here in the Nap. Got my carpenter's certificate too. Should be rolling fat, long as I keep my nose clean, and it's staying clean. Believe that.'

'Good on you. Seriously.'

'Thanks man.'

Anderson won't do. With only one year left on his bit, only an idiot would take the risk. I'm disappointed.

For some reason I thought he had a lot more time left. Damn, and he was at the top of my list.

Next, I stroll over to that scrawny white kid with the braids, the one I was telling you about, White Boy John.

'Huh-Oh. Here come the po-lice,' he feigns alarm, just joking around.

'What's up Cohen?'

'Chillin.'

'How'd your holiday visits go?'

'They was straight. My moms picked my boo up from B-town and brought her up.'

'That was nice of her. You get to see your son?'

'Naw, that little bitch wouldn't bring him in. She trippin.'

'Hey. I hear ya.'

Nope. This guy seems too immature. He might run his mouth.

Suddenly, I am reminded of Goldie Locks, what with the first bed being too hard and so on. Indeed, the third time might be the charm...I think I see Mr. Right, washing the windows. His moniker is Grandpa for the obvious reason that he's the oldest guy in my unit. He's at least sixty, with a receding head of curly white hair and a matching beard, both of which contrast sagely against his dark brown skin. He must've been around my height at some point. Now he's hunched over a bit. A significant potbelly detracts from an otherwise muscular frame. He wears rectangular wire glasses that make him seem more docile than he is, according to his reputation. He's sort of a kingpin, as far as trafficking contraband is concerned. As far as I know, he's not closely affiliated with any one gang. He just has a lot of friends. I think he sort of floats above all that stuff.

Here's his story. Thirty-something years ago, he followed a girl up to Indianapolis. He played the sax but couldn't get gigs, not enough. He had a heroin habit to feed. So one day he walked into a bank dressed as an employee and approached a meek brunette behind the counter.

He said, 'I'm here to rob this place.'

She handed him the bag, the one they set aside for robbers.

'Naw, give me *all* the money bitch.'

She said she was about to faint.

'Don't do that,' he urged, and then he confessed, 'Look, I don't even have a gun. I only want the money.'

The young teller was confused. He talked her through the process. Eventually, Grandpa got what he wanted. Sixty grand. Not bad. Outside, he hailed a taxi and was gone...

Grandpa hit a few more banks and then went back to Baton Rouge where he had some people to look after him, a place where he could lay low for a while. Of all the shit luck, a relative turned him in for the reward...a cousin, I think.

Here's the part I find interesting. Because he didn't use or even possess a gun during the robbery, he was only sentenced to eleven years, of which, he'd have to do five and some change. But he got to the state farm up north and fell in love with a punk, an effeminate male. This punk had a 'wolf,' a pimp of sorts, who wanted the punk to keep turning tricks. Grandpa didn't like that too much. He was in love with this punk. So he stabbed the wolf to death and picked up twenty more years on top of his five.

It's astounding, how many guys like Grandpa come in here with a three-year bit, or a four-year bit, and wind up trapped in the system for decades. He's a genial, likable man. You'd never guess.

I walk up to the window that he's wiping with a squeegee.

'What do you know Grandpa?'

'Not a damn thing. Too much,' he says, not bothering to turn around, 'How bout you?'

'Same I guess. I never see you play chess anymore.'

'Mosley and Jones both left. Since then, ain't been nobody worth two shits up in this bitch.'

'That's true,' I say, growing increasingly nervous about what I'm planning to propose. 'What a waste, you're not half bad. Wish we could have a go.'

'Me too CO, you been talking all that shit.'

'We'll see. When do you get out?'

'Six years and some change…long as you don't write me up again. That was some trifling-ass shit, boss.'

'You were smoking on the toilet, that's a little flagrant.'

'Shit…'

'I don't hold grudges Gramps, how about you?'

'You know better. We're cool-in-the-gang. Hey, I been thinking…You oughtta play my son, he plays on the web, on one of those Internet chess sites, said he's gonna show me how when I get up outta here.'

'I'd like to but...'

'Suppose that kinda stuff is...'

'Anyway.'

'Yeah.'

'All right then Gramps, I better get a cup of coffee. I'm whipped.'

So far, Grandpa has the lead.

AT one thirty in the morning, I count the prisoners again.

I walk down each corridor of bunks and, where possible, look for flesh, bearing in mind that I've screwed up before and counted a wad of bedding in which there was no body because an inmate had been across the hall when he shouldn't have been. When I found him—accidentally, just by doing my rounds—I stripped him down and found a makeshift tattoo gun comprised, mainly, of parts stripped from an electric fan. Vickers. I still remember his name. He would've done six more months except that Big Ed decided to go off on him instead of writing him up...Instead of taking time from the man, Big Ed simply reeducated Vickers, trained him to think differently. And it worked. We never had problems with that guy again.

Two years ago the same thing happened in another dorm, only it turned out that the missing prisoner had escaped in a garbage truck. The trash is always compacted inside the fence so he should've died. But the garbage guys didn't keep the compactor going long enough. Two days later, the cops found him in his mother's attic, half-loony. He needed his meds, that's all.

I think about this stuff as I count the prisoners. Their bedding area makes my stomach queasy. I'll never get used to the concentrated funk of butts and balls, of unconscious bad breath and spunked up sheets. If a Y-chromosome has a scent, this is it.

When I exit the bedding area and enter the hallway, I hand my count slip off to Johnson, who's been picking his nose all night. He looks at each booger before pasting it to the underbelly of his desk, leaving it for the next guy.

The light in the library is on. Perfect. Grandpa's in there cleaning. He's the 'night sanitation' guy, a very industrious fellow, by the way, who would still clean this place if the State withheld the eighty-five cents a day it pays him for his services. He likes to keep busy.

'Long time no see,' I say and shut the door.

'Shit CO, you scared the hell outta me. Don't you know I got a bad heart?'

'Really? You seem so...'

'No. And if I do, I don't wanna know.'

'Fair enough.'

'What can I do for you?'

I pause. Pause? I space out so long that Grandpa clears his throat.

'Boss?'

'Sorry...Have a seat, Grandpa. Tell you what, let's both take a seat for a second.'

'Am I in some kinda trouble?'

'Nope. I am.'

I sit down on a plastic chair and smile. Why the hell am I smiling? I don't know. You ever feel so strange you smile? It's not happiness. I know the difference. Okay, if it's happiness, it's not like any happiness I've ever experienced.

Grandpa sits down close to me. Maybe he can sense something, the aura of a conspiracy. I say that because he speaks to me in hushed, worried tones.

'What's going on?'

'I don't know where to start,' I say, feeling strange all over.

Grandpa studies me a while. 'You wantin to bring something in,' he says, 'make some money on the side? That it?'

'No. But thank you, I guess.' I can't believe he just asked me that. Normally I'd lock him up for even approaching me. He knows better. I must really have him confused. He pushes his glasses back to the bridge of his nose. I start to speak but can't. He looks at me and goes, 'You startin to worry me.'

'Let's see. I guess...I guess everybody's life has certain, I don't know, low points. Right?'

'Uh-huh.'

'Everybody gets down sometimes.'

'That's true,' he says, puzzled.

'Grandpa you uh...ever thought about taking your own life?'

He looks at me like I'm crazy. I rush in to fill the gathering silence.

'Well...have you?'

'Every man's wanted to die, one time or another. What's up with you?'

'Okay, out with it, I guess. Gramps, I want you to kill me.'

'Say what??'

The old man finds his feet a lot quicker than you'd think. I coax him back down.

'Keep your voice down, will you?'

'My bad,' he says, 'Now let me get this down right. You want me to kill you?'

'That's right.'

'Is this for real?'

'Yep. I'll pay you, of course.'

Grandpa contemplates this for a very long time.

'How much we talkin bout?'

'Two thousand. Cash. Or check, whatever. However, wherever. You tell me.'

'Two grand? Man, you off your nut.'

'Okay, what'd you have in mind? How much do you need?'

'Shit, what I need is…I need to think this over.'

I've never been a salesmen but I know enough not to let him go and think things over.

'No,' I tell him. 'Either you're going to do it, or you're not. Either way, it's cool. But I need an answer.'

He cracks his knuckles in an unorthodox fashion, smashing each sizable finger against itself.

'Tell me something boss.'

'What's that?'

'Why you wanna die?'

'No, huh-uh. See, you're trying to make the call. That's not your call. If I say, I don't know, it's because I have AIDs...then maybe you'll do it. But if I say what the hell, it's because I wanted the Mets to win the series...well then, you won't do it. But that's for me to decide. I just want to know if you're in, if you'll help me...Do you want the cash? That's the question.'

He starts to speak, 'The thing is, is...it's...' then he grows befuddled.

'Gramps,' I say, 'There's nothing to worry about. I'm looking at your face. I understand you're afraid, and that's natural.'

'Hell yes I'm afraid. You know I've croaked a few jokers in my day. But never no man in blue. I could get done real bad for that. So yeah. Hell yeah, I'm afraid.'

'Naturally. But see, there's nothing to be afraid of. Sure, killing somebody who wants to live, well, that's tough. That's messy. Real risky. Not me. You'll get no resistance. I'm easy Gramps. I'm complicit. I mean, I'm with you. We're a team on this one.'

'I got that part.'

'I don't think you do. I don't think you see how easy this money is. You don't have any cameras to worry about. What, you think somebody would snitch on a guy who killed a CO? Get real.'

'Shit, quit playin. We'd be on lock down for a year.'

'You're connected, no one's going to snitch.'

'I know that. I'm talkin bout I don't wanna be on lock down for a year.'

'Ah. Then make it worth your while. Let's say I offered you a million, would you do it?'

'Damn straight.'

'Exactly. How about for a dollar?'

'Quit playin.'

'See, so we just need to find a price. How about three grand?'

That puts me short a grand but I can just skip child support for a month. For the first time, he makes eye contact with me.

'What's the plan?'

'Well, honestly, do it however you want. I have some ideas. But the main thing is, you're driving the bus. I don't want you to do anything you're not comfortable with.'

'Comfortable?'

'You know what I'm trying to say. You can get me in one of the toilet stalls. I won't make a sound, I promise. Or I could leave a door open...see, you can slip out after count and do it outside. At night. I mean, if you want. I'll wait behind the dumpster. Those are just details. We can nail all that down later...Don't worry. What I need to know is, are you in?'

He doesn't say yes or no, so, anxious to end this conversation, I nudge him.

'Three grand. What do you say?'

'Fifteen.'

Fifteen!

'Ten,' I say with an air of conclusiveness.

He looks at his watch. Yeah right...like he really gives a damn about the time.

'Some place you need to be?' I stare him down, interrogation-style, Johnson style. He nods his head up and down. But I want a strong commitment on this. No ambiguity here.

'Was that a yes?'

'Yeah,' he says, 'That's what that was.'

'Good.'

'Shit. Good's ass. My hands, they shakin like a motherfucker. I need a drink.'

'Tell ya what. I'll throw one into the deal. Seriously. What's your pleasure?'

'Okay then...Seagram's finest. But I wouldn't go so far as to say—'

'Seagram's then. Consider it done. Likewise?'

'What kinda...when you thinkin bout...'

'Oh, I'm not in a rush. I guess by the end of January would be nice. I'd rather not know the exact day, if you don't mind.'

I walk out of the library, beaming, right past Johnson's desk and into Protective Custody, where I find B-Ray sleeping at her desk. There's not much else to do; the inmates here are locked away in their cells for the night. Snug as a bug.

Startled, she jumps up, then looks comforted to see it's only me.

'You just pinch my toosh?'

I can't write the Oklahoma accent very well but it's there.

I shrug.

'What?' I say, but not as in What?...as in So what.

'I oughtta wup you,' she laughs, showing me a silver tooth, halfway to her lower molars.

'Go ahead,' I say. 'Whip me. I wouldn't mind. Neither would you. Maybe there's an empty cell we could use. What do you say?'

'Lordy Ba-gordy, what's got into you?'

'Coffee, too much of it.'

'I'd say.'

'I'd say you're lucky you're married. You've been looking sexier by the day. Have you been going to the gym? A little Tae-bo?'

'Dieting, more like. Been tryin real hard. Can you tell? Honest?'

'Can I?' I say, and then, leering at her, I make a cat noise.

'You're sometin else Doc. It's real good to see ya smile.'

'Ditto. What kind of perfume is that?'

'Elizabeth Taylor's Passion.'

'Wow, now that's a lot of passion.'

She doesn't get the weak pun, so I leave. Next I come to the sergeant's desk, where Johnson's flipping through last month's issue of *Maxim*. I rap my knuckles on his desk. 'Got a joke for me Sarg?'

His moon-colored eyes look glassy like mine. It's late. This is how eyeballs usually look around here. He turns the magazine over, marking his place. He gives me an ornery grin, 'Why is it pussy hairs are short and curly?'

'I give up.'

'So they don't poke your eyes out,' he grins and tells me two more groaners. I laugh like hell. Simple courtesy, that's all.

Christman's hunched over the desk inside the hazmat room with some article he printed from the Internet that looks like something about black holes, time, origins of the universe and whatnot. I've never met a man who read more and retained less. His shit-colored, red-rimmed eyes swim behind the substantial lenses of his glasses like two moribund fish trapped in twin aquariums.

'Learning anything?' I say, which prompts him to yammer on, quite cheerily, for the better part of an hour while I say uh-huh and wow and jeez and so forth. In a way, I love this crazy bastard.

THE prison yard feels peaceful, quiet and unsullied.

Snow falls softly on the power lines, on the steaming manholes and razor wire. It's beautiful. The whole way home, I'm smiling. Really smiling. And laughing too. I'm happy. Crazy, but happy. There's no mistaking what it is this time. It's happiness.

Consider...It's summer, and you're ten years old, and you're at the local swimming pool, and you've trapped yourself at the top of a diving board—the dreaded high dive. Eight other kids dangle from the ladder behind you...they call you names and tell you to jump. The water didn't look so deep, didn't look so far away from the board a few minutes ago, when you were chomping on a corn dog with your friends and judging the high dive from ground level. Wow, the water's so deep! It'll never end...you'll drown! You're convinced of it. But you've backed yourself into a corner. You have to jump now. Or do you? You turn around to leave, to clamber back down the ladder in shame. Retreat? That's the only thing worse than jumping off the goddamn thing. Can't do it.

You return to the edge of the board and, sure enough, out of nowhere, you find yourself in mid-air. Had you jumped? You must've. It didn't seem like a conscious choice but, well, it's amazing, the things we carry around inside our heads. Heroism springs from a dearth of options Yes, in some nether region of the brain, some forgotten cellar, a choice must've been made. Now you're in the air...free from the monstrous pain of indecision. Naturally, you're happy.

I'M driving home.

For once, the strip-malls fail to turn my stomach. They seem neither more nor less consequential than anything else. In a thousand years, that Wal-Mart will be forgotten rubble, but that's also true of the Notre Dame.

I call Gretchen. She's in some boisterous arcade at the mall with her friend Melissa. I can't hear. Neither can she. We cut it short.

'Bye Daddy. Love you.'

'Love you more,' I say, which might be true. Life itself seems easy enough to let go of, but love's another matter. I've never stopped loving anyone I've ever loved. Maybe that's my problem.

Walking through the door of my shitbox, cockroaches scatter across the kitchen floor, one them looking a little lost, unable to find an exit.

I don't care. Jimmy crack corn, and I don't give a fuck. It'll all be over soon.

Happy New Year, 2005!

MY New Year's resolution is to finally kill myself.

Meanwhile, I still have to work, which has turned into a major inconvenience...Some corn-fed kid named Ryan Hasbrook called in sick in order to celebrate his anniversary, so the Central Dorm is short two officers, seeing as Jeff Weiser just got picked up by the Coast Guard and didn't bother with a two-week notice.

Hence, I've been assigned to a strange dorm that operates differently, with a different cast of characters, all with unfamiliar foibles. It also means I can't read because Long, the Sergeant, is a bit of a stickler, a square. My entire routine is shot to hell.

Central Dorm is built differently than what I'm used to...it's built for a rougher crowd. There are two units, each one separated from an atrium by two automated doors that are controlled from 'The Bubble,' which separates these two units; it's where the Sergeant stays all night, working the doors...calling workers out and letting students in...passing out meds through a little slit.

I check into The Bubble and grab my radio...head back into a tiny atrium. Sergeant Long hits a button, opens one door and then the other...let's me onto my unit for the night. There's a central day room with a TV and a bunch of tables but the room is empty. Here at

Central, all the inmates are locked in their rooms during count. Two inmates to a room. I walk the bottom range and then the top, looking through tiny slits in the blue metal doors, recording my count.

Unfamiliar with this place, I fuck up the count and have to do it again, thereby feeling like a rooky. Or more like a senior citizen...Past my prime.

Count clears and all the convicts come out. I get the cleaning crew going, while enduring a barrage of complaints from a yapping throng of sniveling thugs.

'CO, look. I need new linen.'

'This shirt don't fit.'

'Naw man, I ain't got no extra-duty left on the books. Check with Long.'

'CO! CO! Somebody done stole my radio!'

'My room's too muh'fucken hot.'

Finally, I snap.

'Everybody shut the hell up! Or I'll do shakedowns till sunrise.'

Apparently Hasbrook, the guy who I replaced for the night, he must be a total soft ass; I mean, to let them get away with all this crying and sniveling. He doesn't have them properly trained yet...he's failed to inculcate them with The Lazy CO's Creed...Don't fuck with me and I won't fuck with you. Either that or they're testing me. In any event, I just don't feel like being dicked with all night. And besides, if I wanted to actually work, I'd be on the day shift.

Having established myself as a grumpy no-nonsense curmudgeon, I sit down at the desk and wish I could read a book. But I can't, because of Long. So I take out a blank count slip and start doodling. After a while, I look down at what I've written.

Suicide
Suicide
Suicide
Suicide
You hate yourself.
You know you hate yourself.
Destroy yourself
You are nothing
The world will be better off without you.
So kill yourself
Kill yourself
Kill yourself
Kill yourself
Kill yourself!
Kill yourself!!!

Strangely, this reminds me of Sirhan Sirhan, the guy who bumped off Robert Kennedy. After RFK's assassination, the CIA dug up Sirhan's diary. In it he had written 'R.F.K must be assassinated.' He had written it over and over again, as if preparing himself mentally.

I look at what I've written and I think about Sirhan Sirhan, and I wonder if I might be crazy. And then I think...if so, how would that change my decision? It wouldn't. It's like wondering if there's life on other planets, a ba-zillion light years away. It has no fucking bearing.

And yet, if my kids are to get the life insurance, I'd better not let anybody find such an incriminating piece of paper. I take it to the staff bathroom. Close the door. Rip it to pieces. Run water all over it.

I'm about to flush it down...then I think, fuck that, it might not go down. So I wad it all up into some toilet paper and stuff the soggy wad into the front pocket of my polyester pants, which sag off my ass because I used to actually have an ass when these dorky pants were issued to me.

ONCE again, I count the prisoners.

I can smell dope in one of the cells but I couldn't care less. I take the count slip to The Bubble, push it through a slit, and return to my desk, forcing myself not to scribble any more weird shit that might be found later.

The count clears and I go back to the cell where I had smelled the dope, and where I now cadge an old Hustler Magazine from a young white kid who's wearing a doo-rag; I then stuff the porn mag into a DOC folder, so that Long, looking out from The Bubble, can't tell what I'm looking at. I keep the folder below the desk.

Opening the magazine while shrewdly wearing latex gloves, the first page I come to has a giant spooge stain, right on some blond's face. It's very off-putting.

AROUND midnight, as I'm fighting sleep, the radio traffic goes berserk.

'Signal Ten! We have a Signal Ten in East Dorm!'

'Away the Quick Response Team! All First Responders report to East immediately!'

Fuck. Just what I needed. Tonight, I'm supposed to be a First Responder.

I grab my gear and go...

I'M the second First Responder to make it to East Dorm, which I guess makes me a Second Responder, technically speaking.

That numskull Swann is already on the scene. His face tells me that he's already shat his pants. I walk into the K-Unit, not really caring what happens. There's a young black kid on the floor, writhing in pain. And there's a tiny white kid who's been knocked the fuck out. There's blood spurting from his forehead.

Bunk beds have been turned over and everybody's shit has been spilled all over the floor...Pop corn and shaving cream and porn mags. The room seems to have divided itself into black and white and this crazy-looking white guy with a black eye is brandishing a shank the size of a battle axe, screaming his ass off.

I've been around long enough to know that it could really go south from here. I leave Swann at the door and hustle to the cage where there's a CO/senior-citizen working the desk.

'Tell the Captain to activate the E-squad. Just in case.'

The old guy's face is blank, like he's totally in shock.

'Call him up,' I say, then I return to the fracas, remaining just wise enough not to enter the bed area; I stay on the edge, by the door, watching. My goal isn't really to intervene, per se...I'm just letting them know that I'm watching, that if there's more violence, I will see, and I will report, and they will stay in prison longer, and they won't have visitations for a while, or recreation privileges, or phone calls...that's pretty much how it works at this point in the game. I'm so outnumbered, there's not much else I can do.

But then the crazy white kid starts screaming bad shit.

'I'll kill these fucken niggers!'

'Fuck you, cracker! Lil' white-ass bitch.'

It dawns on me that if I don't do something, we'll probably be looking at a hostage situation soon. That crazy white kid will nab somebody and then we'll all be stuck here for the next twelve hours, filling out paper work, waiting for the negotiators to get here and all that jazz.

So I say fuck it, and I pull out my pepper spray. I figure I can close on him and a least take out the main idiot, so long as one of his buddies doesn't jump on me.

But luckily, I don't have to do anything. Just-in-time-Johnson shows up with the rest of the Quick Response Team, armed to the hilt with everything but guns. Johnson lives for this shit. For him, this is self-actualization.

He's got a scuba tank full of CN gas...it's some really nasty shit. If he opens up, it'll fog out the entire joint...everyone will get hit. They'll have to fumigate the whole place.

Johnson pulls the pin and points the hose in the general direction of the crazy white kid. 'Okay,' he says, 'Who wants to play?'

And like clockwork, two other white kids take the crazy kid down. It's perfectly coordinated, like something we would show in one of our training films.

Some seven-foot tall CO wanders over and cuffs him. A tenuous calm settles over the dorm room. Two guys from medical walk in and cart away the black kid who's sobbing on the floor.

Johnson goes, 'Okay, everybody. On your bunks. Like it's count time. You know the drill. Come on. Let's move! You...Cornrows, on your bunk! You too Smiley, bunk the fuck down!'

Everybody obediently shuffles into place. Johnson yells some more.

'Shirts off, girls! That means you, too, Bed Head. Everybody! Shirts off!'

The members of the QRT stand guard with pepper spray and batons and stun guns. Meanwhile, me and a couple guys who normally work this dorm, we go around to each bunk and look for signs of struggle. One by one, we identify the five men—three black, two white—whose knuckles appear to be damaged. One at a time, we escort them from the dorm, and then we cuff their asses up.

Strange, I don't even feel a drop of adrenaline. I task myself with escorting a huge white guy out of the dorm...a fucking ogre. But soft looking, like he's never done a push up. Like he grew up on Nintendo.

I take him to the hole...

DU, short for Detention Unit, is a squat little building sitting all by itself, in between two manholes that belch steam into the crisp December air all night.

It's good duty, to work in DU. The Captain can't just walk right in here. It has a controlled access point. So you can play cards and read and do whatever you want all night. Sergeant Lenderman, the OIC, he spends half the night chatting on the phone with his Haitian wife, a real stunner. He and I go back...like, back to when I was normal. We've always had a good rapport.

I take the ogre into the atrium and Lenderman comes over...helps me pat him down for weapons. His assistant remains sleeping in the bathroom. Probably has a day job.

'How ya been, Wes?'

'Not bad. You?'

'Not bad,' he says, sounding a little distant, which is the way Lenderman has sounded ever since coming back from Iraq, where he worked as a corpsman in Baghdad. An affable guy, but also an erstwhile Golden Gloves boxer. Not to be fucked with.

Swann brings over this guy's property box and we go through that, finding a wad of tobacco hidden in a Bible, the pages of which had been carved out in order to accommodate more contraband.

Lenderman verbally hazes Swann for just standing around 'like a useless head of cabbage,' so Swann takes off, pouting his way out the door. We take the ogre into a side room and strip him down. The ogre continues to talk massive amounts of shit, like so many of them do, when they're handcuffed, when they know we can't really do anything.

He goes, 'We know all about you, Weimer.'

'That right?' I say, 'Turn around.'

'Yeah, we know you're married to a black lady,' he says, getting the story wrong, not knowing that I'm divorced, presumably relying on dated intelligence.

'Turn around,' I repeat.

'You fucken nigger lover.'

'That's enough,' I say, reflexively looking around for an object to hurt him with.

Lenderman gets my back, 'Shut your fuckin cum-catcher, Scooter.'

Scooter growls again, full of misplaced hate, 'Ya fucken goddamned nigger lover.'

'Turn the fuck around,' I say, 'And show me your asshole. That's how this works.'

'You can tell your nigger wife and nigger babies to kiss my big white dick,' he says, and then he gathers up a wad of saliva, preparing to spit it in my face.

'Do it,' Lenderman says, 'And I swear to God…I'll knock your fuckin teeth in, then I'll say you fell.'

'I'll report you for this.'

Lenderman turns to me, 'Know how to tell when an inmate is lying? His fuckin lips are moving.' And then he turns back to Scooter, 'You think anyone would believe your lying ass over me? So do you want to keep your teeth or not?'

It all sinks in. We're about to treat his body like a flesh-covered piñata. We're about to have a field day with his ribs, and maybe his head, and he knows it. As a result of this sudden realization, the fat bastard's face changes completely. Checkmate. Solidarity! Workers of the world, unite!!

We finish searching this sloppy moron, and then I adjust his handcuffs for him...I crank the cuffs as tight as I can get them, until he screams. I know I'm leaving marks but I don't care. I never act like this, I never get all petty and emotional, which means I can get away with it once or twice because no one would believe the truth....so, if my conduct gets reported to the Disciplinary Review Board, no one will believe a word he says. Lenderman, he's right about that. You can't get away with being an asshole all the time, but if you've got a hard-on for someone, you can usually make the system work to your favor, if need be, as long as you, personally, don't go after the same inmate more than once.

I walk him down to the Green Range, twisting his wrists behind his back, right before the point where I can do any real damage. He gasps, even though he's trying not to. I throw his ass in the clink and slam the door.

'Turn back around,' I say, preparing my key in order to remove the cuffs.

He bolts to the back of the cell, 'I'm filing a grievance, CO. You can bet your ass on that!'

'Go ahead, you fucken redneck piece of nothing. Now if you want those cuffs off, you need to stick them through that little hole, genius.'

'Fuck you! Eat a dick!' He screams. And then, using his cuffs to vandalize the cell, he starts banging them against the stainless steel sink, doing more harm to himself than to the sink.

'Destruction of government property,' I say, 'Insolence. Fighting. Keep going. Let's see how long we can keep you here.'

This makes him pause, but not for long.

'Hey,' he says, 'I bet you got yourself a bunch of little nigger babies running around the house right now, don't ya? Buncha jigaboo space crickets, stinkin up the place!'

'I'm leaving,' I say, 'Good luck with those cuffs. Doesn't seem like a big deal now, but we'll see how you feel about that in an hour or two, when you can't event scratch your nuts.'

He starts going ape-shit again. This time on the toilet.

'Listen,' I say, and then I scream. 'Listen! You keep it up, and I'll have your ass in four-way restraints all night. Is that how you want it?'

He thinks about this.

'Okay,' I say, 'Now let me get those cuffs off so I can go. It's the last time I offer.'

Finally, I get the cuffs off, noting with pleasure the bruised and bloody ring that they leave around his wrists. But he still won't shut up. Lenderman finally puts down his crossword puzzle and comes over.

'That's it,' he says, 'You're going on Yellow Range.'

Yellow Range is where the lights stay on 24/7. Eventually, they either go crazy or soft. I appreciate the support that Lenderman has given me. He's old school that way, and I feel indebted.

There's a CO still sleeping in the bathroom so, out of courtesy, I pinch it, fight back the urge to shit. Instead I sit in The Bubble and drink coffee with Lenderman for a while, catching up on how he's been since getting back from Iraq. He spits his tobacco juice into a Styrofoam cup and tells me the story. Turns out that, while he was over in Baghdad, his wife made friends with some guy at the electric company where she works. He doesn't think they've actually been engaging in the formal fucking process, but he's nevertheless consumed with paranoid jealousy. I get the impression that I'm the first guy he's told this to. I feel bad for the guy, but I can't find much to say other than 'You could hire a private dick, I mean, if you really wanna put the question to bed. Bad choice of words but...'

While we're sitting there, the phone rings. It's the Captain, looking for me.

I go down Medical where Briggs, the young black kid from earlier, is sprawled out on a bed, quietly groaning. He is completely and utterly fucked up. Smotherman, the guard working Medical for the night, he fills me in on what happened.

Earlier a kid named Daley, the young white kid who I found in a state of being knocked-the-fuck-out, he had sold a bunch of tobacco to one of Briggs's buddies; the tobacco, apparently, had been cut with something, like, I don't know, lint, or whatever. So Daley is sitting there in the day room, watching ESPN with a bunch of other guys. Briggs walks up and demands Daley's seat.

He punks him out. In front of everyone. Just to show him what's what. Daley, being much smaller than Briggs, he acquiesces. But then some Arians get a hold of Daley; they ridicule the young kid, call him a pussy for not standing up for himself. Etc. Etc.

Daley thinks about this. He goes to his bed. He gets some baby oil and a cup of sugar. He mixes it up together in a bowl. He walks over to the microwave, nonchalantly. He heats it all up for three, maybe five minutes. Then he walks back over to the chair that had been stolen from him, and he dumps the boiling baby-oil/sugar concoction down the back of Brigg's neck. It goes all over his back, down his ass crack, and eventually to his balls. A little bit hits his throat, too. The hot oil burns and the sugar makes it stick to his skin. That's when all hell broke loose at East Dorm.

Over the phone, the Captain gave me the task of transporting Briggs to the hospital. As for a sidekick, I get stuck with Humphrey, another genius. Humphrey will be my driver. I, being senior, shall be the armed escort.

THE ambulance shows up...makes it through the gate as we halt all movements.

I go according to the book; I chain Briggs to the gurney, despite the fact that he is all fucked up and could not possibly escape or even resist. They hoist him up, into the back of the ambulance, which waits for us as we draw our weapons and check out a van, which we will use to escort the ambulance.

ON the way to the hospital, Humphrey talks about his favorite pastime...wife-swapping...He tells me about these seedy little joints, buried in the crevices of conservative Indianapolis, where he and his hairy-faced wife go and pick up other couples...so he talks about how he enjoys watching other men fuck his wife, how *exciting* it all is, how it makes everything new. I can't take it anymore.

'Humphrey...I am *begging* you, will you please, *please* shut the fuck up and just drive?'

'You're weird,' he says, all wounded, 'People been sayin' you turned weird, and they're right.'

I don't know what to say in response but I'm glad to have a moment of silence as we pull into Wishard.

WE get Briggs out of the ambulance and get him moving toward the ER. Humphrey leans over the gurney and goes, "Offender Briggs, if you try to run, we will shoot you.'

'Give it a rest,' I say.

'Well,' he says, 'they need to know you mean business.'

'You really think this guy is in any condition to run?'

'Stranger things have happened.'

'Look, just...Whatever. Stay with this guy while I take a shit. I'm dying.'

WHEN I get back from the bathroom, I find that the doctors have removed Briggs's shirt...they've gotten most of the cotton out of his skin.

I've been doing this a lot of years and yet, to me, what I see is still pretty sick. His dark black skin is covered with huge blisters that have popped and opened up, revealing the pink meat beneath. Personally, I would be screaming my ass off...I would be screaming off other asses than my own...I can't understand how he's even dealing with this. But he just quietly sobs as the nurses dab some brown liquid over his wounds.

ONE by one I watch with a sad twisted sense of amusement as the ER gets flooded with a tide of wounded prisoners from East Dorm.

First it's Daley with a concussion. Then a black kid comes in with his nose flattened against his face. Next it's a white kid who had taken a padlock to the forehead; and then the chin; and then the bridge of his nose. I notice that he's holding his teeth in his hand. He offers them to the nurse, as if she'll put them right back in.

It goes on like this until three in the morning, until the ER is overcrowded various idiots and racists, bent on smashing each other up...until all the real fighters are either in the ER or else down in the hole...until the dorm has lost its collective will and strength to fight. Finally, they must be tired and worn out...like the rest of us, they just want some sleep.

I get back to the joint, fill out all the paperwork, and go see the Captain, who's playing solitaire on the computer with his boots up on his desk.

'Pretty bad night,' he says casually, looking up with a pair of watery eyes.

'Captain, don't ever stick me with that idiot Humphrey again. *Please.*'

'Here's a little secret. Between me and you?'

'Sure.'

'He's got a sexual harassment charge against him. A real one. I don't think he'll be here much longer.'

'One of the nurses?'

'Kitchen staff. Speaking of, I need you to help me feed this morning. We're short handed.'

SO I go to the kitchen and pretend not to see the prisoners stealing oranges and bags of milk.

I don't feel like doing any more paperwork. And besides, after what I saw earlier, theft doesn't seem like such a big deal.

Instead, I shoot the shit with a young officer named Bennion, a devoted Mormon with brains and looks and a heart of gold. For God's sake, I hope he doesn't stick around here long enough to become another me.

While lecturing Bennion on his latent potential, I spot a middle-aged cho-mo with bad skin, walking up with his tray of slop, still wearing his headphones, which is forbidden when outside one's dorm.

Like so many child molesters, he looks like an older David Koresh, or a young Stephen King...super-thick glasses with those squareish, 1980s frames. He's from my dorm, but out of Christman's unit. Just arrived last month. An obvious baby-raper, he fits the mold perfectly.

'Hey,' I say, 'Take off your headphones.'

'What's up, CO?' he says, looking offended. 'I heard you were one of the good ones. Did you turn all Robo Cop all of a sudden?'

Fuck him. If he wants to play, we can play. I'm in no mood. Besides, a part of me enjoys torturing cho-mo's, whenever I can get away with it.

He's older. This has to be his second bit. Or his third. By now, he should know better than to yank my chain, so I say 'Come with me, offender, we need to have a chat.' And then I lead him back into the kitchen, into a meat locker.

He goes, 'What's got up your ass?'

'Give me your ID,' I say, closing the door to the meat locker as my breath spurts out in front of me like a frozen cloud of smoke.

'Fine,' he snaps at me, 'here.'

'Now, give me your radio.'

'Whatever. Give me a confiscation chit first.'

I smile, examining his ID. 'So, Drexler...what are you in for?'

'Drugs.'

'Drugs, huh?' I snort, already knowing what he's in for because he has to attend these pervert classes once a week. 'More like you drug a kid off a playground.'

'Hey, that ain't cool.'

Hmmm...Drexler...Drexler. Name sounds familiar. Michael Drexler...it rings a bell.

'Wait a second,' I say, 'Are you from Danville?'

'No, why?'

'Were you arrested in Danville?'

'Why's that *your* business?'

Yeah, that's him. Read about it in the papers. He raped his three-year-old step-daughter...couldn't get it in, so he took out a box cutter...made one slice, connecting her tiny vagina to her tiny anus. And then he raped her. Fortunately, or unfortunately, depending on your viewpoint, she lived.

My voice starts to shake as I speak, almost in a whisper. 'Give me your radio. Now.'

His face goes white, sensing that the situation has changed, has become personal. He hands it over. I look at it. 'Interesting. The DOC number on your ID doesn't match the DOC number on your radio,' I observe. 'Hmmmm. So...is this stolen, perhaps?'

'I bought it.'

'Oh. You've been trafficking with other inmates then? Either way, it's a Class B offence.'

'Shit, man. Are you serious? Come on...You're gonna write me up for this...this weak-ass shit?'

'You're a pervert and coward, Drexler. Ok, so you picked up the tough guy language around you. Well, I'm not impressed. And I'm not fooled, either. I read the papers. You're a high school janitor and a goddamned degenerate, not a tough guy. Not a drug dealer, either. You're a fucken baby-raper. Now did you steal that radio or did you buy it?'

'What's it matter? Like you said, either way, it's a Class B.'

'Tell you what,' I grin satanically, 'Smash it up. Right here. Right here in front of me. Smash it up and I'll let it go.'

'Ah...that's...that's real messed up. Look, I don't know what happened in your personal life. But leave me out of it. I ain't gonna bust up a perfectly good radio.'

'Up to you. I can't make you do it. You know that. But I can take out my pen and start writing...I've been at this a while. I'm pretty sure I can keep you here for at least another year, if I throw in enough detail. Like how you just physically threatened me.'

'Man I didn't threaten...' then the light bulb goes off.

So. I watch with twisted glee as Drexler smashes the radio into a billion bits, obliterating one of his few possessions...It's the most valuable thing he owns in the entire world, and I watch with great pleasure as he smashes it to pieces...I watch, thinking about my daughter and my son, and I feel happy for a moment as I realize something; namely, for the first time in a very long time, it's not me I want to kill, but someone else. For an instant, here, I actually value my life more than someone else's, which I find puzzling and strange. I know that I want to kill. I know that I could kill, too, that I have it in me. And I know this would be a noble act, that sexual predators nearly always re-offend, or try to...odds are, snuffing out his life would be no worse than shooting Hitler, say, in 1935. It would be doing the world a favor and the only thing that stops me is the law, the prospect of having to share meals and a bedroom with these bozos and degenerates. Jesus, the monsters we have to work with...it's hard to fathom...it's a wonder you don't read about prison guards killing these perverts more often...Cops, they just drop them off. Here ya go! We have to *live* with them.

WHEN I get back to the desk in the cafeteria, arriving with a little pep in my step, elevated from my low-grade torture session with Drexler, I find Bennion standing there expectantly, holding up the phone.
'You gotta call,' he says.
'Captain?'
'Don't think so.'
It's Big Ed. I recognize that Barry White voice right away.
'Bizzle,' I say, 'What's goin on?'
'I gotta gig for you, if you're interested. I can't get people to work over the fricken holidays.'
'Sure,' I say, 'I can be there.'

ON the way to the gig, I think about the shift...about Briggs and the pink open blisters on his back...about Lenderman and his wife...about the racist ogre I locked up...and about that cho-mo, Drexler, and the pieces of his radio, scattered on the floor of that chilly meat locker. He looked like he was about to cry and this brought me a flash of happiness.

I was an unprofessional prick all night and I vaguely wonder...If I keep it up, how long would it be until they would have to fire me?

And then I get a tremendous case of butterflies in the stomach because I realize that, unless Grandpa backs out, I should be dead before the State could cut through enough red tape to get rid of me. I wonder how bad he'll hurt me...if he'll be too nervous...or if he'll be as steady as the executioner in that old movie, *A Man for All Seasons*.

My hands are shaking. I feel sort of numb as I slide the Civic into a metered slot along Pennsylvania Avenue, downtown, right in front of the armory, where a line of young partygoers wraps around the building, forming and L.

All the buildings and even the park across the street are painted silvery gray from the streetlights and the moon. I hate to work these underage clubs...they always fight too much. But, at twenty bucks an hour, cash in hand, no taxes, who can say no?

Big Ed is standing outside the armory wearing Roca-wear jeans and a new red hoody...diamonds in each ear...tight little waves in his short-cropped hair...a thin little mustache above his upper lip, which he constantly treats to chapstick in the winter. He nudges the promoter and says something into a radio, probably a comms check, and then our eyes meet warmly. I walk over. He gives me a bear hug.

'Damn, Wes! You lost some weight, bro. You been doing a lot of cardio or something?'

'Yeah,' I agree noncommittally. 'When I can make time. How's the fam?'

'Good, man. Good. Shantel's about to start high school next year, if you can believe it. You outta pop over more than once a year.'
'I know that's right. It's just…'
'How's the kids?'
'Okay I guess.'
Awkward silence.
'Well,' he says. 'Let me go check on the guys inside. Make sure they're in position.'
'You want me to come with?'
'Naw. I want you out here, searching all these youngsters. I need somebody who knows how to do a proper pat down,' he says, which could also mean, and probably means, that he no longer trusts me inside, where things might get rough, where you might need a little beef and at least one ounce of testosterone.

FREEZING my ass off in the breezy foyer of that old stone building, I perform my menial duties perfectly. Mostly because of the respect I have for Big Ed and the crushing amount of guilt I would feel if somebody got into the club with a weapon and started shooting up kids.

I'm reaching up now, along some big dude's crotch, when my phone rings. I ignore it. A second later, it rings again. A minute later, same thing. I check the phone. Cooper. Well, I decide, I may as well call him; otherwise he'll keep it up all night.
'Coop, I'm workin a gig. What's up?'
'Tomorrow night is New Year's Eve. Don't forget.'
'How could I?'

'And no excuses.'

Cooper hangs up. Big Ed comes outside to check on me.

'How's it going?'

'No drama.'

'How 'bout them Colts?' he says, making the well-intentioned mistake of attempting small talk with me. I used to follow the Colts and the Pacers and IU basketball. And Big Ed used to read, back before he opened up two businesses, and adopted two kids from his crack-head sister, bringing the total population of his brood to six.

He stands out there in the cold, and he tries and he tries to re-connect with me. But we just don't have anything to say to one another anymore. There's a whole history between us that neither one of us can seem to draw on. We can't tap into it.

Back when we were both on the E-Squad, we went on a bunch of runs together...wild shit...and we went through the annual Chemical Day, where we spent eight hours getting gassed and sprayed as we shot at targets, fought each other with batons, and tried to complete the land navigation course while our skin sizzled with pepper spray and our mouths went dry with dehydration.

And I remember the day we locked up Vickers because I caught him with a tattoo gun, and the guy went off on us. We took him into the office. Cuffed him up. Vickers yelled at me, 'You a cracker. And your boy Smithe there...he ain't nothin but a motherfucken graham cracker!'

Big Ed went ape-shit. He walked up to Vickers and took off his cuffs.

'Do something now! Do something now, bitch! You ain't shit! You wanna talk all loud when you're cuffed up. Say something now!'

This went on for a good long while. For about twenty minutes, give or take. Vickers finally broke down...started crying...

'It's just this place...and, and my mom and...It's been like this my whole life!'

Satisfied with the outcome, Big Ed threw the tattoo gun away, let Vickers walk back to his cell, humbled, and we never had another problem with him the whole time that Big Ed and I worked together. That man is a master of male psychology. And what struck me as funny was, not five minutes later, I walked back into the office and found Big Ed on the phone with Nia, his youngest daughter; he was talking to her like he was Mr. Rogers.

'Hey sweetie....Daddy was just thinking about you. I love you, you know that? You know that, girl? ...Now you be a good girl for Mommy, okay?...Because you have to take your medicine or else you'll have problems breathing again. Please? For Daddy?...Thatta girl...Okay...Let Daddy go. He's gotta work,' he said, and then he made sweet little kissing noises into the phone. He looked up at me and knew he was busted, knew that I had seen his inner-Teddy Bear.

We laughed about that night for several days after, about me hearing the kissy noises he made into the phone, and so on. We laughed about everything. We never ran out of laugher and conversation. We talked sports, religion, politics, books, family. And now, there's nothing. Our entire friendship is a shell. Or maybe more like a ghost. Anyway, it's spent.

I get home around two in the morning and let Cleo out.

Hunkered over the particleboard desk that I picked up on sale from Staples, I down a fifth of bourbon while cruising the Internet...jerk off...eat a baloney sandwich...then look around the house for more bourbon, but don't find any.

A little after four in the morning, I collapse in my unmade bed, snuggled up with Cleo.

Then I sleep for fourteen hours.

AROUND eight in the evening, I hop in the hooptee and head east, then north, feeling completely different. Happy, I guess. By this point, there's been a total shift in my mindset...

I mean it's like...at long last, you've finally made a decision; you've committed yourself....so now you're focused...alert, yet no longer jumpy. At peace. You putter along, with your collar up and your face down, trying not to think or reconsider matters, allowing inertia to do the work, letting the momentum of your decision carry you through the last colorless season of your life while you wait for it all to end and end quietly, without much of a splash. I am ready for my close-up. I am ready for my exit.

NEW Year's Eve? Another year in the toilet.

It all started at Average Joe's. Cooper and company had rented out a bar in Broad Ripple. A standard bar, pretty run of the mill. Average Joe's. Aptly named.

That's what you do when you're too young to stay in for the night but too old for the diehard mobs. You throw a party or, as a compromise, you rent a bar. I think they sold around three hundred tickets to this thing. Unlike the other bars in Broad Ripple, you could actually breathe in this place; you could move around without having to wade through drunks and vomit. The ratio was favorable. I saw more women than men, despite the abundance of cops, the abundance of mustaches. Tons of chicks. Lots of eye candy, which I wasn't used to. Highly titillating.

Justin Brace, Coop's old college buddy, he was the first guy I ran into. That was around eight thirty. Justin works as a retail guy for the Bank of Indianapolis and, as Chance would have it, he happens to work with Cassandra, my ex-wife, who's a teller there. She finally quit the prison gig.

'Sure,' he said, 'I know Cassandra.'

'She used to be a lot smaller,' I assured him while elbowing Cooper for bringing it up, for pointing out the fact that I had once been married to woman who now has an ass that resembles a mountain of chewed Wrigley's.

Justin, though I don't know him well, always struck me as phlegmatic and decorous. Inherently likable. Used to be a nose-tackle for IU, back in the glory days. A gentle giant. He has a kind, smooth-shaven face and an unassuming way about him. I guess he wanted to be a kindergarten teacher or a social worker or something (I forget which) but he didn't like the income, or lack thereof. So he's a banker.

It's strange, though, how even the nicest guys are still just fucking animals underneath. I watched his eyes follow this young woman's ass...I followed that crude stare...I watched his mouth start to open instinctively as the PROCREATION program started spinning up on his hard drive, triggering off one more process in that meat-covered machine called Justin Brace, whose reptile mind was slithering toward her sex as naturally as a snake or an earthworm might thrust and crawl toward a warm hole in the ground. She turned the corner and, as his desperate gaze lost sight of its prey, his teeth perceptibly snapped against each other in a micro-expression of angst at having failed to seize the prize, the young flesh. Fucking animals...All of us.

Into Justin's hovering gaze walked Leonard Mailer...Leonard, the redheaded retard cop; it's good to know that the DOC doesn't have a monopoly on idiots. Auto-theft, that's his thing...somehow he got promoted...Detective Mailer. More like Detective Moron. He's at least as stupid as anyone I work with, and I mean on either side of that thin blue line. But Coop maintains a certain sentimentality for the poor dolt, I guess because they'd been assigned to the same unit, or team, or whatever, when they first started out with the police department. The whole primacy effect.

The Mackay brothers showed up and rescued me from Leonard. Both cops. Good guys. This was the springtime of the evening, the budding time, when people were still showing up and everyone was glad to see everyone. I was hopelessly underdressed in my Levi jeans and my zip-up black thingy from Old Navy.

Billy Braun—such a suitable name!—showed up already drunk. He's a firefighter...as wild as Coop but with a mean streak. Nonetheless, a good guy.

All the wives were there. Except mine of course. I should've brought Cleo...put her in a blond wig, give her two pair of stilettos...size threes. She deserves a nice night out.

I'm kidding of course but that reminds me, there's a guy in jail who got caught screwing a chicken. That alone is sick and hilarious, I know, but it's the details that get to me. He was busted in a hotel room...I think it was at the Embassy Suites up on the North Side. Why the hell would anyone get a fancy hotel room for a chicken? That's what I want to know.

Anyway, I know one of the turnkeys assigned to this guy's unit. He said he shook-down the chicken-fucker's bed area and found what we in the industry refer to as a 'fee-fee,' an improvised prosthetic vagina (IPV), most often constructed from one cotton sock, a few rubber bands, and some unwitting prison-guard's latex glove, which serves as a condom; throw in some microwaved hand lotion and there you go, you're ready for hours of scintillating self-love. Well, this chicken-loving pervert just couldn't let it go; once in jail, he'd gotten a hold of some construction paper and then he proceeded to fashion a chicken beak for his fee-fee.

I was so drunk I shared this anecdote with a group of cops, which would've been no big deal, except their wives were present. I was that drunk. What can I say, it was an open bar. Sixty bucks bought all you could drink, and that's what I drank. Started off with Red Bull and vodka, then passed desultorily through every imaginable option. New Year's Eve, I thought, would be my last night on the town. One last drunk...a good one, I had decided. Eat, drink, and be merry. That old time-tested sentiment.

Swept up in the urgency of my final days, carnal impulses announced themselves boldly. I simply had to get laid. At all costs. I was prepared to mount just about anything...the blind, the crippled, the crazy. Bring it on! I was committed to the mission. Go out with a bang! Why not? But something happened.

Coop spotted me near the bar, ordering a Nevada Pale Ale, which was not part of the open bar, and which I paid for with a nearly maxed-out credit card. He came over, dressed as a priest, alongside Sarah, his pregnant wife, who went as a nun—he'd obviously put her up to it. Mind you, this wasn't a costume party. He just dressed up, had gotten a wild hair, so to speak. He ordered up two shots of Jäger and proposed a toast.

'Here's to you, and here's to me...forever we'll friends be. But if we ever disagree? Fuck you buddy, here's to me!'

We clanked glasses, spilled liquor, did our shots. Cooper patted me on the back and vanished. He had a rigorous social schedule to maintain, hopping and whooping from group to group, backslapping and howling, exchanging friendly insults with other cops.

That left me with his wife, Sarah. She's quiet. Tender and kind...but quiet. There's only so much conversation you can manufacture for a quiet sweet woman with whom you share no direct intimacy. I was doing all the talking. And I'm no talker. Well, as I'm straining to keep the conversation going, this vision walks up in a crushed red velvet dress, which was stretched and swollen by her young and sizable breasts.

'Sarah,' she said, as she approached, 'Gee, I didn't know you'd be here.'

'Oh hi...' Sarah said, looking uncomfortable.

'You can't remember my name. That's okay. It's Darshanna.'

Darshanna! Can I so much as adumbrate her perfection? Impossible! She was from Livingston, New Jersey. And she wielded the razor-edged accent to prove it. Her parents were originally from Northern India, somewhere near Agra, she said. Her last name was Petal. I worked with a Petal once...only other Indian I've known. Maybe over in India, Petal is like Smith or Jones. Her parents were engineers. One older brother was an architect and the other was in medical school. Not that she blabbed. I pulled the information. So, I deduced, she came from money. I didn't hold it against her...people don't ask to be born rich any more than they ask to be born poor, or black, or white, or pigeon-toed. Still, I find rich women daunting.

Jesus. She had the body of a twenty-year-old gymnast. But these dark circles around her velvety eyes, they put ten more years on her face. She was twenty-three but with a face that could've passed for thirty. Her body and face were conflicted. I loved that. Right away, it struck me. She seemed elegant yet bold, slightly intimidating...like a woman's riding glove, perhaps. I remember how Sarah introduced us-- awkwardly.

'This is my husband's best friend. Have you met Chris?'

'Hi, Chris.'

'Actually, I'm Wesley,' I said, feeling stupid.

'Sorry. Chris is my husband,' Sarah said, and then she further clarified, 'Wesley is Chris's best friend.'

It sounded weird, at my age, to be introduced as someone's best friend. Juvenile. And yet pleasurable, in a way.

Apparently, Darshanna was a 'student teacher,' a teacher in training at Sarah's high school. With all that success buzzing around the Petal household, Darshanna was free to study whatever she wanted...which turned out to be English literature.

Ah yes...Desire's impatient rhythm took possession of my heartbeat. I had no saliva in my mouth. For the first time in months, I felt alive, which was a feeling I wasn't ready to deal with. It was too much. Sensory overload. I needed a drink. In the middle of my second shot of Absolute Currant, this gal with big blond hair accosted me from behind...she apparently put on makeup with a shovel...a hairdresser...hair and nails...originally from Kentucky...said she lived down in Bedford...just up to the city for a few days, for the New Year.

Her acid-washed denim skirt was so short she almost needed two hairdos. Her laugh felt forced. So were the smiles we exchanged. She wore a painted smile on a painted face, the kind that makes you wonder what kind of skin is under there. I forget her name. At any rate, I got rid of her somehow, made my way back to Sarah and Darshanna.

Pretty soon, it was like Sarah had faded into the background, into the dark pink wallpaper. Darshanna and I, we hit it off instantly. In a highly sarcastic fashion, she employed banal space-fillers like Golly, and Gosh, and Gee. Hard to explain, but it was funny, the way she did it.

I can't help it, sarcasm draws me in immediately. It seems to ridicule the absurdity of life while at the same time allowing everyone to share a laugh along the way. Sarcasm says hey, this is all pretty pointless, but we may as well have some fun with it.

With a few of the comments she made about our fellow partygoers, Darshanna seemed to embarrass if not offend Sarah, who I guess you might call demure, since I'd never call her downright prudish. She said a few things that made Sarah blush...something about rumors of impotence and the gym teacher and his wife, who taught sociology.

To be quite blunt, I don't have much of a bladder...especially if I'm out on the sauce, pissing it up. So, having to go, but not wanting to lose

Darshanna in the mix, I went to the bathroom as quickly as I could...pushing, squeezing it out until my urethra burned, like I was pissing butane.

Washing my hands, I noticed the reflection of my face in the soap-splattered mirror. As Douglas Coupland has pointed out in two or three of his nearly perfect novels...eventually, you wind up with the face that you deserve, a face that sums you up. Just as Cooper's face says Incautious Exuberance, or Justine's face says Reserved Longevity, or Christman's face says Lifelong Disappointment, I saw my reflection and knew that my face had Broken Loser written all over it. I have Failure coming out of my pores. I exude failure. It's in my pheromones.

Looking in the mirror, I tried to match up this simple fact with a less simple fact...that for some inexplicable reason, Darshanna seemed to be into me. Usually, there are only two groups of people that are drawn to failures....other failures, and those who want to rescue failures; among this second category there are two subcategories. The first group is afraid of commitment; the second and murkier group, well, they actually want to help people, for one reason or another. I wondered which category or subcategory she might belong to as I rushed back to the very floorboard I had left, relieved to discover that she hadn't moved. She even wore what I would call a cheerily expectant look upon her perfect face.

'Sarah tells me you're a writer,' she said, chomping down on an ice cube. 'Gosh. Nothing sexier than a struggling writer.'

'I wouldn't say I'm a struggling writer. I'd have to be writing something, something worth reading, you know. I'd say I'm struggling to be a struggling writer.'

'Me too,' she said, 'I'm struggling to be a struggling writer.'

'That's a lot of struggle to have in such close proximity.'

'It is, it is. But that's a good thing, isn't it? You'd never have a plot without a struggle.'

'That's true. Then I guess my life's been heavily plotted. What are you writing...or what are you struggling to write?'

We laughed a little. And ok, we made eyes. Sarah disappeared without my noticing. Darshanna was so beautiful, I couldn't believe she was talking to me longer than five seconds. I don't just mean beautiful as in some standard physical, photogenic runway beauty...I mean she was radiant...I mean if the Earth could clone more of her the world would be happy.

'The rub,' she said, 'is that everything I write turns out like a poor imitation of an American Zadie Smith.'

'You could do worse.'

'I could do better.'

'There you go, confidence is everything.'

'That's not what I meant,' she kicked me in the shin. Not too softly.

She said, 'I'm just not a huge a Zadie Smith fan.'

'Oh,' I said, as though I hadn't understood.

She said, 'What about you?'

'Me? Zadie's okay I guess.'

'What do you write?'

'I thought we'd already established that I'm only struggling to struggle to write.'

'And?'

'I like stories about sheep,' I said, 'Sheep and the men who love them. I've been thinking about moving to New Zealand. Or Scotland. You know, just for the research.'

'Plenty of sheep.'

'More sheep than people, I hear.'

'It's gorgeous,' she said.

'New Zealand?'

'Scotland.'

'Oh, you've been?'

She'd been everywhere...So not only was I financially poor, I suddenly felt impoverished in terms of life experience as well. It was humbling. She was younger by years yet older by life.

We found ourselves in a booth. It must've been pushing ten o'clock by then. I noticed with disappointment that she only drank Diet Coke. Some helpful advice? Never drink more than the beautiful woman you're hoping like hell to seduce. I know that now.

'You're not drinking?'

'Urinary tract infection,' she said rather nonchalantly.

'Oh. Wow.'

'It happens,' she said, sipping cola through one of those tiny, flat brown straws that are usually reserved for mixing, not drinking.

'You have a killer smile,' she said, then she flashed me her own.

Darshanna was forward. And nearly a decade too young for me. *Perfect.* I needed a forward woman. I was too bashful and out of practice. Without a forward woman, I could never climb outside myself long enough kiss, let alone screw. Plus, an older woman usually wants security, tangibility, something more than just potential...an older woman doesn't want bullshit, promises, and maybes...an older woman would never put up with a flop like me. Youth, however, will sometimes take chances.

I loved Darshanna. Instantly. Of course that's not true. I mean the sensation I experienced, the rush of chemicals in my brain, or whatever, made me feel like I was in love. Good enough, I say. *Good enough.*

We talked about books, naturally, as well as films. In the whole of my adult life, since Claudette left me, I had never had the chance to discuss literature with another woman. So on New Year's Eve, it was as if a dam had broken, and words were gushing out of me, untamed. I blabbered on about dear friends whom I had never met...Milan Kundera and Iris Murdoch and Joseph Heller and André Gide and Douglas Coupland and Irvine Welsh on and on. I think she was impressed, which was a first for me. Not that we agreed on everything. There was some verbal fencing going on for a while, prompted by Darshanna's unyielding defense of Jane Austin, for whom I've never found a use.

'She was subjugated, Wesley. Don't you see? Why wouldn't she obsess on what we have the luxury of regarding as "trivialities," as you put it?'

'Maybe so. I just don't like the fact that she writes in a passive voice. It puts me to sleep.'

'A passive voice reflects her condition. Have you considered that?'

I changed the subject, to what I can't recall. I must've said something that she found to be funny because she laughed like hell and, as she did so, her breasts shifted and bounced in such a way as to suggest their epic firmness. Slowly but steadily I was caressing her with words, wearing her down with them, wrapping her up in them, as if forming a bouquet...serenading her with well placed lines, ensnaring her with the tenderly crafted phrase. For once, I brought my A-game. I pressed my fingers lightly on her elbow, establishing my right to touch her, gently taking possession of her as I spoke.

'I love your dress, it's perfect.'

'Oh? And what makes a perfect dress?'

'I guess one that actually puts on display what it pretends to conceal.'

'I see.'

Without thinking, I removed my fingers from her elbow and looked at them, as if expecting to see drops of sunshine there. Abruptly, she excused herself to piss. Meanwhile, I found Cooper in a corner without his shirt. He slung a naked sweaty arm around me and kept it there.

'So fucking good to see you out, man. Man...Hey, are you hooking up with that Chinese chick?'

'She's Indian. And I was going to ask you, is she some kind of a...escort?'

'Escort?'

'A pro.'

'A hooker???'

'Yeah. Did you hire this gal for me or what?'

That's how perfect she was. That's how drunk and suspicious of life I was. When Coop realized that I was serious, he pissed himself laughing.

'Maybe not,' I said and walked back to the booth. Three corporate guys had taken it over. Darshanna was waiting for me. We stood, leaning on a banister, and continued to chat. It was all too perfect for real life; even then, I could see it all in words, written down.

Well I gave her a very condensed version of everything I've told you—the divorces, the kids, the prison—minus the suicide bit. Then I tacked on a disclaimer.

'So run now, if you feel like it. I wouldn't blame you a bit. Granted, I wouldn't be happy. But I truly wouldn't blame you for a second.'

'I like you,' she said, wrapping her slender arm around my waist, 'I like you a lot.'

'Really? Why?'

'Why would that matter?'

'I know what's going to happen. We're going to end up wasted and—'

'I'm not drinking.'

'Okay, I'm going to end up wasted...'

'You already are,' she tried to kick me in the shin again, but I was too quick.

'Just give me your phone number now, before I forget.'

'Jeeeez,' she rolled her big brown eyes, 'You'd forget?'

'I can see it happening.'

She gave me her home phone, her cell phone, and two email addresses...she wrote it all out on a beverage napkin and handed it to me. I was stunned. She smiled. I smiled back.

I said, 'That's weird.'

'What?'

'I'm happy.'

'Me too,' she said, looking away as if she wanted to say something else, something more effusive. Out of the blue, I thought about Grandpa, who, within the next thirty days, was supposed to stab me or strangle me or do something else more creative yet nevertheless lethal.

When Darshanna went to the restroom again, I called her cell phone and reached her voice mail. I had expected a fake phone number.

So. She wasn't a prostitute hired by Coop to cheer me up. And the phone number was real. Strange. I wondered if she was a transsexual or something. Maybe I would reach down later and get a gigantic handful of sweaty balls.

I just couldn't figure out what such an intelligent, beautiful young woman could possibly want from me. Pity fuck? I thought that was a myth, an urban legend.

When she emerged from the restroom, I pieced a bit of it together. She wasn't covering up her forearm anymore. Until that moment, she had concealed it with her hand or else kept it behind her back. Now I could see that it was badly burned. Or rather, scared from an old burn. It looked horrific.

'It's bad,' she said, 'I know. When I was a kid, my brother's friends used to call me Freddy Kruger. So, um, it's your turn to run.'

'Are you nuts?'

'Who isn't?'

'Who are you here with anyway?'

'My cousin,' she said, 'we had a tiff. It was nothing really, but she went home without me.'

I knew that was a lie...I could tell by her voice and the slightly pained aversion of the eyes—I've been working with professional liars for years and years. So what if she was lying? I didn't mind. We hadn't known each other long enough to expect much truthfulness, not of that nature. I knew the score. She'd either been stood up or else she'd had a fight with her steady man.

If she didn't feel like confessing that some fool had left her there all alone, that was fine by me. Like Chris Rock once said, what are you gonna do, put a flag on it? *Exactly*. She could've shown up still dripping from her last amorous engagement, and I would've been smitten just the same.

In the moments that followed, autumn settled over the evening; everything bright turned brown. Something terrible happened. I didn't puke on the dance floor or forget her name or do anything quite so banal and forgivable. I wish it were that simple...

MIDNIGHT was approaching.

By midnight, my lips had to be wrapped around Darshanna's. Or somebody else would beat me to it. That's how it works in a bar at midnight on New Year's Eve. I'm no Casanova but I know that much.

But Darshanna had disappeared, allegedly to call her brothers and wish them a Happy New Year. So she said. Well, she hadn't returned. I couldn't find her anywhere. She'd been gone for over thirty minutes. By this point, I assumed that she'd left me...that she'd reunited with whomever had brought her to the bar in the first place. Or else she had wised up, and had no wish to waste her midnight kiss on a frog of a prison guard who had no hope of turning into a prince.

The countdown was in full swing...couples were kissing and groping and arguing all over the place.

'Ten...nine...eight...'

I called her phone. No one answered. I was talking to her answering service, blubbering something, probably something moronic. Who knows. Keep in mind, I was so drunk that I could barely walk, let alone reason.

'Three...two...one...'

Then something grabbed me, that goddamned hairdresser from Bedord. She kissed me, and I mean she really laid one on me. My hand moved up her plump, quivering thigh. It was instinctual. I was so drunk! It had been so long! When my eyes popped back open, an angry gaze was burrowing into me.

'Darshanna...' I said feebly.

She huffed but didn't say anything. Not one word. At least she didn't bolt. She was waiting on an explanation. No doubt a good one. I first turned to the hairdresser.

'Um, could you uh...give us a moment? Thanks.'

I took a step forward. Darshanna took a step back. I tried to explain myself. 'It...it was midnight. You were gone. I thought you left me.'

'I don't mind that you were kissing her.'

'You don't?'

'Not so much.'

'That's good.'

'I mind, Wesley, that your hand was headed for her crotch! What kind of a slime ball are you?'

'A...drunk one? I'll get down on one knee. That's no hyperbole. As long as you don't leave me here, I'll do it.'

The ordeal of groveling, well, it's never pleasant. But I was wholly poised to face it. I gave self-respect the heave-ho years ago. Roll me in my own shit, fine. I don't care, so long as you'll agree to love me for a while or at least pretend...just don't get me down on my knees for nothing. But before I could supplicate myself further, the next terrible thing happened. A big drunken oaf stepped up and interfered. It was Coop's buddy from school, the banker. Justin. But he seemed like such a nice guy! So mild mannered...How could he?

'Wesley,' he said, 'I think you should walk in the other direction.'

'Thanks Justin. Thank you. I appreciate your concern, but I've got a handle on this.'

He entered my personal space and all those prehistoric primate cylinders started firing. But I kept my cool. He was big...built solid. Besides, it was Coop's friend. I didn't want a scene. Not to mention—since killing a man and since Big H had given me the ass-drumming of a lifetime—I'd been shying away from violence whenever possible. Way the hell away.

He was taller and, looking down on me, he used this genetic fact to his psychological advantage.

'What'd I say?' he snarled, 'Walk away.'

'Yeah...listen, you know, I really don't need any more advice. But thanks.'

'That so? You wanna fight about it?'

'No. Not really.'

How drunk was he!? I was terribly drunk, as I've mentioned, yet I could still tell that Justin's speech was slurred well beyond normal New Year's limits. Cold stones had replaced his eyes. He was subhuman.

I heard Darshanna groan 'For the love of God,' in a tone that, while clearly meant to transmit disgust, may've contained a shred of sarcasm.

That's right before Justin inexplicably punched my forehead. What an idiotic place to punch someone. I bet he broke his hand. That wasn't enough to satiate him. He grabbed me by my Old Navy pullover, at which point there was little choice in the matter.

When the bouncers arrived, I was on top of Justin, steadily choking him. It felt so good, so damned good to unleash all those barbaric juices. You figure, in such situations, the drunkest guy will usually lose. I happened to be a tad more sober, that's all. I still think that somewhere in my drunken brain, I knew better than to punch his face in, which I had no desire to do in the first place. I was only subduing him, preserving my safety and maybe a little pride.

Cooper, I tell you what, he's always maintained a canine's loyalty. He sent me to the bathroom...ordered me, more or less.

'Stay here till I come for you,' he said, still shirtless...all back hair and man-tits.

While I waited, I read the graffiti inside the stall and then my entire life came rushing over me in a series of images; I belong to the first generation raised on MTV, and that's how my life presented itself, in bytes, in third person clips shot at strange angles, as though the cameraman's hand were shaking ...meanwhile, judging from what I later pieced together, Coop flashed his badge and had his buddy tossed out of the bar. Poor bastard. A waste of sixty-bucks...that's how much it cost to get in.

Eventually, maybe ten or twenty minutes later, Coop came to the bathroom and knocked on my stall. I opened the door. He had his priest shirt on but not the jacket. He seemed more sober than before.

'Okay Rocky,' he said, licking his dry drunken lips. 'Coast is clear.'

'What'd you do?'

'Took care of it.'

'Is he still out there?'

'Huh-uh,' he said, 'Justin's gone.'

'Brother, I owe you a million apologies. I promise I didn't meant to uh...'

'You don't have to explain shit to me.'

'Can I come out?'

'Yeah, yeah,' he said. 'That's the good news.'

'Oh. What's the bad?'

'Your chick split,' he said, with a big sloppy grin. He underestimated his bad news. He thought it was humorous. He went on, not knowing any better...

'Yeah, she told me to tell you to fuck off. That's a quote.'

I came unglued. Unhinged. Un-everything, and all at once...

My soul has cancer, it's got Lou Gehrig's...It has full-blown AIDS...Gulf War symptoms and festering buboes. It's sick, infected. And without warning, it started oozing out, suppurating.

It dawned on me, as I sat there shaking on the toilet, that not only was Chance a sonofabitch, but so was I. Granted, I suspected it all along, but suddenly I knew. When random Chance didn't shoot me in the foot, I did it myself. And here I had presented myself to myself as a victim, when, all along, I was only a fool. I'm not blind or lame or retarded; I have no excuses. I've brought it all on myself. It was me. *Me*. Me, all along.

I did this to myself. I have wasted my life, *all of it*. Self-sabotage. There's nothing worthy of less pity. That didn't stop me. I wept and sobbed and shook with thunderous implacability. I jammed my fists into my eyes sockets. I winced and slobbered.

Cooper stood there, stunned, like a stretcher-bearer deciding whether or not to run into a burning house. Then something yanked him from his daze. He had to block the door to keep guys from coming in for a piss.

'Out of order,' Coop said to the door. 'Use the lady's.'

'What the hell's going on in there?'

'Hey, dickhead, I said use the lady's!'

It's staggering, the degree to which alcohol amplifies the melodrama of our lives. For the first time in years, an irresistible woman had shown some interest in me and I had cocked it up completely. That's all that happened. So what. It's not like I lost a leg or something.

Yet booze is a funny-mirror for misery; booze stretches it, twists it, magnifies and distorts it beyond its natural borders until, for whatever reason, you're convinced that the world is ending. Sure, you wish booze were an upper. And we attempt in vain to use it like one. Nevertheless it's a depressant, a downer. There's no getting around it.

Well, amid my drunken bout of self-pity, my gasping ululations...I did something even more idiotic than molesting a hairdresser from Bedford. I opened up my mouth and spoke.

'Coop...man I'm...I'm all fucked up. I..Jesus I..'

'What? What is it?'

'I hired some guy to croak me.'

'Hold up,' he said, bending down toward me. 'Did I hear that right?'

'Yeah, you heard me. I paid a prisoner to cut me open, carve me up. I'm fucking through with all of this.'

'Are you shitting me? When??'

It seemed like a typical cop reflex. Before anything else, he wanted to know how much time he was working with. I answered most of his questions. Then he asked me the doozy.

'Why? Why would you do something so stupid?'

Why? Good question. I didn't answer. I didn't look at him. I couldn't. I sat on the toilet with my face in my hands.

'Why?'

I didn't answer.

'*Why?*'

'Guess it's simple. I don't want to live anymore. Why else?'

And at this point, Coop changed. Completely. He boxed my ear...could've been with an open hand or with a closed one. I don't know. It felt somewhere in between. The blow didn't wake me up, so to speak, or jolt me into a new awareness of my folly or anything like that. It stung like a bastard and drew my attention to the absurdity of the evening, of the moment. I had to laugh like hell. Which I did, until Coop looked as if he might strike me again. He was fuming.

'Think this is funny, dickhead? You were going to fucking *leave* me?'

'It's not...Don't take it personally. This isn't some spur of the moment kind of...'

'People love you!'

'Yeah?'

'*Yes.*'

'Maybe but...I don't know, there's only so long you can hang on for other people.'

'Well fuck you too,' he launched into me for a while, cursing, spitting, vituperating, shoving. Drunks kept coming up to the door.

'Guess we shouldn't stay here, Coop.'

'Fuck 'em.'

'I'm fine now.'

'Yeah,' he snorted, 'You look fine. You look great buddy.'

'I'd better get home.'

'You're crashing at my place.'

Because of our jobs, we had had the same kind of suicide prevention courses, Coop and I. He was trained not to leave me alone. A compromise was reached. I was hustled out the back door so as to avoid any further embarrassment. We shuffled across the street to Coop's car, a gigantic champagne SUV provided by the city; it was supposed to help him look like a big-time dope dealer. It was parked illegally along the yellow curb.

He started up the V-8 engine...got the heater going. I gazed at the crumpled fast food bags on the floorboard. He lit a cigarette and cracked a window. His face became adult-like, with sparsely a trace of the childhood friend with whom I'd once shared a paper-route as well as every boyhood secret.

'Weimer, here's what we need to do. We need to pick this thing apart, all right? Let's separate what you can change from what you can't. Right? Okay. Then, so, you want your kids. That's out. Not gonna happen. Sorry. And you're broke. Okay. We can work on that. And you want to go to school. That's what I'm hearing, right? That's what you've been saying. That's what I've heard you say, right? These are the issues.'

Here, his clinical tone vaporized and he took the whole thing personally again.

'I'll send you to school, you dick. How much could it cost? Move in with me, you won't have any bills. Zero man. No grocery bills. No utilities. Nothing. All you'd have to do is get your ass to class.'

'Can't do it,' I said, feeling lower and lower. 'I know the score. I don't want that.'

'You don't want what? To try??'

'No, charity.'

'Beats suicide,' he said, a point that I considered open to debate. We sat there for a while in silence. Then he pleaded with me to stay the night at his pad. I told him I had to run an errand for my mother in the morning. He asked if that was bullshit. I said it wasn't, which it wasn't.

'Promise?'

'Promise,' I said, holding back the bizarre impulse to smile.

'Swear to God?'

'Swear to God.'

See, Coop knew my relationship with God was queasy at best. But, as an old childhood hangover, we never lied about anything when we swore to God. Ever. It's just a habit that stuck. A sort of absolute. He put the SUV in drive.

I said, 'Is this a kidnapping?'

'Better believe it. Unless you swear you won't do anything at all until after we talk again. Anything. Fucking anything. We're gonna fix this. I swear. We're not done, okay? Run your mom around tomorrow then come right over.'

'Those are the uh...terms of not being kidnapped?'

'Yeah. Where's your car?'

'By the Wellington.'

'You swear to God, right?'

ON the way home, my exhaust system went to shit.

The pipe underneath ripped open and fell down...sounded like a B-52...sparks went flying up behind me. I don't know why I didn't get pulled over. I certainly deserved it. I looked at the sparks in the rearview mirror and I had to laugh.

When I got back to my dump, I couldn't sleep. More than anything else, I felt foolish...crushed by the full weight of my confession...suffocated by embarrassment. I didn't know if I could ever look Cooper in the eye again. I would forever feel naked around him.

Why'd I do it? Why'd I blab? I don't know. At first, I blamed it on booze. But what was underneath? Or was there anything underneath? I tried to piece it together. Maybe it was the dishonestly of it all. I mean, if everything went according to the plan, then, by the end of January, once I was 'killed in action,' people at work would herald me as a guy who 'took one for the team.' A martyr of sorts.

Granted, prison guards are never regarded as heroes. But if you die in the line of duty, it's bound to make a ripple. It would show up in the papers. Guaranteed. Gretchen, Mom, Cooper...everybody would get the wrong idea. I wanted one person to know the truth; I wanted my best friend to know that I had lost the contest with life, or, to be completely honest, that I had simply given up.

No, it was more selfish than that. I wanted Coop to know that I didn't do it irresponsibly, that I took out a million dollars in life insurance and saw to it that everyone I loved could live a little easier in my absence. Or had my confession been a cry for help? How cliché!

I don't know. Maybe it was something else entirely. When we make our intentions known to the people we love most, action tends to follow. Maybe I was still teetering on the edge and needed to reinforce my commitment. If this had been my motive, it certainly worked. I mean, there's no way I could live day to day as Cooper's emotional charity case. That's how it would end up going down. I knew the score. Cooper has a good career and a family of his own, I thought, there's no reason he should have to change my diapers too.

I was going through with it after all, I decided, and it made me feel a little giddy. Still rather intoxicated from the night before—and possibly going crazy—I sent Claudette a cryptic text message, borrowing the title of an old song by a band, The Verve Pipe, that had been popular during our time together, "We were merely freshmen."

A little after six in the morning, I drank the last of my coffee and spaced out on the couch next to Cleo, who kept using her paw to drag my hand down to her belly. There wasn't a sunrise. It was as though some master switch had been slowly cranked up...The Near West Side was gradually filled with dead, leaden light.

I drove to a hardware store on Thirty-Eighth Street with my exhaust pipe sparking along the asphalt. It should've fallen off, but didn't. In the parking lot, I slid underneath my rust-bucket and fastened the tailpipe back together with a C-clamp. While under there, tinkering and cursing, I wondered how the hell I was going to get my mitts on the eight grand I needed for Grandpa's help. I had made a down payment but I needed the rest and didn't know how to get it. For obvious reasons, I couldn't ask Cooper. I thought about prying the money loose from Claudette with some expertly fashioned guilt-trip. It would take one hell of an acting job and a lot of self-denigration. That didn't stop me. I decided against it because she's sharp, far too bright. She might piece everything together. Doubtful. Less than a one percent chance. Still.

Fine, I decided, I'll have to hit Mom up for the money. It'll clean Mom out, I thought; but then again, she'll get paid back times a hundred, just as soon as the insurance comes through. I was simply helping her to invest wisely, I decided.

Such were my thoughts as I picked Mom up with a hug and a kiss and a 'Happy New Year.' It was good to see her. As you progress toward oblivion, it's a bit like knowing that you're going to move soon. You really appreciate the little things and certain people—though not enough to keep you from packing up and moving out.

We went grocery shopping. Always good fun with a quasi-blind woman. She smacked the hell out of everything with her cane, knocked over a cardboard kiosk of hand lotion. She held oranges right up to her face and squeezed them such that if they weren't bruised before, they certainly were afterwards. In the frozen section, I started to launch into an ill-prepared spiel.

'Mom...'

Then I realized how stupid it was. I was going to tell her that Cooper blew all of his money in Vegas and I needed the eight grand so he could pay his mortgage and some medical bills.

She'd say 'What? What? You're off you're rocker. You want me to pay for your friend's gambling habit?'

I'd say 'Ma, I know it sounds weird. But I already promised. Come on, have I ever asked for money before?'

To which she might say, 'Actually, son, you certainly have.'

No. I'd have to think up something better. I was in the middle of fetching a bag of celery when my phone rang. Unidentified number. Ooooo. Could be Darshanna. My heart-rate went through the roof…I couldn't remember giving her my number, but it was certainly possible.

'Hello?'

'Wesley?'

It wasn't her. It was Sarah, Cooper's wife, calling from her cell phone.

THE Coopers live in a tall, narrow, pumpkin-colored brick home with weeping mortar, over near Butler University, in an older part of town sprinkled with pubs and cafés and poor folks and rich folks and lots of people in between. It feels like a city or a town, not a suburb. In short, it's not depressing.

What is depressing, is the way I always feel like a third wheel whenever I go to their house. When I was married (both times), I loved coming over. We'd grill out, watch a little football or sit on the balcony and drink wine. Play chess. Shoot pool. Standard stuff. Coming over as a thirty-three-year-old bachelor feels odd, a bit uncomfortable. Either Sarah feels like a third wheel or I do. Or I perceive it that way, which is all the same.

When Sarah called she had sounded exacerbated, at her wit's end.

'I can't handle him. I need your help. Come as soon as you can.'

So I did.

COOPER had lost it completely.

The night before, Cooper's Dad, a successful detective himself, had consumed more than one or two pints at the Rathskeller downtown. No big deal. Cops don't get DUIs unless they're driving drunk outside the margins of their jurisdiction. Everyone knows that. However, something happened.

On the way back to my neighborhood, where Harold Cooper and his wife Mimi still lived at the time, the bumper of his Cadillac Seville collided with a motor scooter. This wouldn't have been much of a problem, had an eleven-year-old boy named Danny Stuart not been riding it.

Danny screamed. Then Harold Cooper did the stupidest thing imaginable. He hit the gas, thereby dragging this boy and his scooter the length of two city blocks. A stupid mistake became vehicular manslaughter and fleeing the scene. I know Harold well enough to know that he'd never do that sober. It was a drunken mistake, exponentially compounded by the idiotic drunken impulse to abscond. This time, he had really put his foot in it.

So. When I found Cooper on Forty-Second Street, he was naked except for his cowboy boots, a cowboy hat, and a black leather utility belt with a holster containing his police-issue, nine-millimeter pistol, which, according to Sarah, had been discharged into the air more than once. I stepped out of the Civic, warily. His eyes looked sightless. Cooper wears contact lenses and seemed not to have them in. Also, according to his infantile gait and the reddish sheen of vomit down his chest, he was blind drunk. Apparently, he had taken the news of his father's arrest rather harshly.

I was afraid. Best-friend or not, the man was drunk and he had a gun. Add too much booze, and guns tend to discharge on their own. I hollered from a snow-covered yard.

'Cooper!'

He made a megaphone with his hands and yelled back.

'Help me out bro, I'm outta ammo!'

At that, I closed on Cooper, imploring him to come along. He sat down in protest with his balls dangling over the curb and wouldn't budge. My first thought was 'What the hell did he eat to make his puke so red?' Naturally, my second thought was, 'I need to get him home, but how?'

I got a hold of his thick, pale wrists. I was uselessly trying to jerk him to his feet, when a white patrol car rolled onto the scene. An unbelievably short policeman hopped out with a crew-cut and a scowl. Obviously, he hit the weights. He looked nearly as thick as he was tall. A pocket Hercules.

The kid was a rookie, as evinced by the fact that he didn't recognize Cooper. On one hand, I thought, that's good, because he won't be able to run his mouth at the FOP lodge. On the other hand, he might not cut us a break. I didn't wait for the muscular hobbit to ask me his obligatory questions. I rushed to explain.

'Officer, my brother's diabetic. I need to get him home so he can have his insulin.'

'Smells like your brother's been drinking.'

'I know,' I said, 'I've told him. It aggravates his diabetes. You know, the whole blood sugar thing.'

'You can smell him from a mile away. He's drunk.'

Cooper spoke up. 'Hell yes I am.'

'He's drunk,' the officer concluded and then, ignoring me, he brought his skin-colored lips to Cooper's ear.

'Stand up,' he said. 'Up, up, up.'

Suddenly, the cop caught sight of Cooper's pistol and leapt back.

'Put your hands on your head!,' he drew his piece. 'Both of you. Now.'

We complied. Cooper played the card he's used to playing.

'It's okay man,' Cooper slurred, 'I'm a cop.'

'What's that?'

'I'm in your friggin department.'

'You have some ID?'

I said 'Are you serious?'

He said 'Put your hands back on your head.' And then, 'Sir, what's your badge number?'

It didn't work. At any rate, not in time to spare Cooper from humiliation. Another cop car pulled up. A huge black man emerged and recognized Cooper. The three of us hauled him back to a bedraggled Sarah.

Somehow she and I coerced him into the tub, which barely accommodated his wide drunken ass. Sarah and I, we tried to laugh about the whole affair, but didn't succeed. It was Coop's turn to break down...

But instead he went to sleep. No tears. Nudity and gunpowder had been enough, apparently. No surprise.

The last time I saw him cry was when his mother's mother had finally given up her fight with some chronic respiratory disease. He was tight with all of his grandparents. Like I said, it was a close-knit family. Anyway, he didn't cry when the first three grandparents died. But when the last of them left for good, he finally broke down, like he was saying goodbye to all of them.

Sometimes I think that men like Coop and me, men who hold back too much and too often, are prone to these maudlin eruptions. You make a mental list of all the things you should've cried about but didn't. Then, one day, the dam breaks and you have full license to back-pay yourself for tears owed. You go berserk.

In any event, I passed out on the recliner in his study, which is really only a home for his computer since he never reads. I awoke, once, when Sarah placed a blanket over me, and again when I intuited that it was time for work. I called in sick and went right back to sleep. Again I was awoken, this time by the phone.

'Daddy?'

It was Gretchen. She was drunk. My fourteen-year-old daughter was drunk.

'Gretchen it's…four in the morning.'

She said something. The room she called from was so loud that I couldn't hear what she had said, so I asked her to repeat it.

'I miss you, Daddy.'

'I…miss you too. Are you being good?'

'No.'

'Have you been drinking?'

'Will you be mad?'

I thought about this for a second and took a diplomatic tact.

'If I were mad, would you keep it a secret next time?'

'Probably, yeah.'

'Then I'm not mad.'

'Yes you are.'

'No, I'm fine.'

'You promise?'

'I'm concerned.'

'I finally got invited to a party. Isn't that awesome?'

'Isn't the party a day late?'

'Yeah but...Courtney's Mom and Dad didn't leave town till this morning.'

'Who's Courtney?'

'A new friend. You don't know her.'

'Oh.'

'I better go. Only I wanted to say how much I love you, and plus how much I miss you.'

'Well, sweetie I—'

'Gotta go.'

'Okay, don't drive.'

Click.

Don't drive? Was this really the only sage advice I could offer a kid who didn't even have a driver's license yet?

I couldn't sleep anymore. I thought about my daughter. I don't know. If she lived with me, I would've grilled her...I would've come down hard, all right. Fourteen? It's too young for wild parties. At a minimum, she would've been subjected to a long, guilt-inducing sermon. But she doesn't live with me, so what could I do? Besides, what can you really say to teenagers...except hurry up and enjoy a little happiness before it vanishes, before it all gets swallowed up by the innumerable dead-ends and dark alleyways, before it all disappears into the blind spots and pot holes of life...because in time this youthful love of life will pass through so many spiritual black holes, get gobbled up by so many supernovas left over from self-aborted dreams...until the only thing left of your love of life is a wistful echo that tortures your subconscious, like some long ago and forever dead romance that was made possible only by your childish ignorance.

I got up, pissed, and tried to check on Cooper. The door to the master bedroom was closed. Not wanting to intrude, I drove home.

Happy Birthday!

WITH Cooper's dad going through hearings, and trials, and suicidal ideations of his own, I couldn't exactly leave my best friend in his darkest hour, as it were. So I caught Grandpa hunkered over a deep sink in the mop room.

'Gramps,' I said glibly, 'change in plans.'
'What plans?' Pause. 'Oh, those plans.'
'Yep.'
'You backin out big daddy?'

'Yeah, for now.'

'Shit, congratulations boss. You want your cash back?'

'Yeah, I'd sure appreciate it. Unless you feel like going to the hole and staying there until you leave.'

'Okay. I'll get it to you tomorrow then. Or at least by Wednesday.'

'Thanks.'

Grandpa poured some bleach over the mop head, 'So what happened, you meet a girl or something?'

'Something.'

I handed him a plastic Gatorade bottle filled with Seagram's, along with a hundred bucks for his silence. He looked askance at the bottle.

'This what I think it is?'

'Yep. You know, for mental anguish.'

'I read you, boss. But I wouldn't run my jib no how.'

'I know. Still...I felt bad, backing out and all.'

'Okay then,' Grandpa shrugged, 'Let me know if you change your mind.' He winked. He fucking winked. What a natural killer.

'Will do,' I said, leaving him to clean up the sink, suddenly realizing that I had forgotten my dinner, and wondering what kind of an ordeal I would have to go through in order to have a pizza delivered to the front gate.

ADMITTEDLY, I strained a metaphor earlier.

I likened people to ceramics. I said you can't make an ashtray out of a poodle, or something like that.

Well I'd like to go a little further and say that, while you can't make an ashtray out of a ceramic poodle, you can certainly knock it off the shelf and watch it shatter into pieces, until all that's left is entropy. And that's what happened to Cooper, more or less. His nearly indestructible optimism was eroded by the tragedies that one by one befell his family.

BY the end of February, when by all rights I should've been good and dead, Harold Cooper found himself in the Greenborough Correctional Diagnostic Center, where I used to work with Big Ed. Coop's family was falling apart.

His mom, Mimi, was so flummoxed and ashamed of her husband that she left him, moved to Avon (a Westside suburb), and for the first time in her life she took a job—I think at a Target, if I have that down right.

Coop has two older sisters. Angela, the oldest, she sided with Mom. Madison, the youngest of the three, she sided with Dad. Coop tried in vain to remain neutral. But battle-lines had been drawn...there was the Mom Camp and the Dad Camp...cousins and nephews and aunts and friends and so son, they all segregated themselves along these party lines. In the end, Cooper's declared neutrality was as repugnant to each side as either side was to the other. The Switzerland act, it couldn't last forever.

Something tipped the scale and, by the middle of February, Coop found himself aligned with Harold, who by then had been transferred to the GCF. Apparently, Chance has a sense of humor.

Harold was first housed at the PQ Unit and then at the West Dormitory, where he worked as a hazmat clerk, dispensing cleaning chemicals to prisoners from various dorms. Thirty-five cents an hour.

None of this matters.

What did matter, at least to Harold, was that Harold Cooper, while serving undercover for some twenty years, had spied on and infiltrated various white supremacist groups—chiefly the Aryan Brotherhood, though the Klan and a few minor players had also been vitiated over the years. Like all cops, Harold had enemies.

ON Valentine's Day, we were short several officers. Maybe nine or ten. It's not a national holiday, so you can call in sick without getting in trouble. We use our sick days as if they were vacation days.

Anyway, it was Valentine's Day and Harold received a present that night while he was sleeping. Someone put a padlock in a gym sock, swung it around a few times, and connected with Harold's face, thereby splitting open his brow. Twelve stitches. 'Lock in a sock,' we call it. Inelegant, perhaps, but effective.

They caught the guy. The attack had been part of his initiation rite. He was proud and didn't try to hide what he had done. I forget his name but I remember him being transferred to 'The Farm,' a Level-5 prison.

I met Cooper at the Hooter's on West 38th Street and broke the news.

'But he's okay?'

'Sure,' I said. 'Your dad's a tough old bird. Twelve stitches, that's all.'

'Was it a one-off thing or...Will it happen again?'

'Yeah, if he keeps refusing Protective Custody.'

'He refused?'

'Of course. What, are you surprised?'

'I'll talk to him,' Coop said. 'I've got a visitation scheduled for next Tuesday.'

'Yeah. Do that,' I said, and then, when the bill came, I let Cooper pick it up because I had just paid to have my exhaust system fixed and my alternator replaced. As usual, I was broke.

DURING my next shift, he was attacked again. Somebody stabbed Harold in the back when he was coming out of church. Superficial wound. Nevertheless, the word was out, obviously, and Harold was in danger. His days were as numbered as a piglet's.

Cops don't fare well in prison and successful detectives do even worse. 'Walk in one side of the jail and get drug out the other.' So goes the saying.

On the up side, Harold finally did what he should've done in the first place...he requested Protective Custody, which was granted immediately.

The next morning, a drizzly March morning, I met Cooper at Dancer's. He really looked like hell. For the first time, Coop appeared to be close to my age, which he is. His eyes were sunken into doughy nests of purplish flesh. He smoked one cigarette after the other.

He wouldn't shake my hand or accept a clumsy man-hug or anything. He didn't want to be touched. Peering through the hood of a Raiders sweatshirt, Coop looked at me with his road-mapped eyes. Sad and desperate.

'Will he be safer now?'

'Safer? Sure. Of course.'

'But will he be *safe*?'

'I don't know,' I said, which was the honest truth.

'You don't know, or you don't wanna say?'

'The way it's set up, he should be fine but...'

'But?'

'Some prisoners do have access. Limited access...to mop the halls and stuff like that. They do have to feed them, you know. And, well...'

'What are you saying?'

'Well, here's an example of the way it could work. Let's take a prisoner. We'll call him Ralf. If Ralf pretends to be threatened, then he can request Protective Custody. Then Ralf would be in Protective Custody...right next to your dad. It's easy enough to fake it. You can geek the system. Someone who really wants access can get access.'

'So...he *is* in danger.'

'Listen. I'm not gonna blow smoke. It's...I don't want to slam my brethren, but not every CO stays awake on the job. State pay doesn't always buy the most devoted employees, that's all I'm saying.'

'So he's definitely in danger.'

'Possibly.'

'Can you...is there...there anything you can do?'

'Yes. And I already did it.'

Coop lit a fresh Marlboro Light with the ember of a dying one.

'What? What'd you do?'

'We got lucky, Coop. The gal who works Protective Custody, she has a thing for me. I'm not sure exactly what kind of thing, but it doesn't matter. She said she'll let me work her unit from now on...I didn't tell her why...if they find out I know your Dad, we're finished. They'll move me out of there...

'So what'd you tell her?'

'Told her I needed the seclusion so I could finally start working on a novel.'

'So...it's covered?'

'Actually, it's far from covered. I mean, I work one shift. One out of four. We have three other shifts to worry about. It's the other night shift. That's the one that's really...'

He looked pensive. Thoughtful. Me, I wasn't pensive. I was nervous. I astonished myself by reaching over and grabbing one of his cigarettes.

'Can I pinch one of these?'

'You have to ask?'

He removed the hood of his sweatshirt and examined me. 'What's up Weimer? What is it??'

'I might have a plan,' I said, choking on smoke but also feeling pretty good. Nicotine. Jesus. What a drug.

I explained to Cooper that there's no way one CO can keep a wanted inmate safe, not twenty-four hours a day. The key, I thought, was to make Harold indispensable to a coterie of influential inmates. In short, I proposed to Cooper that I traffic massive quantities of tobacco and hand it over to Harold. This, I hoped, would serve more or less as protection money. He could placate the folks he had pissed off over the years, namely the Aryan Brotherhood. Also, if he was worth something to the right person, everyone else would steer clear. Such were my thoughts, such was my rationale.

Coop liked the idea. He's always been a Boy Scout cop. Straight as an arrow. Well that shit was out the window. It was time to save Dad's neck.

Tobacco is bulky, as drugs go. It would've been easier to smuggle in sheets of LSD or crack or just about anything else. Yet Cooper and I would only take this thing so far. For one thing, it was a matter of degree. It may be unethical to smuggle tobacco insofar as it's illegal but it doesn't threaten the safety and security of the institution in the same way that, for example, crystal-meth might. No one smokes a cigarette and feels suddenly compelled to whack somebody or start a riot. In fact a cigarette, if anything, might actually subdue a prisoner, especially if he's already hooked. There was also a more pragmatic reason for not smuggling a harder, more convenient drug. If I got caught smuggling tobacco, I'd probably just get fired. That's usually what happens.

But if I got caught smuggling something else, I'd be done. I'd go to prison, get caught trying to hang myself, end up on some suicide watch for a long time, then I would finally snuff it in jail. And that's after being forced to toss more salad than an Olive Garden. A former CO in prison? No thanks.

Also, if hard drugs were involved, they'd take a close look at the case, and the money trail could possibly lead back to Cooper. True, the chances were slim to none. But still. I needed a foolproof smuggling device, a violin case for my tommy gun, as it were. I'm a thinker, if I'm anything, but I've never been a doer.

Coop's a lot better with his hands than me. Over the weekend, he came over with a twelve-pack of longnecks and he soldered a partition into a giant stainless steal thermos. We called this thing Max, short for Maxwell House.

'Yep,' Coop said, 'Max should do the trick.'

'Maybe you got in the wrong line,' I said, 'You would've made an excellent crook.'

Now that I had Max, if the COs up front, the lobby dorks, well if they opened up my thermos to investigate—as they periodically do—the only thing they'd see and smell would be the bottom-shelf coffee that I subject myself to. However, the other ninety percent of the thermos would be stuffed with contraband. Max, God love him, was damn near foolproof.

AFTER a while, I decided against tobacco. Like I said, it's bulky. Also, it's conspicuous; both visually and aromatically. When we do shake downs, we know how to look for it. When an inmate gets caught smoking, he sometimes snitches on his source in order to reduce his penalty. Because of the odor, inmates frequently get caught. Such an unfortunate occurrence might lead back to me. My hands had to stay lilywhite.

So I decided to go with Nicorette gum. It's smokeless, for one, which minimizes the chance of detection. Also, it can be easily disguised as regular old gum. COs aren't looking for it. And it's dense stuff. In one thermos, I can smuggle in the equivalent of four hundred and twenty cigarettes. Such a quantity of gum costs $69.30 but goes for a lot more in jail. Moreover, prisoners can use it all day long, whereas tobacco has to be consumed furtively, thereby artificially reducing demand.

IN the middle of March, I first approached Harold. He really looked like shit, gazing numbly back at me through a small, mesh-wired window in his blue metal door.

I studied his face...I think because it dawned on me that the physical similarities I'd always perceived that Harold and Chris Cooper shared could not possess a genetic basis. After all, Harold wasn't really Chris's father.

No, I decided, they really don't look similar at all. The shared mannerisms had fooled me into equating them with physical congruities. They scratched their faces the same way, with a palm dragged across the cheek. And they had both developed the habit of coughing into their hands before saying anything serious. But, unlike Coop, Harold had imperious moon-colored eyes similar to Johnson's, though less near-set.

Harold's eyes had always struck me as fierce. But when I looked him in the face for the first time since he'd been locked up, his eyes appeared heavy and sullen...two frosty windows into a broken spirit. His handlebar mustache was made less prominent by the recent appearance of facial scruff, the color of cigar ash. He was shorter than me and had lost weight, and for the first time I wasn't afraid of him. If anything, I pitied him.

We'd never been close. We were neither on bad terms nor good ones. He was taciturn, removed, crotchety. He only smiled at his grandchildren and, if no one was looking, his wife...I mean before they started having problems.

Anyway, I sidled up to Harold's cell and tapped a knuckle on the door. He came to the window.

'Wesley.' He used my name as a somber greeting. 'They got you working over here now?'

'Officer Weimer,' I corrected him. My face was supposed to explain the situation but I guess it didn't. 'We've never met, Offender Cooper. We don't know each other. That's important.'

He didn't get it. 'Whatever you say boss man,' he sneered.

'So. How you getting on?'

'You don't want to know.'

'I can guess.'

'Can you now?'

Somehow, we'd gotten off on the wrong foot. I knew small talk was useless. I cleared my throat and lowered my voice. 'Harold, I'd like to help you out with something.'

'Can you get me some pants? Some sonofabitch ripped off my pants. I put a request in three days ago. How am I supposed to get by on just one pair?'

'We're still out of pants.'

'Then what do you want?'

Suddenly, he checked his gruffness. 'How's Christopher?'

'Worried about you.'

He looked away, guilt-ridden as hell. I handed him a Ziploc bag full of nicotine gum. I didn't feel like explaining. 'Know what this is?'

'Am I supposed to?'

I was paranoid. His cell was the last one on the block but there was one cell across from his and one to the left. I couldn't believe he wasn't catching on. I did my best to remain adequately cryptic, yet get my point across.

'Try a piece,' I said. Harold was a smoker, so I knew he'd finally get it.

'What is this stuff?'

'Just try it.'

'That a order, boss?'

'*Yes.*'

Skeptically, he plunked a piece of gum into his mouth and, as the nicotine found his bloodstream, his face glowed like I'd never seen it. *Jackpot*, said his face.

'Good Lord,' he said, 'do I ever owe you one.'

'It's not for you. Sure, you can have piece. But it's not for you.'

He looked at me through the chicken wire with bitter incredulity. 'Son, are you *trying* to confuse me?'

'Keep your voice down.'

I explained the situation as quickly as possible '...and you guys always buy those soups on commissary...those fucking ramen noodle packages....Look, soups are like currency here,' I explained to him, 'they get passed around all the time. It's common. It never raises an eyebrow, when a guy hands somebody a soup. So. Put what I give you in the soup.' Then I whispered 'You picking up what I'm putting down?'

'No. Yes but no, I don't want any part of this.'

'Harold, you're being ridiculous. Just do what I tell you.'

'My ass. Who do you think you are?'

'A guy who was sent here by your son.'

'Christopher's in on this?'

'It was his idea,' I lied. 'Think on it. Sleep on it. I'll see you tomorrow night. If your answer is still no, I'm washing my hands of the whole goddamn thing. If you don't care, I don't care. I'm just trying to do your son a favor. Seems like the least you could do is stay alive. For him, if for no one else.'

Harold had been sentenced to twelve years, which, in Indiana, could be reduced to six years with good behavior. If he obtained a skill, say, the auto-body trade, he could have his sentence further reduced.

True, he had killed a child...but he still might get out in five years, if all went well. That's simply how the system works. My only point is, he wasn't a hopeless case. He wanted to live. He hadn't thrown in the towel. Not yet.

THE first day I smuggled this stuff into prison, I nearly shat my pants...that's not an overstatement. I had Max in one hand, fully laden, and I nearly dropped him in the lobby, right in front of everyone...My hands were sweaty and shaking. I thought I might be having a heart attack.

The lobby dorks, as well as Johnson, and B-Ray, and almost everyone else on camp...I was convinced that somehow they all knew what I was up to. My pulse went through the roof and stayed there. My palms went from sweaty to slimy as I walked through the yard toward my dorm.

It was time for count. I could just barely write numbers down on the count slip. I handed my slip to Johnson and slinked away, convinced that he had read my face perfectly, that he had smelled my guilty, brick-shitting fear.

After count cleared, I killed time with a Vonnegut novel. I think it was *Sirens of Titan*. Vonnegut is one of the only authors I can still read when my mind is fucked sideways. I guess some people love him and some think less of his work. Say what you want, but he has to be one of the most readable authors ever, which I guess is worth something all on its own. Vonnegut brought me comfort through those stretched out hours of anxiety.

Immediately after the midnight count, I went to the bathroom...unscrewed Max...took out the goods...put on my coat. And then I walked down the range to Harold's cell. I hurriedly jammed both baggies through the handcuff porthole in his door.

'Find a friend, Harold.'

◎

THE next few days were smeared gray with insomnia, and needlessly expanded by the acuity of anxiety. It was all very Dostoevsky. Clearly, I was Raskolnikov. And Razhumikin was there to play his part. But Petrovich never took the stage. The struggle was internal, nothing more. The dipshits in the lobby went through my bag a few times but they never even gave my main man Max a second look. In the end, there just wasn't much drama, which I guess is how a well-planned crime is supposed to go.

After a while I adjusted, both to the sense of risk, which quickly diminished, and to my sudden moral flexibility, which seemed enough to my emotional advantage that I quit worrying about it. I felt good. Vital. I wouldn't say I was completely free from guilt. It was more like...the guilt was far outweighed by something else. I was needed. After all, a human life directly depended on me. Such was my perception, be it accurate or not. Also, Coop had contributed a lot to my life over the years, and I felt like all I'd given back was misery and worry. Finally, I was worth something to someone.

More than once, Coop tried to give me a cut, tried to give me some money.

'For all the trouble,' he said, while we were shooting pool at his house.

'Brother,' I said, 'If I do this out of friendship, it makes me one thing. If I do it for money, that makes me something else.'

He gave me an understanding nod. Even though I was happy to help out Cooper, in the back of my mind, I figured it couldn't go on forever. Eventually I'd get caught. And when I did get caught, I'd revert to Plan-A, only I'd have to figure out a way to pull it off without Grandpa, seeing as I would be fired the same day I was caught.

It would still have to look like an accident if my family and friends were to get the insurance money, which was costing me a pretty penny in premiums. I figured I could always get myself locked up, and then, the first chance I got, I could run for the fence and get shot down. Why not stick with what you know?

@

THREE or four days a week, all the way up through April, I smuggled nicotine gum via my thermos, Max, and then I passed the stash to Harold, who never once even muttered his thanks, the ungrateful prick.

We rarely spoke at all. He resented my necessity, I believe, and I resented his ingratitude. But this was all done quietly...including our tacit though mutual resentment.

Everything was done very quietly.

In truth, smuggling this gum, which would've been legal anywhere else in the world, gave me no anxiety whatsoever after a while. Sometimes I'd forget that I had it on me. I left work one time without having passed on the booty. I'd simply forgotten. Like all work, crime eventually becomes mundane.

HAROLD came to look increasingly haggard.

For as long as I had known him, he had never taken care of himself but hardheadedness had carried him through until now. Now he looked terrible, worn out, like an old man before his time.

After several curt, cryptic conversations, I was made to understand that Harold was under pressure—exactly what kind, he wouldn't say—to traffic more gum and other things (drugs and knives and so on). Once he'd been marked as someone with a connection, they wouldn't leave him alone. I guess I hadn't considered this possible externality.

To Harold's credit, despite whatever pressure he'd come under, he told me that he never once revealed his source, which I believe. I wanted to help the man, but there was only so much I could do. I refused to bring in anything that wasn't related to nicotine or porn, and I couldn't smuggle much more of the gum. I started bringing in two gum sandwiches to augment Max, the thermos. That's where I drew the line.

Matters must've reached an equilibrium because Harold never approached me again, at least not regarding our operation, though on occasion he'd want me to pass a letter to his son, who was drinking even more than usual.

In any case, the one thing Coop had going for him, throughout this mess, was Sarah. She maintained graciously low expectations of her husband...He loved her and he paid the bills, and took out the trash and fixed the pluming when it needed fixed...she could put up with the rest, apparently...with the growing army of empty beer bottles...the overfilled ashtrays...the way he would sit on the couch for hours at a time, watching sports or re-watching movies that he'd seen a million times before. Maybe she was getting used to it—but I was getting worried.

ASIDE from the mind-numbing guard towers, the Protective Custody Unit is widely considered the most painfully boring position in the prison. After lights-out, it's just you and a long smothering silence, intermittently ruptured by snores and farts, and the occasional weeping convict.

While working there, I would read three, four hours during every shift. I would've read more but you still have to do your rounds, even when prisoners are sleeping, because if someone escapes undetected, it'll be on you; or, more likely, if the doctor finds out that someone in your charge has been dead for several hours—because of a suicide, or a heart failure, or whatever—the first thing the doctor will ask is, 'how is it that the patient had been dead for three hours when you're required by DOC regulations to make your rounds every fifteen minutes?' It's hard to get fired from a government job but there are, in fact, a few ways you can do it.

When B-Ray worked here in Protective Custody, she would sleep intermittently (using a wristwatch alarm to wake her up in order to do her rounds) and she would often consume an entire book of crossword puzzles on a single shift. Also, she frequently left her post to sneak cigarettes, to get more coffee and visit with other COs. As for me, I fought back boredom and the urge to sleep by writing, by getting out what was in my head and putting it somewhere where I could see it, examine it, possibly diagnose and fix it.

That first night in Protective Custody, I didn't have any paper. So I used official forms. PROPERTY CONFISCATION, SANITATION INSPECTION, DISCIPLINARY REVIEW, and so on. I didn't bring paper the second night either. I never brought in paper. Everything you've read so far has first appeared on the back of some form provided by Indiana's Department of Corrections.

ON the 5th of May, I got a phone call around eleven in the morning.

I was nursing my hangover with a can of Red Bull that I hadn't yet paid for, waiting in the checkout line at the CVS down the street, preparing to buy another installment of Nicorette gum as well as Nicorette lozenges, which had grown more popular at the prison.

In the checkout line, I was looking at all the magazines designed to make us feel like shit, to remind us of all the things we'll never have, never be, the people we'll never screw or even meet, the cars we can't drive, that places we'll never see, the clothes we can't wear, the homes we can't afford. The lives of the upper point-zero-zero-one percent.

I was pondering the societal impact of these trashy magazines when my cell phone started vibrating in my pocket. It was Cooper.

He said 'Dad just died.' And then he hung up.

ACCORDING to all initial reports, it appeared that Harold Cooper had been murdered. His death remained under investigation for some time, but has never been resolved.

Here's how it happened, I mean how Harold's tongue swelled up so much that it split right down the middle, and how he suddenly quit breathing and so forth.

As it turns out, Harold had an allergy to peanuts. I didn't know this. And I didn't know it was such a common food allergy. And I didn't know it was potentially lethal, either...Though apparently it is.

The inmates assigned to PCU, they never go to the chow hall with the other inmates. Their meals are brought to them on mushroom-colored plastic trays to be shoved through slits resembling mail portholes, located beneath the chicken-wired windows of their blue metal doors.

It was later discovered that Harold's meatloaf, or more specifically, the brown meatloaf sauce, which should've been red, was laced with concentrated peanut oil. Concentrated peanut oil is not a stocked item in the kitchen, so someone must've brought it in from the outside.

Cooking the peanut oil into the meatloaf sauce might've degraded the structure of those lethal proteins so, not surprisingly, investigators discovered that the peanut oil was uncooked, that is, it had been mixed in with the sauce *after* the sauce had been cooked. This diminished the ability of investigating authorities—GPD, and GCF 'Internal Affairs'—to pinpoint who had contaminated Harold's last supper.

Though much has been done to limit access to knives and cleavers and so forth, the kitchen crew itself isn't highly regulated. Meaning, any of the seventeen cooks could've laced the sauce that day. As well, any of the four food handlers could've laced the sauce. Either of the two inmates who had pushed the two food carts from the kitchen to the PCU could've likewise laced the sauce. Last but not least, the CO who shoved the tray of toxic meatloaf through the slit of Harold's door also could've been the one to taint the sauce.

How did the murderer or murderers discover that Harold had a peanut allergy? Clearly, one of the thirteen members of the medical staff with access to his records must've divulged this information, or created a security breech that allowed some inmate to gain access to this information.

Good luck getting to the bottom of that one.

Given that all of this happened in prison, it's not particularly remarkable that Harold's death should forever stay a mystery. A former cop was killed in jail, a cop-turned criminal. So what. Case closed. Murders happen all the time in prison, and at least half of them go unsolved.

The CO on duty that night, Tony Cheetums, managed to keep his job. He did so by telling what appears to be the truth, that he had been stricken with a ruthless bout of diarrhea. He'd been given a prescription. It was all well documented. So when he was asked 'Mr. Cheetums, why were you away from your post so long?,' he had a plausible defense.

Upon returning from the toilet, purportedly, Tony was beckoned to the end of the darkened hallway by a din of excited whoops, emanating from within the cells of Harold's neighbors.

When Tony keyed into the cell and found Harold, the latter was still breathing but unconscious. He was on his back, fully clothed. His lips were visibly swollen.

'Thirty-three, eighty-eight,' Tony called over his radio. 'We have a signal-three-thousand in PCU. Man down.'

Judging from experience, it probably took the medical personnel at least five minutes to react. Probably more like ten. Or fifteen. Most of the calls they receive turn out to be frivolous, or, at any rate, not emergencies. Usually a diabetic needs a piece of fruit or an unfortunate loudmouth needs a few stitches in his face. I'm sure the male nurse on duty was not in a terrific hurry to respond.

Harold was wheeled up to the medical station, still unconscious. While having his vitals taken, he died of anaphylactic shock. So it seems likely that Harold

Cooper was murdered. Either that, or he took a page from my plan, and had done himself in. Who knows.

How did Cooper take the news? He's never been the same of course. Blow by blow, he suffered through that winter and into the spring. Each blow changed him, deforming his character a little more.

Over the coming weeks, he became a quiet, brooding man. He got rid of all his costumes. He sold his Mustang. He barely did his job. He was barely a husband. Barely a father. Given my own history, who was I to say *snap out of it*?

But it didn't stay like that forever. For one thing Mimi, Coop's mother, took it upon herself to forgive Harold all trespasses and in fact she guards his memory with an eerie religiosity, which, to focus on the positive, has done much to repair the relationship between mother and son, between sisters and brother, and so on.

In short, Cooper got his family back, minus his father. Oddly enough, I pray for the Coopers every day. I don't know to whom or what I am praying...and I don't know if every prayer simply bounces back like a returned email sent to a bad address...but I know I feel a little better, and I know it can't hurt.

THESE last few pages have been written much later than the rest, and they were written in a much different state of mind. I guess the result, in part, is what English teachers call 'an uneven voice.' I don't sound like the same person because I am not the same person.

And I've gone back over what I've written and it feels strange, alien, and a little bit spooky to read what I was thinking back then...how I was feeling...what I was considering. I've done my best not to change one word, even though I have.

I read this stuff and I think, was I really like that? Could I really not find an exit? A way out? A way up? Considering who I am today, I find it strange.

YESTERDAY was my son's ninth birthday and I threw a huge party for him. Much in my life has changed since Harold's death. And all for the better, more or less.

For starters, I now have custody of Shane. We live in a white row house in Broadripple. We live with my mother and a boarder named Jeff Liong, a physics graduate student at IUPUI, originally from Singapore, a country I couldn't find on a map until Jeff moved in and we became fast friends.

Looking back on the blue period of my life, I see now that much of my sadness had been caused by habit and routine...Repetition erodes life, chips away at it until hardly anything is left because one day or week is interchangeable with any other, as if the days were coming off the assembly line...readymade, identical, and therefore pointless.

I've started doing different things, eating different foods, going places, meeting people. And I think it's these differences, these enemies of routine, that ultimately fill life in, that fill life up and give it weight. Things are looking up.

Now I drive a new Toyota. And I've had a girlfriend for a year, Fumiko Saito, an exchange student from Japan, a beautiful youngish woman whom I met in class after retrieving a pen that she'd dropped on the floor. I'm back in school now, with three more semesters to go.

Fumiko and I are getting close. This summer, if all goes well, we'll fly to her hometown of Nara, near Osaka, where apparently we'll meet the parents, and I guess there's a temple we're supposed to see with some deer running round nearby.

Her English isn't the best but that's okay...it beats my Japanese. She's kind. She's smart. She's patient. She likes to screw, which is also a plus.

We watch movies with subtitles. It all seems to work. Things are really looking up.

BUT things weren't always looking up.

When Harold died or got killed, or whatever...when he expired, the situation changed. With good old Harold out of the picture, my raison d'etre was back on shaky ground.

True, I worried and genuinely mourned for my friend. Yet soon enough, my thoughts inevitably returned to me. Because that's what people are really all about.

So once again I wasn't sure, exactly, why I was sticking around, slugging it out, taking up space unnecessarily.

Then something occurred to me, as I stared at the boxes of Nicorette gum sitting next to me on the passenger side of my rusty Civic, something simple yet profound...My misery, at least a good chunk of it, could be liquefied with money. I make no apologies. I'm not a Buddhist, I'm an American; why shouldn't it all come down to money?

AFTER my next meeting with Grandpa, after we had shored up the terms of our business arrangement, it struck me that I had worked with prisoners for twelve years without ever really relating to them.

For the first time, I was able to fully empathize with their criminal impulse, the need to meet desperation on your own terms, the passionate will to improve your lot—at great risk and potential sacrifice, if need be.

The money was good. Really good. Here are the numbers...I brought in an average of 460 pieces of gum three times a week (factoring in sick days and so forth), which brings it to 5,520 pieces a month. It cost me $227.70 for 1,380 pieces of gum each week. Such a quantity sold for a flat rate of $3,450. Rounding off, I kept $2,230 of that. Meaning, I made over two thousand tax free dollars every week.

The key, I knew, was to pocket every dime. I'd only spend my salary, none of my ill-gotten nicotine money. I had learned something important by working with convicted felons...Don't get greedy.

Some prisoners get caught because of bad luck and/or stupidity. However, most of them aren't stupid. Uneducated, perhaps, but not stupid. They're in jail because they didn't set a limit to their appetite for more—and if they did, they had surpassed it.

You could set up a robbery or meth lab tomorrow morning and, if all you want is a quick ten grand, chances are you'll never get caught. But that's not how it works. Convicted felons, for the most part, are locked up because they are creatures of habit, because they kept going back to the same well, which eventually dried up on them. If a deer keeps going back to the same stream at the same time every day, after a while, the poor bastard gets a 306-round in its neck. Or it's stomach. Creatures of habit die.

All those prisoners had taught me a lot. I had learned from their mistakes. I set my limit. I didn't eclipse it. I didn't follow the formula. By the middle of August, I had saved just over one hundred K. Right at $117 K, if my math is decent. I quit my job to start school. Actually, I had myself fired by calling in sick on three holidays. This allowed me to collect unemployment for six months.

Being an impoverished father of two, and unemployed to boot, the federal government was kind enough to give me a sizable chunk of student aid. My child support payments to Gretchen's mother continued unabated through my first year of school because child support is calculated by using the previous year's tax information. By the time school started, however, I was no longer paying child support for Shane, who'd been living with me since June.

LAST April, about a year after Harold's death, a few months before I quit the prison gig, I made a midnight drive through Haughville, which is, hands-down, the scariest neighborhood on the West Side of Indianapolis. It's not far from my old dump, right across the railroad tracks that separate the poor white-and-brown folks from the poor brown-and-black folks.

At first, I was going to ask Cooper for advice. But I thought better of it. So I called up Big Ed and met him in the back of his sporting goods store, where he was clamping chinstraps onto football helmets.

'How's your sis doing since she got out?'

'Pregnant. *Again*.'

'Sorry.'

'I could kill her. Man, she's like a womb without a brain. I love her but...'

He didn't finish his sentence so I changed the subject. 'Eddie...brother...I need some crack.'

'You mean, some ass?'

'No. Some crack cocaine. *The rock*, if you prefer.'

'Please don't tell me you're a crackhead too.'

'Are you insane? I just need to set somebody up. You remember me telling you about Yellow?'

'Uh-huh.'

'So I need a few grams, or whatever it comes in.'

'Oh.' Pause. 'That's real fucked up. But okay. Yeah, we can hook that up.'

I was the only white guy I saw that night. My pistol, a piece of crap .380, stayed on the passenger-side seat with a round in the chamber. I was nervous but determined.

With a Colt's cap pulled down over my eyes, I turned off North Holmes Avenue, and onto a side street resembling an alley, up near the projects. A young kid walked right up to the car. I said what Big Ed told me to say.

'I need some butter.' Then I flashed some bills and got exactly what I needed, twenty rocks of crack cocaine.

In the morning I picked up Shane and brought him back to house. As he played video games, I slipped on a pair of latex gloves and dragged his tiny purple backpack into the bathroom where I sewed the cocaine into his bag, sewed it in a way that would keep it hidden and secure, so he couldn't get into the stuff and harm himself.

The next day, after I dropped off Shane, on that rainy afternoon in April, I drove directly to a pay phone outside the 500 Liquor on Tenth Street.

I dropped a quarter, I 'dropped a dime.' The phone rang interminably. Rain pelted the phone booth. A CVS shopping bag floated by. Finally, a young woman answered the phone. Her voice could've cut a diamond. I told her I had information. She asked what kind.

So I told her about Yellow, about how he was selling drugs again, and how he smuggled his cocaine in a young boy's purple backpack from time to time, or so I had heard. I gave her the address, the details. Child Protection would not be happy. If nothing else, they would find all the weed that he and Cassandra consumed on a daily basis...Soon enough, I knew, I would have custody of Shane.

I guess when it comes to Survival—emotional or otherwise—sometimes you have to pick your own over everyone else's. I know that now. Sure, I've really gone downhill, ethically speaking, since my younger days. But if you kept the uncompromising spirit of your youth, you'd never forgive yourself for what you eventually become, which is bound to be a disappointment, especially if you never lower your standards.

In fact, much of coming to terms with life is lowering your standards...the standards to which you hold others and, more importantly, the standards to which you hold yourself.

Life as I live it now meets my lowered expectations. Granted, I had to undo over thirty years of indoctrination, of optimistic brainwashing...it starts with Disney and the bible and Aesop's fables...stories like The Tortoise and the Hare. Okay, the tortoise won the first race. But who do you think won the second, third, and fourth race? The hare, always the hare. The world belongs to the hares, the Winners, so you're better off realizing this fact early on, and throwing away your shell in exchange for a good pair of sneakers.

Presently, as I write this, I'm not completely happy...at least not in the Hollywood sense. But I don't think anyone is. Of course I've had to relearn lots of stuff that I'd forgotten...like how to take pleasure from the smaller joys with which life presents us. There are oodles and oodles of these smaller joys, I'm just discovering.

And even though it wasn't easy, I've reattached myself to the masses. I watch Monday Night football, and I read the paper, and I even flip through the channels once in a while...not because I really care about that stuff...but just to keep myself connected to everybody else, to swim in the common soup, to speak the commercialized language of modern society. These things are important. The only alternative is loneliness, isolation, despair... and I'm never going through that kind of self-imposed torture ever again.

Like you...like everyone...I don't have everything I want. But I have a lot more than I did. And that's really what it's all about, getting what you want. Everyone knows that.

So then...I don't know. Perhaps we really are just meat machines with hard-drives we call brains. Maybe. If so, I simply could not override the program for Survival.

CPSIA information can be obtained at www.ICGtesting.com
Printed in the USA
LVOW08s0746181214
419342LV00004B/98/P